FALCONER'S TRIAL

Further Titles by Ian Morson

The Falconer Mysteries

FALCONER'S CRUSADE
FALCONER'S JUDGEMENT
FALCONER AND THE FACE OF GOD
A PSALM FOR FALCONER
FALCONER AND THE GREAT BEAST
FALCONER AND THE RITUAL OF DEATH *
FALCONER'S TRIAL *

The Medieval Murderers

THE TAINTED RELIC
SWORD OF SHAME
HOUSE OF SHADOWS

The Niccolo Zuliani Mysteries

CITY OF THE DEAD *

* available from Severn House

FALCONER'S TRIAL

Ian Morson

This first world edition published 2009
in Great Britain and 2010 in the USA by
SEVERN HOUSE PUBLISHERS LTD of
9–15 High Street, Sutton, Surrey, England, SM1 1DF.
Trade paperback edition published
in Great Britain and the USA 2010 by
SEVERN HOUSE PUBLISHERS LTD

British Library Cataloguing in Publication Data

Morson, Ian.
  Falconer's Trial.
  1. University of Oxford – Fiction. 2. Falconer, William
  (Fictitious character) – Fiction. 3. Great Britain –
  History – Henry III, 1216–1272 – Fiction. 4. Detective and
  mystery stories.
  I. Title
  823.9'14-dc22

ISBN-13: 978-0-7278-6826-8   (cased)
ISBN-13: 978-1-84751-196-6   (trade paper)

Severn House Publishers support The Forest Stewardship Council [FSC],
the leading international forest certification organisation. All our titles that
are printed on Greenpeace-approved FSC-certified paper carry the FSC logo.

Mixed Sources
Product group from well-managed
forests and other controlled sources
www.fsc.org Cert no. SA-COC-1565
© 1996 Forest Stewardship Council

Typeset by Palimpsest Book Production Ltd.,
Grangemouth, Stirlingshire, Scotland.
Printed and bound in Great Britain by
MPG Books Ltd., Bodmin, Cornwall.

*Dedicated to my wife, Lynda,
without whom none of this would
have been possible.*

PROLOGUE

Old Sekston woke from his slumbers, uncertain of the sound that had roused him. He looked cautiously round the mistress's physick garden to make sure he had not been spotted, but could see no one. The weather had been too good to sit indoors cleaning Sir Humphrey's silver, so he had sneaked off from his duties to sit in the sun close beside the apple trees that hid him from the house. He resented the demeaning tasks they had found for him since he had been removed from his previous responsibilities. And he hated his master's wife for being the instrument of his downfall.

Mistress Ann Segrim's fate had once been entirely in his hands, for he had been tasked by her husband to keep an eye on her every move. He had been particularly warned about a master in Oxford, who sniffed around the mistress whenever she went to town to shop. Sir Humphrey suspected the master of breaking his vows of celibacy with his wife. Sekston had taken great pleasure in never allowing that to happen when he was present. But the mistress had at last had her revenge. She had finally convinced the master that he, Sekston, was too old to look after her when she went out and about. Sir Humphrey had had him replaced. Having for so long enjoyed the freedom of following her from place to place, he felt betrayed. Now he was confined to the estate at Botley polishing silver and chivvying lazy serving maids.

He eased back against the knobbly trunk of the old apple tree and sighed, half forgetting the noise that had roused him. He closed his eyes and revelled in the sun warming his wrinkled old features. Then he heard the noise again. He started up and cupped a hand to his ear. It had sounded like a low moan but he was not certain whether it was a human or animal sound. Then he heard it once more. Definitely human, and coming from just outside of the walled garden that was Ann Segrim's pride and joy. Fearfully, he pushed himself up on all fours, and levered his creaky limbs so he was finally standing. He tiptoed towards the door in the south side of the wall.

When he got there, he pressed his ear against the weather-beaten wood. He was sure he could now hear some muttering. It sounded like a prayer. Carefully, he inched the door open.

On the path outside that led back to the manor house, he could see a man kneeling down with his back to him. A tall man dressed in a shabby black robe. He looked vaguely familiar to Sekston, but his eyes were not so good and he couldn't make him out properly. There was also a shape at the man's feet that looked like a bundle of clothes. He began to creep towards the man, who seemed engrossed in his prayers. If that's what the muttering was. As he got closer, Sekston realized the bundle of clothes looked quite like the dress that he had seen his mistress wearing that morning. A fine blue robe that had looked well with her pale-yellow braided hair. In fact, he could now make out her long braid lying across the path. A small broken pot lay close by with some nasty-looking fluid dribbling out of the shattered base. What had happened? Had Mistress Ann been carrying the pot and fallen? Then he saw the bloody flux that pooled around her mouth and head. He let out a sudden groan and the man turned abruptly round.

At that same instant, Sekston saw the bloody stains all over the man's hands. And he knew why the figure had been familiar. It was the man Sir Humphrey had warned him about, the Regent Master of the University of Oxford. William Falconer.

Thomas Symon was seriously contemplating his future. Now that he had passed all the required examinations at the university, he had to decide how he was to earn his keep. Henry Ely, the parish priest of his local village who had supported him at Oxford, would want to be relieved of his burden. After seven years, it was time for Thomas to repay his debt. But he desperately did not wish to return to his family's village. His eyes had been opened to the full panoply of knowledge that the university offered. He could not go back to settling petty disputes between neighbours and teaching illiterate children their catechism. But what else could he do? He sighed and stared out of the narrow window that looked out on to St John's Street. The view, like his future, seemed dark and restricted. Then the main door of the hall swung open with a jarring crash. Startled, Thomas stood up and turned to see

who had so abruptly broken into his thoughts. The crooked
figure of Peter Bullock, the town constable, stood framed in
the doorway.

'Peter? What on earth has happened?'

Bullock stepped into the hall, his hand clutched tight on
the hilt of his old sword that hung at his waist. Thomas could
not recall ever seeing the constable without this weapon by
his side. It was his badge of office and, though the metal was
rusty and the edge blunt, it served Peter well. Many a fight
had been broken up by the judicious application of the flat of
the blade on a drunken head. Bullock was clearly in a hurry
and his answer came between pauses to catch his breath.

'Master Thomas, you must come. It's William.'

Thomas Symon felt a cold chill run down his back. William
Falconer was his mentor and friend. What could be wrong?

'Is he hurt?'

Bullock's rheumy old eyes closed and he shook his head,
not believing what he was about to say. When he spoke it was
in short gasps as though he was forcing the truth out from
between his lips.

'No, he is not hurt. It is far worse. He is taken. For murder.'

Thomas followed the constable to Bocardo, the jail set in the
thick town walls beside North Gate. The heavy oak door had
an iron grill set in it and anyone could look inside to see
whoever was interred within, the intention being to show
everyone who passed what the fate of a malefactor was like.
The cell was bare of any comfort, even decent straw for the
floor. Thomas now peered through the grill. He saw Falconer
sitting on the slimy floor, hunched up against the cold and
damp of the cell. Bereft of any expression, his eyes stared
dully into space. Thomas had never seen them so empty before.
Falconer's gaze was usually so piercing, often with a hint of
mischief in the eyes. Thomas recalled how he had looked at
his Inception when Falconer had played that trick on Ralph
Cornish. Now his eyes were voids, as if his soul had been
taken and his body was only waiting for death.

'He has been like this since he was brought here.' Bullock's
voice was low, as if in the presence of the dead. 'He will not
talk to me. And he apparently offered no resistance to the
labourers who were called by Sekston to help take him.'

Thomas frowned, puzzled by the reference to the old retainer from Sir Humphrey Segrim's estate in Botley.

'Sekston? What had he to do with this?'

'It was he who found William. And the body. He called for help, fearful for his own safety. But as I said, William waited patiently until the field labourers who responded to Sekston's call came and bound his wrists. They brought him here without any trouble. He didn't even object when my watchman locked him away and went off to fetch me.'

The constable squeezed hard on Thomas's shoulder. 'See if he will talk to you.'

Thomas peered once again into Bocardo. It was clear Falconer had not moved an inch since he had last looked.

'Master Falconer . . . William . . . what has happened here? Will you tell me?'

Despite his wheedling tones, Thomas could not get a response out of the prisoner. He turned back to Bullock.

'Who is it he is supposed to have killed, anyway? You did not say.'

Bullock swallowed hard, as though he were choking back tears.

'It's . . . Mistress Segrim. Ann.'

As though Ann's very name had penetrated into his daze, Falconer's voice could be heard echoing from his cell.

'Thomas? Is that you? For God's sake, take care of Saphira.'

PART ONE
THE CRIME

ONE

A week earlier

Young Thomas Symon raised the long knife blade uncertainly, hesitated and looked at his mentor. The older
man nodded grimly. Thomas gritted his teeth and
plunged the knife into the pale-pink flesh stretched out on the
table between them. The taut skin yielded beneath the cruelly
sharp blade, and peeled apart as Thomas drew the blade down
his victim's belly. Surprisingly little blood oozed out of the
wound. But then the subject of their attention was already
dead, and much of the blood had previously been drained
from the incision made in the neck region. Thomas was encour-
aged by the first cut he had made and proceeded to enlarge
the opening. His aim was to reveal the viscera lurking within.
His mentor had killed their victim in some unspecified way
earlier that morning. It was now his job to uncover the cause
of death. Soon he had a shimmering, greyish-pink mass of
organs revealed as he pulled back the resilient flesh.

He was already sweating, and made to wipe the beads of
sweat gathering on his upper lip with the back of his hand.
The older man grabbed his wrist in a steel-like grip.

'Stop right there, Thomas. Remember what happened to
Richard.'

Thomas stared at his blood-smeared fingers, which he had
carelessly almost wiped across his mouth, and shuddered. He
nodded in acknowledgement, and crossed to the barrel of water
on the other side of the cellar where they worked. He plunged
his hands into the icy water, vigorously washing them. Then
he lowered his face into the water, cooling both himself and
his nerve-endings. Lifting his head up, he flicked the water
off his dark locks and looked across the well-lit basement
room at William.

'I will not forget in a hurry.'

Master Richard Bonham – the man of whom the two spoke
– had on the surface been a quiet, grey figure of a man.

Apparently a deeply religious and conventionally-minded teacher at the University of Oxford, he had hidden a secret in his heart, and in the cellar of his house close by St Michael's at North Gate. When Thomas Symon had first come to Oxford as a student clerk more than seven years earlier, he had seen something that made him think Bonham was a murderer. He had stumbled on the man with a wicked blade in his hand and a corpse in his cellar. Bonham had turned out to be innocent of murder, though his secret was almost as dangerous. What he was revealed to be was no more nor less than an anatomist. His obsession had been to understand God's work in the form of the human body. An obsession he had to hide as anatomizing bodies was largely proscribed. Unless the body was that of a murderer, in which case the offender had forfeited any right to have their remains treated with reverence. Bonham's obsession had come to the attention of Regent Master William Falconer, who himself had an unhealthy obsession with death, and Bonham had ended up helping William in establishing cause of death in many strange cases of murder.

But in this fifty-sixth year of Henry of Winchester's reign, the third king of that name, in the year of Our Lord 1272, Bonham had contracted a dreadful disease due to some carelessness on his part when handling a body. When his house had burned down with him inside it, everyone had lamented the tragic accident. But William knew Bonham had sacrificed his life, and perhaps his immortal soul, to prevent the spread of typhus to others. Now, as Thomas Symon learned the skills of anatomy for himself, William was determined that a similar act of carelessness should not befall him. Regent Master William Falconer patted Thomas on the shoulder, drawing him back to his task.

'Come. This elderly pig, which only yesterday was rooting in my backyard, calls for your attention to establish how I so foully slew her. And do hurry – my students are impatiently waiting for a good meal made from its carcass. Moreover, I have matters to attend to before you and other students of mine undertake Inception.'

Thomas smiled secretively. He knew what was on the regent master's mind; it had been the talk of the university for days now. Inception was the final step in the young students' process of qualifying as a Master, where they had to maintain a thesis in debate against any opponent. But on many occasions older regent masters used the days of the ceremony to throw out challenges to their peers by questioning the skill of their students. Just such an encounter was predicted in two days' time. The rumour abroad was that Regent Master Ralph Cornish was preparing to debate with Falconer. Thomas didn't reckon that such a public debate between William and Ralph could hold any fears for Falconer. Ralph Cornish was a regent master who stuck to the orthodox views on everything, whereas Falconer's mind ranged freely on a myriad subjects. Thomas was sure his mentor and regent master would run rings round Ralph in a debate. And he told William so.

'Master Ralph will be humiliated.'

Falconer smiled at Thomas's confidence in his abilities, and certainly he was not afraid of the impending encounter. He was only worried that he might speak his mind too openly. He had a habit of getting into trouble with the establishment of the university, and in consequence the Church.

'I have prepared my debating points. And anyway, if matters should go against me I have a little surprise in store.'

Thomas Symon raised a quizzical eyebrow, but Falconer would say no more. Turning back to the beast on the table, the young man pointed at a small tear in the pig's heart.

'This pig was killed by a thin blade being pushed through his chest and into his heart.'

Falconer patted him on the back.

'Very well done. Now wash your hands in the vinegar water and we will eat.'

Sir Humphrey Segrim held on grimly to the gunwales of the little cog that had carried him across the Channel from Normandy. As it beat its way up the Thames on the incoming tide, he held his heaving stomach in check. He reasoned that it was the pork he had eaten in the dingy harbour tavern at Honfleur that afflicted him. It must have been bad. Now, he calmed the bubbling surge in his belly by scanning the level mud flats of the estuary. Then he cast a fearful look behind him to once again convince himself that the Templar was no longer on his tail. The broad, brown waters of the Thames Estuary bore only small craft dodging from shore to shore and into the various inlets. He breathed a sigh of relief.

'Thank God my ploy of leaving from Honfleur has got rid of him.'

'What's that, Master?'

The whining Essex tones of the little vessel's skipper reminded Segrim that there was precious little privacy on the small boat. Indeed, he had not realized he had expressed his relief out loud. He covered up his slip.

'I said – when will we be landing?'

'Not long, Master. The tide will not be at the full for a long time and we shall be at Shadwell steps soon. But are you sure you wish to disembark in the middle of nowhere? We will easily make Queenhithe before the tide turns.'

Segrim shook his head vigorously.

'No, no! The middle of nowhere suits me fine.'

The cog's skipper shot his passenger a strange look and shrugged his shoulders. The heavy-set old knight who had sidled up to him in Honfleur harbour had seemed furtive from the start, as though he had something to hide. But if he did, then the skipper cared not in the least. His wish to be dropped outside of London was his own business. Let the man drag his heels through the mud of Shadwell if he wanted. He was paying handsomely enough. The skipper jingled the coins he had earned in his well-stuffed purse and cast an expert eye over the sails of the sturdy cog that was his home from home. He knew a short stop at Shadwell would not delay him much and the taverns of Queenhithe would be all the sweeter for it. A sudden cross-current lifted the bow of the boat abruptly. It lurched, and the passenger threw up the contents of his stomach over the side.

In the end, Falconer eschewed the pork stew for himself. He had decided to call on Saphira that night and did not want the odour of a forbidden animal on his clothes. Or on his lips. It was some months now since Saphira Le Veske, a Jew from France, had surprised him with her forthrightness. For weeks since she had turned up in Oxford, they had performed a decorous dance around each other's feelings. Then she had stopped his dithering by simply offering him her naked body.

He had revelled in her red-haired charms many times since, regularly breaking his notional vow of celibacy. A regent master of the university was supposed to be in holy orders of a sort, but many took the stricture with a pinch of salt. The rules really only meant that he could not marry and Falconer had indeed been celibate for many years before meeting Saphira. Except for the occasional romp with a pleasant whore from the stews of Beaumont, which didn't count. His very public friendship with Mistress Ann Segrim had remained unconsummated, despite what others thought. She was the wife of Sir Humphrey Segrim of the Manor of Botley, and though the marriage was essentially a sham, still Ann held to her vows.

Perhaps that was why their friendship had not withstood the arrival of Saphira Le Veske in Oxford some months ago. The Jewish widow was all passion and fiery charm, where Ann was cool and composed. Falconer had not stood a chance. Yet he regretted the estrangement from Mistress Segrim and resolved to reinstate their friendship as soon as he could. But tonight he was to devote his time to Saphira.

Or so he thought.

Saphira was renting a house in Fish Street that belonged to her cousin Abraham. The front door was noticeable for a gouge in its surface caused by an axe. An axe which had almost split Falconer's head open. It had been during a riot when the Jews of the town had been under attack for an imagined offence against the Christians. Saphira had dragged Falconer indoors just in time to save his brains from being splattered across her doorstep. The door had suffered badly from the blow, however, and the mark still marred the surface. But Falconer did not use this front entrance to Saphira's house. For the sake of her reputation, and not really his own, he used the rear access to her house via Kepeharm Lane. This evening, he did not get as far as the narrow alley, however. As he passed her front door, Saphira came hurrying out, almost bowling him over.

'Whoa!' He grabbed her arm, halting her headlong progress and smiled ruefully. 'I did not think to meet so publicly as this.'

'William! How nice to see you. Was I expecting you? I am in rather a hurry.'

She smiled up at Falconer who was a head taller than her. He grinned and reached out to tuck a stray red curl back under the modest snood she wore in public. As a widow and a Jew, there were certain niceties to observe. Niceties that had no place in the privacy of her home, however. He had felt the lithe form of her body as they had collided, and marvelled again at the sleekness of her shape even though she was forty years of age. A twinge of disappointment shot through him.

'You are going somewhere? I had thought we might . . . talk.'

Saphira pulled a face, expressing her regret.

'I am sorry, William. Truly I am. But Samson has promised to teach me a little more about herbs and cure-alls. He has an alembic bubbling nicely and it will not wait for any man.' She pressed her hand against his chest. 'Even you.'

Falconer felt the heat of her hand through his robe. He was filled with desire for her, but knew that Saphira had recently conceived a desire to learn more about the art of herbs and their use in medicine. Samson the Jew was not getting any younger and had no one to pass his knowledge on to. His only child was Hannah, who though dutiful, had no desire to learn the secrets from her father. And although she had recently married Deudone, her new husband too showed little interest in the esoteric art. Saphira could not bear to let the knowledge lodged in Samson's brain be lost and had spent weeks learning the basics. Now she was entering the next stage of her studies and had become an eager student. She saw the look of disappointment on William's face and squeezed his arm discreetly.

'Come later tonight, if you can. But beware, for I am learning about poisons. Today Samson is telling me how to concoct the most lethal of brews.'

She grinned at him and with a swirl of her favourite green gown, strode off down Jewry Lane.

TWO

Sir Humphrey Segrim had instantly regretted his decision to disembark secretly at Shadwell. Only after the sturdy little cog that had brought him safely across the Channel had drifted away from the dock on the tide, did he look round. There was nothing but a rickety wharf and stinking tan yards. The smell of piss was overwhelming and no one was in sight. He had slumped down on his oak chest that contained all his armour and spare clothes and stared disconsolately over the mud flats towards London. In evading the Templar, he had landed himself in the middle of nowhere. He was safe for now, but could see nothing for it except to trust his worldly goods to luck, and to walk along the bank of the Thames towards Wapping. At least there would be someone there who could arrange his passage to Oxford. He had wearily hauled himself to his feet and trudged off into the mud.

Now, he sat in a dark, low-ceilinged inn perilously perched over the banks of the river Thames, drinking weak ale and eating an unidentifiable chunk of burned meat. All around him sat rough-looking workmen with big beefy hands that bore the scars of heavy rope and manual labour. They eyed Segrim with curiosity. He was a man well advanced in years, with long grey hair and a beard he had cultivated in the East. His skin was reddened by his journey, but he had the unmistakeable bearing of a nobleman. His tunic, though caked with mud along its hem, was of fine cloth. He clutched his purse nervously and cursed the fact he had left all his weapons except a dagger in the oak chest in Shadwell.

'I have arranged a cart, Master. Jed will collect your chest and be back in no time.'

Segrim was startled by the sudden appearance of the scrawny man at his shoulder. He reckoned the fellow must be a thief to be able to pad around so quietly. He had seen Segrim looking lost on Wapping quay and offered his services. With no alternative, Sir Humphrey had given him a small coin and enlisted him in the recovery of his chest. Now, it seemed the rescue party was swollen by another man called Jed, who would no doubt also want paying. Segrim wondered if his purse would stand it, and if he would ever see his property again. Or his home and estate in Botley. He appeared to have fallen from one hot pan into another. Though he acknowledged that Osbert Smith – as the scrawny thief called himself – was to be preferred to the Templar. It might be like having to choose between facing either a slippery snake or a wild boar head on, but Segrim knew which he preferred. Chances are a snake like Osbert would slither into the undergrowth if threatened with a stick.

'Sir, would you like another jug of ale?'

Segrim observed the man, who stood before him wringing a shabby felt hat in his calloused hands. He shuddered at the thought of drinking any more of the stale beer, that he was sure was just dipped directly out of the Thames. It had the same muddy brown appearance as the river.

'No, Osbert. But you can take one for yourself.'

The little thief grinned as another coin was pressed into his palm, and waved his hand imperiously at the innkeeper.

Segrim stepped out of the inn, leaving the odour of sweat and stale clothes, and stood inhaling the less dank airs of the marshy river. As he stood at the quay, he saw a large sailed vessel, its sides black with pitch, drift by. It looked grand and yet at the same time dark and demonic to Segrim. It was no doubt on its stately way to Queenhithe and a more commodious landing than Segrim had found in Shadwell.

As the sun descended in the sky, a golden glow sparkled along the rippling surface of the river. The ship seemed to glide effortlessly over this gilded surface. A beam of sunlight caught on something shiny, high on the stern of the demon ship. It must have been the sparkle of well-oiled chain mail or a polished helm. Segrim screwed up his eyes, which could no longer see clearly over such a great distance. An imposing figure stood at the stern rail of the ship, holding casually on to a halliard that ran up into the rigging. For a moment Segrim was convinced that it was the Templar, and that the man was staring directly at him with those crazy green eyes of his. Then, as suddenly as it had come, the apparition was past. Segrim shuddered, turning away from the river and its traffic. He needed to get to London as soon as possible and arrange his passage to the safety of his estate near Oxford.

Falconer rose early the next day. Despite his dismissal of the importance of his possible debate with Ralph Cornish, he could not stop his brain from scurrying back and forth over arguments and ideas. He had sat through Thomas's simple disputes of Vesperies the night before, after which it had been too late to return to Saphira's house. He regretted the omission at the time but was determined to support his favourite student as he took his final steps to becoming a master of the university. The boy was on the verge of his final test. Boy? Thomas Symon was a young man in his twenties, and far more level-headed than Falconer had been at that age. He had thrown up his studies for a life on the roads and merchant routes of Europe, sometimes earning his keep as a mercenary soldier. It had only been the recollection of the encouragement given him by a certain Franciscan friar that had lured him back to learning. Roger Bacon had been teaching at Oxford when Falconer first arrived and had shown him what a good brain he had. His yearnings to see the world, though, had torn him away from the man later dubbed Doctor Mirabilis. But the bond had always remained. Falconer had eventually settled down to study at the University of Bologna, only to return to Oxford in 1250.

He could not believe that twenty-two years had passed since that fateful day. But scrubbing his fingers through his greying locks and feeling the natural tonsure that was growing atop his skull, convinced him that time was indeed passing. It did not seem seven years since Thomas Symon had arrived in Oxford in the middle of a particularly nasty set of murders. But today he would complete his studies and become a master himself. He would have his Inception into the university. And Falconer would encounter Ralph Cornish. He grinned at the thought of Ralph Cornish thinking he could ambush Thomas with his disputations, merely to humiliate William himself. Ralph's tenet was that, if the student was shown to be foolish, then the mentor must be also. But what Ralph did not know was that Falconer had prepared a surprise for him that had nothing to do with cold intellect. Ralph would be caught like a rabbit in a trap. Falconer looked at the long paper tube lying amidst the jumble on his work table. He tapped it tentatively with a finger and grinned like a naughty little boy.

Morning in Oxford that day was beginning exactly as any other day in the town, except for Sunday, of course. The sun had barely begun to warm the streets before the sellers of fish and meat began to open the shutters of their narrow-fronted shops. Long before being a university town, Oxford had been the marketplace for the region. A crossroads of trade. In fact, the main streets of Oxford were like four arms of a great cross, apparently lying on its side from east to west. It defined the shape of the town. These unusually broad avenues were filled with shops, each with its own customary site on the cross's arms. A traveller entering from the east would stroll past the pig-market, kept close to the edge of town, then wood-merchants, purveyors of earthenware, gloves, bread and dairy produce. From the south another traveller passed first the fire-wood sellers, then fishmongers, tanners, faggot sellers until he passed the crossroads and encountered the corn-merchants below the north gate. Here the impressive gate, stoutly built because there was no protection from the marsh and rivers on this side, housed the Bocardo. The town's prison.

It was as though the sun had stirred an ants' nest with its rays. Townspeople, intent on the business of the day, came scurrying out of the narrow streets that linked the broad avenues. And from the vennel, or passage, set in the narrow frontage of each house, emerged the shopkeepers and metal-beaters, ready for the arrival of their life's-blood. Those with money to spend.

Saphira Le Veske was an early riser normally, but last night she had been awake almost till dawn. So the daily noise of Oxford's market beginning did little to rouse her from her stupor. She stirred languorously in the warmth of her bed, and wondered if William had come to her back door last night only to find her not at home. A momentary regret at missing their assignation crossed her mind. But then she began to mull over what she had learned from Samson. She had not been joking when she had told William that she was learning about poisons. That was the dangerous knowledge that the old man had led her through last night and on into the early hours. She had exhausted Samson and herself with her eagerness to learn. She once again pictured the scene.

Samson had cautiously opened his door in response to her knock, his lined face peering out. The grizzled locks, hanging either side of his old face, gave him the look of the very Devil incarnate. But his strong visage and sparkling eyes did not correspond to the reserved manner that defined the man. And few outside the Jews who lived in Oxford knew of his secret skills, not only in medicines but also in poisons. If the Christians in whose midst he lived guessed at this knowledge, he would have been singled out for special attention and, even worse, persecution. So he lived a secret life inside a secretive community. He was getting old now, however, and Saphira hated the idea of his knowledge dying with him. She had begun to mine that fund of information, and the night was going to be about poisons.

Samson pulled her in by her arm and slammed the heavy oaken door closed behind him. He dexterously slid a wooden bolt across the back of the door; only then did he speak.

'Saphira. Welcome. Come with me.'

He crooked a finger and trotted off down the dark passageway, his black robes billowing in his wake. Saphira, who knew his odd ways, smiled and followed her new master. The room at the back of the house was like her own, at least on the surface. A kitchen with a large open fire dominated one wall, and in the centre of the room stood a well-worn table for preparing vegetables and meats. But that was where the resemblance ended. The table was not set up to accommodate Jewish dietary laws, nor any other form of food preparation. Instead, its surface was covered with pots and jars. Strange aromas filled the kitchen, coming mainly from the pot that bubbled over the fire. Samson had hurried over to it and was stirring gently.

'Forgive me, child, for being so abrupt, but the concoction needs my full attention.'

Saphira smiled coyly at being called a child and even found herself blushing a little. This old man indeed made her feel once more like a child learning its alphabet. Except he was teaching her ways of poisoning people. He pointed to the brew on the fire.

'Albertus Magnus himself wrote down this recipe. It is arsenic boiled in milk and can be used to kill flies. He also recommends a mixture of white lime, opium and black hellebore painted on the walls to the same purpose. This preparation . . .' He took one of the jars from the table and lifted the lid, showing it to Saphira. '. . . This is the herb henbane which Pliny says can be used to cure earache. Though he does warn it can cause mental disorders.'

Saphira peered in the pot and went to touch the contents. Samson cautioned her.

'Beware. Four leaves only shall induce the sleep of drunkenness from which you may never awake.'

Saphira had found herself wanting to know more. And more. Until the lecture had lasted into the early hours of the morning. Finally, Samson had fallen asleep over the big kitchen table and she had quietly let herself out of his house, stepping over the unseasonal frost that coated the cobbled street. Now, she lay enveloped in the warmth of a thick bearskin and played with the names she had learned.

'Mercury, gypsum, copper, iron, lapis lazuli, arsenic sublimate, lead.'

These were all powerful, strong words with powerful effects. But she preferred the names of the herbs and insects. She lay back with her eyes closed and recited her lethal catechism.

'Usnea, hellebore, bryony, nux vomica . . . serpentary. . . . cantharides.'

And the most evocative of them all.

'Cateputria.'

THREE

The interior of St Mary's Church was alive with the excitement of the moment. Twenty or thirty students were incepting today; they were at last becoming Masters of the great University of Oxford after seven years of study, disputation and reading. Far from being a solemn occasion, it was a lively event, and loud voices echoed into the vaulted ceiling of the church, which stood metaphorically at the centre of the university as it did physically in the town. A whole day had passed since Falconer had missed his assignation with Saphira, and he hoped she didn't think he was deliberately ignoring her. She surely understood that his students came first, and the previous day had been spent teaching and organizing the rowdy events that would follow Inception. Looking around him now at the uninhibited behaviour of some, it seemed that many clerks had already started consuming plentiful supplies of wine and ale. Even before they were incepted.

Falconer had to elbow his way unceremoniously through the throng of excited students, and their supporters and masters. He was looking for Thomas Symon, though he was keeping a weather eye for his adversary Ralph Cornish too. He didn't doubt that Ralph would see him first. Despite having a piercing stare that scared many of his young protégés nearly to death, he was very short-sighted and could not see far without eyeglasses. Though he avoided the finery indulged in by most other regent masters, especially on such a day as today, he was himself a tall man and stood out in a crowd.

All around him were masters bedecked in cappas or sleeveless copes bordered with many different types of fur. This they wore over a simple tunic, the colour of which ranged from black to purple and in some cases a less than sombre scarlet. And all wore the square biretta on their head. William was dressed differently. He wore the same black robe he was garbed in every day, its edges fraying and green with mould. Normally, he would be bareheaded too. But today he had given in to formality and wore a simple black pileus over his greying, unruly locks. It amused him that it closely resembled the cap worn by many of his Jewish friends.

'Master Falconer.'

He felt a hand on his arm and turned around. It was Thomas, his face alight with the excitement of the moment.

'Did you see? I have knelt before the chancellor and taken my oaths. All I need now do is to deliver my final disputation in the schools.'

In truth, Falconer had missed his student's presentation to Chancellor Thomas Bek. He had lingered too long under the window of Saphira Le Veske's bedroom, hoping to see her rise. But the shutter had remained firmly closed. By the time he had given up his quest and arrived at St Mary's, he had found himself at the back of the throng, and Thomas had already been presented to the chancellor. He did not want to disappoint the youth, however.

'Yes. You performed well. I am proud of you. And I look forward to your final disputation.'

His piercing blue eyes sparkled and he winked at Thomas Symon. Both were aware what was in store at the schools, though only Falconer knew the full facts. He gingerly touched the money pouch that hung at his waist, ensuring his little secret weapon was still there. Then Falconer took out his eyeglasses and held them to his face. The lenses had been carefully ground to his own specifications and mounted recently in a frame with folding arms that he could lodge on the top of his ears. But he was often too embarrassed to wear the heavy object as he thought it gave him the appearance of a dim-witted owl. A quick scan of the church, however, soon revealed Ralph Cornish. He was lurking on the opposite side of the church, partially in the shadows of the side aisle. He was talking animatedly to the chancellor, but as though he sensed Falconer's eyes on him, he suddenly turned. He stared hard at Falconer, a grim but determined look on his face, then continued speaking to Bek.

William did not seek to provoke him at this stage and took Thomas's arm. The two friends, mentor and former student, strolled out of the church and up the narrow lane by St Mary's western end. This brought them to the rooms that served as schools for the students of Oxford. Here, Thomas Symon would deliver his first lecture as master before the inevitable revelries began. Without looking back, Falconer knew that Cornish was following them, together with a gaggle of students and regent masters who had heard that an interesting debate was soon to be had.

The world of the university was an inbred community, where petty intellectual differences meant a great deal to those who devoted their lives to arguing the proverbial matter of angels on pinheads. Reputations stood or fell on the ability to outmanoeuvre one's fellow masters during convoluted arguments that meant nothing to the average citizen of the town the university infested. Sometimes more than reputations were concerned. If heresies were sniffed in the air, a master's very life might be forfeit. Falconer himself had sailed close to the wind on more than one occasion. He prayed that this time he would not give in to temptation and do the same again. The device in his purse was there to save him from himself.

Falconer rented the ground floor of an anonymous tenement in School Street, on the corner of St Mildred's Lane. It stood opposite Black Hall, where ironically Ralph Cornish governed a group of well-regulated clerks, who were rarely seen to misbehave on the streets of Oxford at night. If any one of them did, they were soon banished from Cornish's glowering gaze. He also recruited his wards from wealthy families, earning a pretty income in addition to the living he made as a priest somewhere locally. Falconer guessed that Cornish's annual remuneration far exceeded his own from his petty charge of six shillings per annum for each student. But despite his own poverty, Falconer had secretly funded Thomas's revels.

He knew the youth was himself from a poor family, and his backer was an impoverished clergyman who liked to help clever boys improve themselves. Henry Ely, though, could afford to help the youth no more. Symon would have to stand on his own two feet from now on. Together, Thomas and Falconer crossed the threshold of the tenement school to be greeted by a gaggle of cheering clerks who had got there before them. Someone had stacked the long benches that normally filled up the floor along one wall to make more space. The single piece of furniture left in place was the high desk where the master sat. Falconer indicated it with a sweep of his arm, and Thomas sat behind it nervously. But then Thomas recalled his mentor's informal approach to teaching, which he had copied on a number of occasions when he had given lectures to younger students as part of his training. More confidently, he stood up and stepped to one side of the desk as he had often seen William do. Like his mentor, he would not have a barrier between him and his students.

He scanned the eager and happy faces, noting that the room was packed tight as even more soberly-clad clerks and masters squeezed into the room. He could not see Ralph Cornish, but William Falconer stood head and shoulders above most of the people in the room. He saw the encouraging look on his mentor's face and began his uncontroversial lecture on the interpretation of Aristotle's teaching by his own namesake, Thomas of Aquino.

In a day and a half, Segrim had only managed to travel as far as the small market town of Berkhamsted before heavy rains cut his journey short. The speed of his journey had been impaired by the necessity of keeping an eye on Osbert. Humphrey now found that he couldn't shake the Londoner off, even if he had wanted to. The skinny man from Wapping had first convinced Humphrey to entrust the conveying of his oak chest to him. The chest held weapons, heavy chain mail and a metal helm, along with extra clothes and a few trinkets from the Holy Lands. So the trust did not go further than Segrim's eyesight. He had watched carefully as the chest had been roped to the back of a packhorse, which Osbert then insisted he lead by its halter. But it was then Osbert's contention that for him to walk, while the knight rode, would delay Segrim unconscionably. His master would have to hire a horse for his servant and Osbert knew just where to get a bargain. So now, Osbert sat himself upon a nag almost as scrawny as he was. But he sat on it proudly. Of course, it was Segrim who had been persuaded to pay for it all.

Still, the nag could not keep up with Humphrey's more powerful destrier and they had arrived late in Berkhamsted, on the afternoon of the second day on the road. Here, the increasingly impoverished knight was lucky to find himself a room in the only inn in the town, as the place was crowded with people who were there for market day. Osbert had to settle for a bed of straw in the stables along with the horses. But Segrim knew he would still find his purse even emptier because of such accommodation.

His fear of the Templar drove him upstairs at the inn, where he spent a long hour staring out the unglazed window at the Norman castle opposite. Perched on the ancient mound across the river, the dark slits in the gloomy stones glowered at him menacingly. But finally he could stand it no more and he decided that he had evaded the man who had dogged him across Europe. He could safely show himself in the inn's main room downstairs, if only for the sake of the fire that glowed there. His room, high under the thatched eaves of the inn, was icily cold and damp. He descended the rickety stairs and surveyed the long narrow room below. The rain had driven many farmers and cattle dealers into it, and the air was thick with damp clothes and animal smells. Segrim eased his way into a corner seat with a high back designed to keep out draughts. He waved an imperious arm at the innkeeper who scuttled over with a jug of sweet ale and some cold meats. Soon he was settled comfortably into the privacy of his secluded corner, and dozed off. But his sleep was disturbed by dreams of the Templar.

To Segrim's fevered mind, the Templar took on proportions bigger than the man in real life. And even then he was tall and imposing. Now he loomed nightmarishly large over Sir Humphrey, who cowered in fear. In his seat in the Berkhamsted inn his sleeping self whined fearfully. Segrim dreamed he was in the Church of St Silvester in Viterbo once again, its nave stretching long and dreamlike away from him for leagues. At the end of this tunnel stood the altar, seemingly high and towering above the heads of the congregation, who were all baying in warlike fashion at the sight in front of them. Kneeling at the altar was the blood-drenched figure of a man dressed in crusader garb, his chain mail rent by long gashes. Still he tried to say his prayers. But his murderers were giving him no quarter. Three men rained blows down on this man and his tabard was made crimson by his own blood. One of the killers finally turned and strode towards the shivering form of Sir Humphrey. His legs ate up the huge distance between them in a trice. His voice bellowed out a threat, as he waved his bloodied sword.

'It's you next, Segrim.'

Sir Humphrey tried to move his limbs but they were frozen. He tried to cry out in fear. His whimpers caused the innkeeper, known by the name of Roger Brewer, to roughly shake him by the shoulder.

'Are you all right, Master?'

Segrim woke up, swallowed the bitter bile that was rising in his throat, and shrugged off Roger's hand. He covered his embarrassment with an angry rebuff.

'Bad memories. If you had seen what I have in the Holy Land, you would understand.'

He left the man to create his own images of battles with the Saracens, of blood in the sand and lopped-off limbs. It clearly worked, for the innkeeper rushed off to bring him another jug of ale, returning to wave off the offer of payment. In truth, Roger Brewer, who had never travelled further than the manor boundary, probably knew as much about Outremer as his distinguished guest. Sir Humphrey Segrim, a man of around fifty years, had taken the cross in a moment of drunken bravado. He had wanted to prove to his cold and uncaring wife that he still had the spice in him for combat. He had soon regretted his actions.

Crossing the channel had been miserable enough, the contents of his last meal on dry land being heaved incautiously into the wind that had sprung up almost as soon as they had left the shelter of England's coastline. He had then tremblingly splashed water from the drinking barrel over his face and clothes to wash his own vomit off him. The rest of the journey he had sat shivering on the heaving deck feeling both wet and miserable. Ahead of him he knew were weeks of travel. So he had been glad to fall in with a robust and well-built bearded man wearing the garb of a Templar. The man had been reluctant to give his name but Segrim felt sure the Templar liked his company. They were both Latins after all, and due to be travelling in foreign lands. Segrim determined to stick with his new companion.

Master Thomas Symon was drawing to the close of his uncontroversial lecture on Aristotle and the interpretation of his views by Aquinas. He had chosen this subject to please William Falconer, who was a devotee of Aristotle in all his aspects. Thomas was a little more circumspect than his mentor and thereby he hoped to stimulate William to expound his own views. But the interruption, when it came, was from another quarter. The crowd at the back of the congested school room moved apart and like a surge on the top of a wave, Ralph Cornish pushed forward. His robe was a sombre black but his cappa was trimmed with dark fur; the traditional biretta set square on his head. His opening words made it obvious where he was going to take this debate.

'And where do you stand, Master Symon, on Averroism?'

There was a murmur of excitement in the throng. It was well known that the Church was perturbed by the spread of what it called radical Aristoteleanism and Averroism in the universities of Europe. There was a conviction that the ideas challenged the very foundations of faith. Thomas gulped and tried to marshal his thoughts. This was deep water for his fresh and unskilled mind. As he took a breath to speak – though he knew not what he would say – another voice, firm and strong, cut through the hubbub.

'Perhaps I might be allowed, as Master Symon's teacher, to elucidate his thoughts for him.'

It was Falconer who spoke and Thomas breathed a sigh of relief, while feeling cowardly at the same time. In the schools there was a hush as Falconer stepped forward. The gathering formed a circle, with the two protagonists in the centre and an open space between them. It was as if the crowd imagined the two regent masters were about to fight each other. And indeed they were – but the only blows landed would be verbal. This is what everyone present had come for, and after a pause, Falconer continued.

'I would hope that Master Thomas, as an assiduous pupil of mine, understands Aristotle just as well as his namesake from Aquino, who learned his Aristotle from Albert of Cologne.'

Ralph snorted in contempt.

'Albertus Magnus was no more than Aristotle's ape.'

'Yes, I have heard that criticism applied to him. If criticism it be. And there is much about Albert's thinking with which I would disagree. But most of what we know of Aristotle comes from him. And from the writings of Averroës.'

'From where we have the heresy of the beginninglessness of the universe.'

There was a hiss from the assembled crowd. Here was the heart of the matter. Ralph's reference to 'beginninglessness' touched on a dangerous conundrum. If God had created the world, as He surely had, then how could the universe have no beginning? Falconer smiled and eased into an argument he had rehearsed many times.

'But since the beginning of the world cannot be demonstratively proved, then the universe could have existed without beginning to exist. If you held an open mind, Ralph, you would perceive that. If you applied reason . . .'

Many of those present began to snigger as Falconer turned the tables. Ralph could contain his anger no longer.

'What has reason to do with an article of faith? Two years ago in Paris, Bishop Tempier condemned the false belief that the world is eternal as to all the species contained in it; and that time is eternal. Or motion, matter, agent and recipient.'

He crossed his arms over his chest, puffed up with pride at quoting the bishop's words exactly. He gazed in triumph at Falconer.

'And as for reason, I know you as an alchemist and a refuter of the mystical in the natural world. As if the world had made itself and operated without God's wisdom.'

'On the contrary, I am inclined to the mystical and the beliefs of the good Abbot Joachim, who saw an age when the Just would rule and the hierarchy of the Church, exemplified by such fools as Tempier, would be unnecessary.'

Some present were now openly laughing at Cornish and Falconer could see that Ralph's face was becoming redder and redder, as if he would explode. But he realized he had once again gone too far and said too much. He had just suggested that the church hierarchy was not needed. It was time to turn the serious debate on its head. He felt carefully in his pouch and positioned himself close to one of the lighted candles that illuminated the room. Ralph was pointing an accusatory finger.

'I knew it. The Synod of Arles declared these ideas heretical. You are a Joachimite, like your fellow scientist, Friar Bacon.'

Falconer held the little paper tube close to the candle flame and watched it ignite. He held it for a few seconds longer.

'And like Roger I understand the physical world. And can control it.'

He tossed the burning tube at Ralph's feet and held his hands over his ears. The paper fizzed for a few seconds, then the package exploded with a green flash and a sound fit to burst the eardrums. Ralph reeled backwards, as grey smoke filled the room. The hem of his expensive robe was on fire and he hopped around trying to beat it out. After the initial shock, and stunned silence, wholesale laughter rang round the room, though few could hear it clearly. Everyone's ears, save those of William Falconer, had been robbed of sound other than a dull ringing. Ralph saw he was the butt of the joke and pointed once again at Falconer.

'Joachimite. Alchemist. Fornicator. You will pay for this.'

On which threat he stormed from the room.

FOUR

'It was merely what Roger calls a firecracker. He played the same trick himself some years ago. But memories are apparently short in Oxford and no one recalled it.'

Falconer was helping Thomas Symon clear up the school room in the aftermath of the celebration. A lot of food and ale had been consumed after Ralph Cornish's disappearance. More than either William or Thomas could really afford, but jollity had ruled for some considerable while. Falconer scuffed his boot over the black mark on the floor where the firecracker had exploded. Thomas had rebuked him for his childish effort. His attitude to the prank had indeed made Falconer feel like a naughty boy and he was now beginning to regret what he had done.

'Blame Roger Bacon. He left me two recipes for the powder. One lists saltpetre, sulphur and charcoal of hazelwood. But there is a more complicated one too. The trouble is he left half the ingredients as a code . . . Luru Vopo Vir Can Utriet.'

Thomas looked quizzically at Falconer.

'What does that mean?'

Falconer shrugged.

'I took it to give the amounts required. Seven parts to five to five. From the strength of the explosion, it looks as though I was wrong.'

The two masters looked at each other and then burst into laughter. Thomas was jubilant.

'Did you see the way Master Ralph danced? Just like he was possessed by the Devil.'

Falconer's face turned quite solemn.

'Let us hope that is not truly so. It is Aristotle's view that evil can be defined as the lack of, or reduced presence, of God. Ralph is a fool but he is not evil.'

Thomas was now surprised at his mentor's mention of God. Just as he had been when during the debate, Falconer had expressed his adherence to the mystic Abbot Joachim. Though he never dared broach the subject, he had always assumed

Falconer lacked any true faith. Now it seemed he was wrong and Falconer had surprised him once again. Quietly, the two Masters, old and new, finished tidying the school room and left for Aristotle's Hall.

The spicer's shop was a great attraction to Saphira. Before coming to England in her search for an errant son who had run off when her husband died, she had lived in France. There, spices from the East were particularly relished when mixed with the red wines of Bordeaux. England was a dour place in comparison, especially Canterbury and London, where she had stayed for a while when first arriving on these shores. It was only when she had met William Falconer, and then had rashly found herself pursuing him to Oxford, that the cold, wet weather seemed to get less burdensome. To find a treasure house of spices in the market in Oxford had been particularly welcome. The spicer, Robert Bodin by name, was a large, red-faced man, whose joviality hid a sharp acquisitive nature. No one would cheat him out of the tiniest part of a pennyworth when he weighed out his precious goods.

Whenever Saphira entered his shop, her eyes roved greedily over his expensive wares. All sorts of goods brought from Syria and Cyprus and the East were on display in sacks and barrels. She sniffed the air and recognized the pungent aromas of cumin, ginger, cinnamon and nutmeg. But the barrels were also stuffed with almonds, liquorice, figs and dates. Though Saphira had now settled in Oxford and employed a maid-servant to see to her immediate needs, she still liked to make her own purchases. Especially at the spicer's, when her newly acquired knowledge of medicinal herbs and remedies for poisons still buzzed in her head.

Today, Robert was dealing with a tall lady whose long blonde hair was bound tightly under a modest snood. Much as Saphira's own flame-red hair was when in public. Though her back was to Saphira, she could tell the lady, dressed in a rich, blue robe, was calm to the extent of coolness. And this was all in spite of her short, stocky maid who fidgeted unmerci-fully and touched everything that the lady made a move to sample. Aware someone else had come into the shop, the servant turned to stare boldly back at Saphira. The dark hairs on her upper lip and chin unfortunately gave her the appearance of one of those monkeys the men returning from the Holy Lands liked to bring home. Saphira suddenly realized she knew her. Her name was Margery, which meant the other woman in Robert's shop had to be Ann Segrim, who she knew was a former intimate of William's. She had briefly met her in the street when walking with William after the end of the bad business over an ancient body found in a demolished building. That original meeting had not been pleasant, as Ann had suggested that Saphira was no more than a strumpet. Saphira, for her part, had responded in kind. They had parted on bad terms. For William's sake, she resolved to try better this time.

'Mistress Segrim, how nice to see you.'

Ann Segrim turned around, a warm smile lighting up her face, until she saw who it was had spoken to her. Her smile froze and her blue eyes turned the grey colour of a well-tempered sword.

'I wish I could say the same to you, Mistress . . .'

'Le Veske.'

'Ah, yes. Le Veske. That name is Jewish, is it not?'

Saphira's heart sank at the same rate as her resolve hardened. She had so wanted to be pleasant to this woman, who had clearly once been very close to William. But the veiled slur had put an end to all that.

'Yes, the name is Jewish, and a very old and respectable name too.'

Ann Segrim ignored the retort and looked over at Robert the spicer. He could hardly hide the smirk that had crept over his face. He was obviously enjoying the discomfiture of the Jew.

'If you could send the raisins and chestnuts to Botley, I would be obliged. I am to celebrate the return of my husband from Outremer any day now.'

Robert bowed and wrung his hands.

'We are all glad of his safe return, mistress. The goods will be delivered tomorrow.'

Without sparing another look for Saphira, Ann Segrim swept out of the shop, her grinning homunculus of a servant in her wake. Margery, however, managed a look at Saphira. It was a gaze of malevolent triumph.

As chance would have it, two men saw Ann Segrim leave the spicer's shop. William Falconer and Thomas Symon, on their way back to Aristotle's Hall, were crossing the High Street just as the incident in the spicer's reached its culmination. Thomas saw Ann first and pointed her out to his mentor, knowing her as his close friend. He was blithely unaware of the recent shift in Falconer's affections.

'Look, it's Mistress Segrim. Shall I call out to her?'

Falconer hesitated, restraining his young friend. And it was lucky he did, for immediately after Ann's hurried appearance, followed by the servant, Margery, another figure emerged from the shop. It was a flustered Saphira Le Veske, who was staring with apparent anger at the retreating shape in the billowing blue robe. Falconer groaned.

'I think not, Thomas. Take it from me, we would do well to avoid both those ladies at the present.'

Thomas shot a puzzled look at Falconer, not knowing the shapely red-haired woman. But the regent master did not seem ready to offer him an explanation. For his own part, William did not think he could supply one anyway. Dealing with two strong-willed women left him with the feeling that celibacy was not such a bad option after all. He took Thomas firmly by the arm and dragged him down a narrow lane in order to avoid being seen going in the same direction as the two ladies. Though neither woman, in their present mood, would have been likely to have noticed Falconer, even if he had stood before them. Saphira, grim-faced, stood in the doorway of the spicer's shop until Ann Segrim had disappeared from sight in the direction of Carfax. Then she walked briskly back to her lodgings in Fish Street, and a cold repast.

Ann, at first, set on returning home to Botley through the little river gate below the castle, but changed her mind once she was in the network of marsh and streams outside the town walls. Where she was inclined to go now first required her to get rid of her shadow, Margery.

'We shall go to Godstow Nunnery now, Margery.'

The stocky servant's face fell.

'The . . . er . . . nunnery, madam? Why is that?'

Ann smiled to herself. She knew that Margery had an irrational fear of being locked away for life in a nunnery. That somehow her employer would trick her into entering the cloister, from where she would never be allowed to return. Ann continued to play on that fear, knowing that she would thereby free herself of Margery's suffocating presence. The little monkey-face took her job of keeping an eye on her mistress on behalf of her absent master too seriously for Ann's liking.

'Oh, no reason, Margery. Wouldn't you like to see inside the nunnery? See how pleasant the life is there?'

'P–pleasant?' Margery's face was as white as freshly washed linen at the idea of entering a nunnery, even momentarily. 'No, madam. I think I had better return to the manor. Old Sekston will need some help in the kitchen garden. He is getting so frail now, he can't carry all the vegetables by himself.'

Soon, Margery was scurrying away down the road to Botley and Ann was left to make her way alone to Godstow. Picking the meandering dry path between the many streams that infested the meadows north and west of Oxford's walls was difficult. But eventually she came to the rickety wooden bridge that led to the gatehouse of the nunnery. Ann had come to like the prioress who ran the nunnery with an iron fist, though it had not been so when first she had met her. Peter Bullock, the constable of Oxford town, had asked Ann to stay at the nunnery after one of its inmates had been found dead. Lady Gwladys had agreed to the subterfuge reluctantly, and had been quite obstructive. But after Ann had winkled out the truth of the mysterious death, she had softened in her attitude to the calm and clever Ann Segrim. They had met on several occasions since then, especially after Sir Humphrey had left for the Holy Lands. Ann had needed someone to confide her troubles in and the prioress had obliged. Even though Gwladys's own rules, strictly applied, made it difficult for a more permanent friendship to blossom.

Before Gwladys's time as prioress, the nunnery had been lax, and men had slipped in and out with ease. She had had the bishop's approval to prevent a nun speaking to anyone without another nun present. And on no account could a nun speak to an Oxford scholar at all for fear of exciting 'unclean thoughts'. Ann had always smiled wryly at that particular injunction, bearing in mind the thoughts that William aroused in her. Now, with the arrival of Saphira Le Veske, she was less amused by the idea.

At the gatehouse, she presented herself to the gatekeeper, Hal Coke. He was a wrinkle-faced, sour old man, who had lost a great deal in income when his trade of passing tokens and messages from scholars to nuns had been cut off. Ann had been surprised that Gwladys had kept him on, but in one of her rare expressions of humour, she had said the penance was good for his soul. Coke saw Ann and slowly pulled himself up from his stool, setting aside his jug of watered beer.

'Mistress. You wish to see the Lady Gwladys?'

'Yes, Master Coke. If you please.'

The gatekeeper mumbled under his breath something to the effect that it didn't please him to be disturbed at his rest, but what was there to be done. Ann smiled sweetly, pretending not to have heard what he said, and followed him into the outer court of the nunnery. On two sides of this court there stood both St Thomas's Chapel and the lodgings for a chaplain and priest who assisted the prioress in her duties. On the third, south, side stood the range that led to the inner cloister and the nunnery proper. Coke led her through this door, having used a large key to open it. Inside, Ann marvelled once again at the calm that prevailed. The inner walls of the cloister bore paintings with religious themes on the white plasterwork. Three sides led into houses where the twenty nuns had their quarters. A slender but dominating figure stood at the northern end of the cloister. Sister Gwladys had anticipated Ann's arrival it seemed, as she always did.

She had one of those smiles that was a result of the corners of her mouth turning down rather than up. But Ann knew she was pleased to see her, nevertheless. At her shoulder stood the familiar figure of Sister Hildegard, who conformed precisely to the nunnery's requirement of a companion when any nun spoke to an outsider – that of being 'an ancient and discreet nun'.

Gwladys took a step forward and raised a hand as if in a benediction.

'Welcome, Mistress Segrim. I am glad you came. I have something quite disturbing that I need to discuss with you.'

*   *   *

Sir Humphrey Segrim guzzled yet another jug of the cheap
ale and settled into the cosy corner he had established for
himself in the nameless tavern in Berkhamsted. He had given
the innkeeper the impression that he was a knight returning
from the Holy Wars in Outremer, where he had experienced
hard times and cruel battles. In fact, he had got no further
than the island of Cyprus, once ruled by King Richard, but
now in the hands of the French Lusignan family. King Hugh
of Cyprus was an obscure offshoot of that family, who also
laid claim to the Kingdom of Jerusalem, though this was
disputed. Prince Edward, son of Henry of Winchester, was
trying to revive the stumbling Holy War, which had been
slowed down by the death of Louis of France. So when Segrim
and the Templar had arrived at Famagusta harbour, they found
that Edward had already set sail for Acre with a handful of
his followers. The knights of Cyprus had refused to fight on
the mainland due, they claimed, to a conflict in feudal laws.
The Templar cursed them for cowards and immediately sought
passage for himself to Outremer. Segrim circumspectly chose
to see what developed over the water first and stayed in
Famagusta. Besides, he had become uneasy about his travelling companion. There had been the strange incident in Viterbo
in March of that year that had worried Segrim. And still worried
him now.

He was about to call for another jug of ale, when the door
of the inn burst open and a man in rough clothes soaked to
the skin rushed in. His face looked grim and the pallor of his
skin was made all the more marked by his black hair that was
plastered down by the heavy rain.

'He's dead! Lord Richard is dead!'

A cry of horror was wrenched from the lips of all who,
until that moment, had been noisily carousing one with the
other. The innkeeper hustled over to the messenger of the bad
news and thrust a jug into his hand. The uneasy silence that
then descended on the inn was only gradually broken by a
growing murmur of worry. All those present depended for
their livelihood on the lord of the manor who had just apparently died. Segrim guessed it had to be Richard of Cornwall
himself, brother to the King of England and lately elected
King of Germany. He leaned towards a sturdy yeoman who
sat near him.

'Is it Richard, Earl Cornwall, he speaks of?'

The red-faced farmer nodded sagely.

'Yes. And mark my words, there is evil afoot here.'

'Evil? Did he not fall ill with the half-dead disease last December? Though I was abroad, I heard he was paralyzed down his right side and had lost the power of speech. Was not his death inevitable?'

The yeoman shook his head vigorously.

'Not so soon as this. It was said he was much recovered and paying attention to his affairs as though he were whole again. No, his death, coming so soon after his nephew's, who was in his care at the time, is a cause for concern.'

Segrim knew what the man was referring to. Prince Edward's eldest son, John of Winchester, had died quite young in August of last year, while in the custody of his Uncle Richard. Now Richard also was dead. But still Segrim shook his head and turned away from his informant, unconvinced of any suggestion of foul play. Death was a normal part of living, and young and old succumbed equally from perfectly natural causes. Life, after all, was a harsh and precarious affair. He buried his face in the ale jug again. It was only later that something occurred to make Segrim wonder if the farmer had not hit upon the truth after all.

It happened after he had retired to his room with a sore head from too much ale, and aching bones from the persistent damp. He was staring glumly out of the unglazed window, holding the sacking aside that was the only protection from the gusting wind and rain. The bulk of the castle opposite looked even gloomier in the darkness. More so, now that it housed the sad presence within its walls of the body of Richard, King of Germany. Suddenly, Segrim was aware of a sound being carried on the wind. A noise that became clearer as it got closer. It finally seemed to be coming from the narrow lane below the window at which he stood. It was the sound of chain mail and sword clanking together, accompanied by the gentle creaking of a horse harness. The sound was restrained but clear, as if whoever was passing by chose to do so secretively. Segrim leaned out of the window cautiously and peered down. He saw a small group of armoured men on horseback passing below. They were led by the robust and upright figure of the very Templar he had been fleeing for weeks. The man even seemed to sense Segrim's presence, as he lifted his cold, calm gaze up to Segrim's window. Sir Humphrey ducked back inside the room, his legs giving way underneath him. He slumped down on to the rush-strewn floor in horror.

FIVE

The following morning Ann Segrim was still mulling over her conversation with Sister Gwladys the previous day. The prioress had been reluctant to divulge what was disturbing her at first. So Ann had begun by confessing her angry outburst in the spicer's shop. Gwladys had listened impassively, but Hildegard had hung on to her every word. The ancient nun professed to be deaf, fulfilling her role as chaperone perfectly in the nunnery. But Ann knew otherwise. Hildegard was a fund of knowledge. Her ears were as sharp as anyone's, and her store of gossip greater for the fact that all her fellow nuns thought her deaf. Because of it, they spoke unguardedly in her presence. Even though she was aware of the deception, Ann still did not mind speaking frankly.

'I was cold and uncharitable to the woman.'

Gwladys made her strange smile, where the outer edges of her lips turned down rather than up.

'And you did this because she is licentious? With a man of your . . . acquaintance?'

Ann truly did not know if Saphira Le Veske had stolen William away from her using the pleasures of her body. But she knew that look in his eye. It was one she had not been able to arouse. She swallowed hard and nodded.

'Yes.'

'Then coldness is appropriate to someone who does not live by God's laws. But charity is another matter. Does not the sinner deserve our charity so that we may bring them back to God?'

Ann spoke through thin, tight lips.

'Even when the person concerned is a Jew?'

She heard Hildegard hiss behind her. But Gwladys seemed unconcerned by the revelation.

'Even Jews have been known to convert. But enough of that. Tell me, does your husband return soon from his sacred duties in Outremer?'

'He does, Sister Gwladys . . .'

Ann knew that the nun was not really changing the subject. She was instead gently reminding her of her own matrimonial duties in the light of the difficult situation that Ann had mentioned. She had no cause to be jealous of Saphira Le Veske, when she herself had a husband whom she owed her affections to. She was going to say some more about her feelings but the door of the prioress's room cracked open. A young and nervous nun stuck her head round the door, silently enquiring with her eyes if she may enter. Gwladys waved her hand impatiently at the girl.

'Come, come, girl. Bring our guest the sweetmeats.'

Emerging from behind the safety of the door, the young nun scuttled into the room carrying a wooden bowl. This she set on a small table beside Ann Segrim, leaving with the same alacrity with which she had arrived. Gwladys smiled and pointed at the contents of the bowl.

'Please don't mind Sister Margaret, she is shy of other people. Take whatever you wish from the bowl. There are dates and figs, revived a little with rose-water from the East.'

Ann was astonished at such sumptuousness in the austere surroundings of the nunnery. Gwladys had introduced strict control and modesty in the nuns when she had arrived some years ago and her standards had never lapsed. Ann took a dried fig while Gwladys explained.

'I keep them only for guests, of course. The Papal Legate who honoured us with a visit last year was known to have a weakness for Eastern fruits. We still had some supplies after he had gone.'

Having been told the dried fruits were months old, Ann hesitated. But she could see that Hildegard's eyes were wide with envy, as the old nun's tongue moistened her cracked lips. Ann bit into a fig, expecting it to be musty, but instead found it most pleasant. She smiled and thanked Gwladys for her gift. Then the prioress got to the heart of the matter.

'What I am about to say must go no further than these four walls.'

'Of course, Mother Prioress.'

Ann had not been expecting what she was then told. In fact, Mother Gwladys's revelations had been unnerving. Godstow nunnery was located in a peaceful spot, with the river on one side and the dark groves of Witham woods on the other. The place should have been a haven of tranquillity, perfect for contemplation and prayer. But it seemed that peace had recently been disturbed. At first Gwladys had been reluctant to reveal the uncomfortable secret to Ann. She had pressed upon her the need to keep silent about it.

'The chaplain who visits from Oxford to advise and guide us is the only person outside these walls to know. But as you were so . . . useful . . . when last we had a similar problem, I would like to ask your opinion again.'

Ann was shocked. Was there a murderer loose in the nunnery again? What had happened? Gwladys explained, while still studiously avoiding any reference to murder.

'I do not think that it is the same as before. After all, lightning does not strike the same place twice. However . . .'

Ann leaned forward and made to pat the arm of the older woman. Then she recalled the proscription on touching that Gwladys so strictly applied to her nuns and drew back.

'Just tell me what has happened, Mother.'

'It concerns one of our younger nuns, like Sister Margaret who you have just seen. She gave signs suggesting uncertainty about her vocation some while before she . . . some time ago. She appeared distressed and upset. I spoke to the chaplain and then to her about leaving the nunnery. That seemed to upset her even more than questioning her vows. I decided to leave the matter for a few days, hoping she would settle down. It seems I made the wrong decision.'

'How was that so?'

'Because the following morning, Marie was found dead in her cell.'

'Dead? How so?'

'That is what I want you to ascertain, Ann.'

Having slept on what Gwladys had said to her, Ann had risen to a clear and bright morning, ready to talk to the nuns at Godstow. Unfortunately, her morning preparations were suddenly broken into by the sound of heavy boots approaching her solar. She knew it could only be Alexander, her husband's half-brother, who had been appointed by Humphrey to run the estate in his absence in Outremer. He was boorish and often intruded on her privacy in this way. He also blundered around the management of the estate in a similarly uncaring way. Ann had let him get on with matters for a while, but it had proved impossible to stand back and accept the mess he was making. She had ended up doing as she always had done when Humphrey was present, and had run the estate herself. Nevertheless, Alexander continued to meddle in matters he had no knowledge of. So, she had often been forced to step in to mollify angry servants and correct bad instructions. She knew for example that, if a recent command of Alexander's had been followed, the fishponds would have been drained and the fish stocks ruined.

When he had realized she had countermanded him, Alexander had ranted and raved at Ann, demanding she obey him as a woman should. He did not realize that she had perfected the skill of running the estate while allowing Humphrey to think he did. She had honed over the many years of their loveless marriage an ability to do just as she pleased, while allowing Humphrey to keep his sense of manhood. Her husband was proud of having only ever read one book, which was a theological treatise by Friar Nicolas Byard. And he frequently quoted his favourite passage from it to his cronies over copious quantities of good wine:

'A man may chastise his wife and beat her for her correction, for she is of his household and therefore the lord may chastise his own.'

In fact, it was many a year since he had dared lay a finger on her. It became obvious that Alexander had to learn the same lesson soon after he arrived at Botley. When he realized he could not dominate Ann, he had turned to drink, working his way steadily through Humphrey's barrels of Rhenish wine.

Now, when he burst unceremoniously into Ann's solar, she knew he had been at his cups for some time. Her brother-in-law's face was flushed and his gait unsteady. He grinned lecherously.

'Ah, there you are sweet Ann. I have been looking for you. Where were you yesterday evening?'

He stood in the doorway, leaning on the frame to keep himself from falling over. Ann forced a maidenly smile on to her face.

'Why, I was at Godstow nunnery, Alexander, talking with the prioress. Would you like to know what we discussed?'

Alexander Eddington screwed up his eyes in fuddled concentration. He was not sure if he should take Ann's words as the unvarnished truth, or if the bitch was in some way mocking him. He never knew what was going on in her mind. But he did recall stories about past goings-on at the nunnery which was situated between his brother's estate and the town. His grin returned and he waved an unsteady finger at his sister-in-law.

'More news about the *affairs* of the nuns, no doubt.'

He fancied he stressed the word 'affairs' in such a way that would cause Ann Segrim to blush. But she merely held that annoying smile on her face and replied as if he had asked keenly about the religious observances of the place.

'Indeed. The way of life and devotion of the nuns at Godstow are an inspiration to us all. The celibate life I have observed since your brother, my husband, went away could have been modelled on theirs.'

It was Alexander who ended up blushing. He had attempted a seduction of his sister-in-law soon after he had arrived. He had fancied she would find his virility irresistible after years of being married to Humphrey, a man many years his senior and probably incapable of satisfying a woman. He had failed miserably in his attempt. Not only had Ann spurned his offer, she had succeeded in humiliating him in the process. Fortunately, the attempt had been in private without the servants there to observe. He had not tried again. Until this morning, when drink had emboldened him. But once again she had seemed to turn the tables on him.

Uncertain how to retreat without humiliation, he hovered in the doorway. He watched as her hand went to a book that lay at her elbow on the table. Ignoring him completely, she opened it and studied with a pious air. That it was not a religious text, but a commentary by the Arab Averroes on Plato, and expressed a view that women were equal in all ways to men, would be unknown to Alexander. Like many of his sort, he was illiterate. He hesitated only for a moment before sighing with exasperation and retreated back the way he had come. He had been defeated again but would not let it rest there. Before his half-brother returned, he was determined to have his revenge for all the times he had been bested by Ann Segrim.

As the evening of that day drew on, and the streets of Oxford began to empty of tradesmen and farmers, a curious sight was witnessed by old Peter Pady. He was one of the constable's watchmen and, like Bullock himself, was advanced in years. In a town thronging with students, in a time when few toilers in the fields lived beyond their fortieth year, Peter – at sixty-one – was deemed a venerable old man. Aged he might be, but he was a sound man to stand at the East Gate and enforce the curfew. Peter Bullock chose his men carefully, with an eye to their experience and steadiness. Pady was a sober man, who took his job seriously. So he knew it was not excess of ale that caused the strange apparition lurching down the dusty road from the Cowley direction.

It could have been a tent except it was in motion. It was adorned with trinkets and scraps of parchment that hung from it, and jangled and fluttered as the apparition swung along. Atop the decorated brown tent affair was a yellow conical capping piece running up to a spike with a knob at the end. It was only when the apparition got closer to the astonished Peter Pady that the cone shape tilted backwards, and a face emerged. It was a dark and dusty face with long locks and a black beard hiding most of it, but a face nevertheless. The brown tent that was a man stopped in front of the watchman and, as if by magic, a smaller figure emerged from behind the first. It too was similarly burdened. The larger of the two travellers spoke in passable English.

'Is the town closed, sir, or may I enter?'

Peter Pady was of a circumspect nature and, not being sure what or who this vision was, he erred on the safe side.

'Closed,' was his gruff reply. Just at that moment, the sound of a galloping horse came from the same direction the tent had come. The thunder of hooves increased with the same alacrity as the cloud of dust that accompanied the urgent rider. Peter pushed the foot traveller aside and stood nervously in the track. As the rider came closer, he saw that whoever it was did not mean to stop. His cloak billowed behind him and large saddle bags flapped maniacally on the horse's flanks. Pady had meant to halt the horseman in the same way he had stopped the traveller, but discretion and self-preservation took over. He stepped sharply aside, pushing back the traveller and his little familiar at the same time.

'Look out!'

The horseman bore down on the group, and with a flapping

of robes and clatter of weapons galloped past. Sweat from the overridden destrier splattered over them and dust flew up in a cloud, but Pady recognized the rider. It was Sir Humphrey Segrim of Botley, apparently back from the Holy Lands. And was, by the pale and petrified look on his face, being chased by a demon from Hell. Pady only recovered himself just in time to stop the swarthy foot-travellers from sneaking into Oxford in Segrim's wake. He did so by swinging the gate in their faces. The taller one with the conical hat reeled back and cried out.

'What's this? The town was open for that rider, why not us?'

Pady bristled.

'Because he is a knight and a landowner here. And you are . . . well, I don't know what you are.'

'I am a saviour of souls and a bringer of cures. That's what I am.'

The man's bold stance made Pady even more suspicious and he closed the gate firmly, drawing the bolt across. Only the wicket-gate stood open and he leaned through it to give his response.

'And a Jew, if I'm not mistaken. So you can wait outside the gate till tomorrow. Then we will see.'

The seller of cures cursed under his breath and turned to his little familiar.

'Come, boy, we will camp out in the cemetery. We've done it before, and it is most comfortable and dry to have a tomb for a bed.'

Pady watched as the two of them walked across the road to where the Jews' cemetery was located close by East Gate. He crossed himself.

'I knew they wasn't of this world. They'll find company with their own kind, I reckon.'

He wasn't quite sure himself if he meant by that merely with other Jews, even if they were dead, or with similar unholy souls that he knew roamed the graveyard after dark. To be on the safe side, he closed the wicket-gate and barred that too.

Despite being only a few miles from home, and at the end of a long, exhausting journey from the Holy Lands, Sir Humphrey Segrim secreted himself in the Golden Ball Inn in the centre of Oxford. The innkeeper, Peter Halegod, had been puzzled by Segrim's desire for a room, and by his fearful demeanour. The ageing knight had appeared in his doorway, his clothes travel-stained and the hair on his balding, bare head in disarray.

'Halegod! A room and don't tell anyone I am here. Understand?'

'Certainly, sir. I have plenty of room with times as hard as they are at present.' He looked at Segrim, who stood before him with only a saddlebag slung over one shoulder. Out in the yard, he could see Segrim's horse being handled by his ostler, but no evidence of further baggage. Hadn't the man just returned from Outremer? 'Where is your baggage, sir? Have you travelled light?'

Segrim, who had ridden hard, spurring his destrier ever onwards, had outstripped his new servant Osbert Smith for once. He wondered if he would ever see his armour again, but the need for urgency had been compelling. The sight of the Templar in Berkhamsted had terrified him. It was as if the man was more a demon than a human being, who knew exactly where Segrim was by some sort of necromancy. And death and mayhem followed wherever the Templar went. Lord Richard's death was further proof of that. He squinted suspiciously at Halegod.

'Never you mind about that, man. Just show me to my room, and keep your mouth shut.'

Halegod had a mind to turn the discourteous knight away, such was his rudeness, but business was business and it had truly been poor of late. Muttering about the wheel of fate's downward turn and having to put up with ungrateful wretches, Peter Halegod led Segrim to his best room. He would have his revenge by making him pay through the nose for his night's stay.

SIX

On the Sunday of that week, the bells of Oxford's many churches called the good citizens to prayer as normal. The Franciscans and the Dominicans both had their own friaries in the town, and the friars had been long up and about their devotions when Falconer rose bleary-eyed from his bed. For those in holy orders proper, the day began at midnight with Matins and Lauds, though the monks and friars were then allowed back to bed until daybreak. That was the first Mass of the day for them, followed by break-fast. Falconer's day was altogether more congenial, even though Regent Masters and students of the university were also nominally in holy orders themselves. Falconer yawned and splashed some cold water in his face from the bowl one of his students had left outside his door. His black robe, when he pulled it on, felt damp and his boots chilly, and he hurried down the creaky stairs to the communal hall where he hoped someone had managed to stir the fire into a semblance of life.

Unfortunately, all he found was a pile of cold ashes. He ventured to the back of the hall, where a ramshackle arrange-ment of wood and cheap cloth divided off the sleeping areas. In there were small cubicles with bedsteads provided by the abbey landlord. The rest of the bedding was the students' responsibility to provide. Falconer poked his head in Peter Mithian's cell. It was he whose duty it was that week to arise first. He must have done so as the regent master's water had been outside his door. But clearly tiredness had overtaken the clerk again as soon as he had performed that early duty. He lay on a bare plank bed innocent of any mattress. On the floor around him were scattered two books, a candlestick bearing the nub of a candle, a gimlet, a hornpipe and a wooden spoon. Amongst all these, his worldly possessions, Mithian was fast asleep. Falconer stirred him with his boot.

'Get up and pay your way, boy,' he grumbled. The few shillings Falconer earned annually in fees for teaching were supplemented by the commons paid for ten or a dozen students lodging in Aristotle's Hall. But even after he had paid his landlord, Oseney Abbey, its rent, the money didn't stretch very far. Especially as Falconer took a few poor students on who had a begging licence from the university. Their passage through the university was made possible by working for the richer students and living off their scraps. Peter Mithian was one of those beggar clerks, and though Falconer hated it, he needed to keep the boy up to the mark. He would find no other way out of his poverty and needed his qualifications.

Peter Mithian yawned, stretched, then realized who had roused him and why. Blushing deeply across his chubby, boyish features, he scrambled off his bed.

'I am sorry, master. I was conning my texts until the early hours with a candle Tom gave me.'

Tom Youlden was one of the rich students in Falconer's hall. His generosity, however, seemed not to run to providing a mattress for Peter. Falconer was mortified that he had not noticed before that one of his charges was sleeping on bare boards.

'Where is your mattress, Peter? Did you not have one when you came?'

Mithian cast his eyes to the ground and mumbled some words Falconer did not understand.

'What, boy? Speak up.'

'I sold it to buy these books.' He snatched the two precious books up from the floor where they had fallen when he had finally lost his battle with staying awake the night before. Falconer gently took them from his grasp and examined them. One was the *Topics* of Boethius and the other Priscian's *De constructione* – both basic texts for the clerks at university. He carefully gave them back to Peter.

'You should have come to me. I can lend you any books you may want. And as for the mattress, I believe there is an old one in the shed in the yard. It will need mending and airing by the fire, mind. And talking of the fire, you had better get last night's embers going before we all freeze to death.'

Peter Mithian responded to Falconer's final peremptory tones and scuttled from his cubicle to attend to his duties. Meanwhile, the regent master foraged for himself and found some dry bread that he moistened with ale from the barrel in the hall. With the fire downstairs not yet providing any heat, he retreated to his own solar, wrapping himself in the still-warm blanket from his bed until such time as the sun struck through the window and warmed the room. Behind him, high on his perch, his owl, Balthazar, ruffled its feathers and stared impassively down. Night-time was its time for activity, and the day was for sleeping.

'You are lucky, bird. You can sleep the day away wrapped in your own down blanket while others have to toil for a living.'

Falconer's grumble was interrupted by a tentative knock at his door. He called out for whoever it was to come in. Peter Mithian poked his head round the door, a scared look in his eyes. He didn't like inflicting his presence on the regent master, preferring to remain unnoticed. By doing so, he was less likely to be picked on when it came to awkward questions about logic and grammar. But this morning had put him in the full light of day, so he had decided to take advantage of Falconer's offer.

'Master, I need also to read the new logic of Aristotle . . .'

Falconer sighed, seeing he was to get no peace today.

'Come in, boy. You need to read *Sophistici elenchi*. Look, it is over there beside the chimney breast.'

He pointed out a toppling stack of his most cherished books and papers. At the bottom of the heap, less used because they were the approved texts, were to be found books such as the rather dull *Historia Scholastica*. Falconer's more esoteric and well-thumbed works lay on the top, amongst them works by the Arab mathematician Al-Khowarizmi, medical works of Galen and a geography text called *De Sphaera Mundi*. The boy tiptoed across the cluttered room, marvelling at the strange collection of objects on the large central table that dominated the space. Animal bones jostled with dried plants and stones which had weird shapes inscribed on their surfaces. Two scrolls lay open, their edges held down with pebbles and a rusty dagger. He could not decipher the writing on them.

'Hebrew. The texts are both Hebrew translations of Arabic works by Averroes. I am trying to discover the true original text from examining the errors in both translations.'

Falconer's explanation of the scratchings on the scrolls was bewildering to Mithian. He was afraid he would never understand the simplest of texts expounded in ordinary lectures at the university. Let alone be able to put into Latin or English a Jewish version of an Arabic work. He sighed deeply.

'Yes, master. I think I had better learn my Aristotle first.'

He turned to the heap of books, not sure where to begin even now. How was he to identify which text was which amidst this pile of paper and parchment? Perhaps he had better first move the pots and vials that lay atop them. He picked up a stone jar and sniffed its contents. Recoiling in horror, he nudged the pile of books, and had to grab at a couple of other pots that began to slide off the top.

'Here, here. Let me do that.' Falconer shrugged off his blanket and leaped nimbly across the room. Though he was a large, rangy man, his footwork was still neat and sure, due to long years spent dodging swords and daggers in his youth. He had been a mercenary in many of the skirmishes that played out across Europe and along the trade routes that he had chosen to explore before settling to a scholastic life. He grabbed the foul-smelling pot from his student and steadied the others. Gingerly, Peter Mithian took one in each hand and transferred them to the cluttered table.

'You need to take care with some of these pots. What they contain could be quite deadly if swallowed.'

Mithian shuddered, stepping away from the pots and vials as Falconer transferred them from the pile by the chimney breast. Then the regent master slipped out a roughly bound sheaf of papers from the middle of the heap.

'There it is. The Aristotle you so wish to consult, Peter. Learn it well, for I shall test you on it when next you are in my school.'

Mithian groaned. What he had feared had come to pass. Master Falconer would now single him out for special attention and he would no longer be able to hide in the shadows.

'Thank you, master. For this, and for the mattress. I have already brought it in from the shed and set it to dry out by the fire.'

'Which I am sure you now have burning well and warmly.'

Falconer's parting shot gave the boy good reason to hurry from his master's presence. He rushed down to check on the fire that he had roused from the embers of the night before. Falconer, meanwhile, picked up one of the pots and peered at the label he had bound around it. The ink had smeared and the label was illegible. Truth to tell, he could not remember what the contents were and why they stunk so much. Perhaps he would take it round to Saphira and see if her new knowledge of poisons would serve to identify it. Insatiably curious though, he poked his finger in, wiggled it around and withdrew it. Tentatively, he touched his finger to his tongue.

Saphira was sure she had seen the weirdly dressed talisman seller before. But the large conical hat hid his features well. She had been crossing Fish Street on her way to Jewry Lane and Aristotle's Hall, when the apparition that had so startled Peter Pady the previous night appeared at the top of the street. The seller had obviously attracted a lot of attention in Carfax because a small crowd of people were following in his wake. Despite the insistent clamour of the church bells calling them, Christians as much as Jews were attracted by magical gewgaws. Everyone believed strongly in the curative powers of talismans and amulets. There were many suffering from all sorts of ailments who would buy from this man. Personally, Saphira would rather depend on the powers of the plants and herbs that Samson was revealing to her. Though, even those held some mystery for her. After all, why should lungwort, whose leaves were supposed to resemble a human lung, ease congested lungs? But it did. Perhaps buying a talisman – a stone or similar with some marks on it – was no less efficacious in the end. Who was to say otherwise? The strangely dressed vendor stopped in the middle of Fish Street and opened the large satchel that hung around his shoulders. From it he pulled out a handful of items dangling on chains and leather strips. Polished stones and silvery boxes glittered in the light. He held the trinkets high in the air and called out.

'Amulets and talismans to ward off all ills.'

The people that had been following him soon gathered around and began examining his wares. Curious, Saphira delayed her visit to Falconer and walked over to the edge of the crowd. At the front of the assembled throng, a boy with sightless eyes was being pushed forward. He held a silver coin in his trembling hand, uncertain where to proffer it. The talisman seller expressed a reluctance to take his money, but then a sceptic in the crowd snorted his derision.

'I might have known. Just another Jew trick.'

Saphira looked closer at the seller. It was true that though his eyes were obscured by the hat, and he had his back to her, his long dark beard and hair locks suggested he was a fellow religionist. He stiffened at the jibe, and held out a bright stone with a peculiar mark across its surface that swung on the end of a cord. He dropped it in the boy's open fist, refusing to accept the coin in his other hand. The boy held the stone to his forehead and slowly his eyeballs, that had been white as an egg's albumen, rotated. He closed his eyelids, and when he opened them, a pair of dark-brown eyes stared out incredulously. The crowd gasped as one, and the boy darted away, crying out he was cured. Suddenly, hands reached out to touch the Jew's wares. A young woman with an ugly boil on her neck fingered one of the small silver boxes nervously. She engaged in earnest conversation with the stranger, who clearly reassured her that the amulet could rid her of her existing affliction, as well as it could ward off future ills and ailments. The woman turned to her companion, who groaned and put his hand into the purse at his waist. Another coin was exchanged and the box was hung by its leather strap around the woman's neck.

As the trader sold more wares, he turned towards Saphira's part of the crowd. When his conical hat tilted back, she recognized him immediately. It was a man called Covele. Several months ago, he had crossed her path when he had come to Oxford offering to carry out rituals that the majority of Jews deemed forbidden. Rituals that could only be carried out in the Temple of Solomon, which had long ago been destroyed. He had scuttled out of town when his actions had seemed to be mixed up with the death of a child. His deeds had caused untold problems for the Jews who tried to live their life alongside the Christians of England. Saphira recalled he had then had his son with him.

'You trickster. The blind boy was your son and the last time I saw him his sight was perfect.'

She only spoke under her breath, so he couldn't have heard. But Covele must have recognized her all the same. He suddenly stuffed the rest of his wares in his satchel and shook his head at his other customers.

'I am sorry but I cannot sell any more today. The time is not propitious.'

Despite the loud protests, he pushed through the crowd and hurried back up Fish Street in the opposite direction to Saphira. She made to follow him, lifting her skirts to keep pace. At first, she kept him in sight because of the strange hat with the spike on the top. But then he looked back at her and realized what was giving him away. He pulled his hat off his head and was soon lost amidst the rest of the people who thronged the street.

Ann woke up that Sunday with a vague feeling of nausea in the pit of her stomach. Was it a genuine illness creeping over her? Or were the events of the last few days preying on her mind? There had been the unpleasant encounter with the red-haired Jew in Oxford, and the subsequent skirmish with Humphrey's half-brother, Alexander. Both had left her with a nasty taste in her mouth, but neither had seemed so extreme as to make her ill.

She had spent three days gathering all the information she could at the nunnery, each day talking to the nuns and taking some sustenance there, then going back to Botley to think. Her encounters with the drunken Alexander had not disturbed her thinking in the least. But she had left it until today before returning to Godstow to deliver her conclusions to the prioress. She had learned enough to know what the poor nun had done, but didn't know if she would tell the whole truth to the prioress. But speak she must. So, though she felt ill, she knew she could not put it off any longer and rode the short distance to Godstow. Shown the same hospitality as before, Ann swallowed her nausea and ate and drank a little. Meanwhile, Gwladys looked at her expectantly, with the wrinkled visage of Sister Hildegard peering over her shoulder. Ann took a deep breath.

'I do not think you have anything to worry about, other than to feel sorrow for a lost soul. If what I have learned is so, no one could have got into Marie's cell the night she died. Every nun is accounted for, and no one else other than Hal Coke can have gained access. And I rule him out, as I was assured he had had too much to drink that night to even stand, let alone walk into the cloisters unnoticed.'

Hildegard's tongue clicked in disapproval at the behaviour of their gatekeeper. Then she realized she was supposed to be deaf to what Ann was saying, and blushed. Ann chose her words before continuing.

'Of course, people – even young people – die naturally in their sleep from time to time. But . . .'

The prioress held up her hand, not wishing to make Ann Segrim state the obvious. Ann breathed a sigh of relief and stood up to go. Gwladys managed a grim smile of thanks, and, by way of recompense for Ann's inconvenience, offered the rest of the dried fruit that Sister Margaret had brought as usual. Ann accepted the gift and left.

The prioress sat down in her room and pondered her choices. The matter was resolved, but in a most unsatisfactory way. Ann had tried to soften the blow, but the conclusion was clear. The implication of Ann's enquiries was that Sister Margaret had knowingly killed herself. And self-murder was just as shocking as a killing by another person. One way or another, the matter would have to be buried. Along with the young nun.

SEVEN

' t's henbane, you idiot. You were lucky you only tasted a little.'

Saphira sat on the end of Falconer's bed looking at his prone form. He groaned and began to sit up. His vision blurred and the room swam. He lay back again. Saphira had arrived at Aristotle's Hall late that morning to find the students who boarded there in a quandary. Their master had apparently not risen at his normal time that morning. And though it was Sunday, it was very unusual for him to miss the first meal of the day. Even though it could often only be pottage, or bread and ale. The trouble was, they were all afraid to waken him. Then one of their number, Peter Mithian by name, returned from church to tell them that he had spoken to Master Falconer that morning early. He had been awake then, and checking on the potions he kept up in his room.

Much to the consternation of the students, who were used to their master's solitude not being disturbed – and least of all by a woman – Saphira rushed up the stairs to Falconer's solar. She had found him apparently dead on his bed. It was only when she felt for a pulse, she realized he was still alive. She had sent the boy Mithian, who had followed her up the stairs, to fetch some vinegar. She would have liked an infusion of mulberry bark too, but vinegar would have to suffice. She trickled it between Falconer's lips, and was relieved when he coughed, and then vomited a little fluid. He would feel vile for a while but he would live.

While he was still recovering, she found a piece of parchment that had been scraped for reuse. In her flourishing hand, she wrote a stern warning and set it by the pot. But then, seeing his hand move with curiosity towards the offending henbane, she snatched the pot up anyway and stuffed it in her purse. She was determined to remove it once and for all from William's unbridled and dangerous curiosity. He sat up again, this time more successfully.

'I remember now. Roger Bacon was experimenting with soporifics that he had read about in Arabic texts summarizing Galen's work. Just imagine – hundreds of years ago Galen was performing surgery on eyes and the brain. We both were sure he must have dulled the feelings of his patients first. So we were looking at what he might have used. It was all a bit hit and miss, though.'

Saphira shuddered at the thought of cutting into human flesh. She wasn't squeamish, but preferred the idea of intervening in a patient's illness with natural herbs. It all seemed less brutal and she resolved to stick to what she knew.

'Well, you would have been very successful in dulling a patient with this pot.' She patted her purse, where the offending article now safely nestled. 'More than four leaves would lead you by the hand into an eternal sleep.'

'Hmmm. You don't think, as Albertus Magnus did, that the effects of henbane were due to the influence of the planet Jupiter?'

Despite the seriousness of the situation, Saphira laughed out loud.

'You must feel better already.'

'Why do you say that?'

'You are applying your enquiring mind to the effects you have felt. It cannot be all that dulled.'

Falconer leaned towards her, placing his hand on her knee.

'And it is not only my mind that is being revived by your presence.'

Saphira laughed again, but firmly removed his hand from its position on her leg.

'William! Not here, and certainly not in such close proximity to your students. We agreed, did we not, that our pleasures should be undertaken discreetly. For both our reputations.'

William pulled a face.

'It is ironic, is it not, that we have preserved our secret of intimacy. And yet I am wrongly reckoned to have broken my vows of celibacy with another lady whose reputation should be spotless.'

'Ah, yes. Mistress Segrim. I saw her the other day at Robert Bodin's shop. It did not go well.'

Falconer forbore from telling her that he had guessed as much when he had seen the aftermath of their encounter. He might not have been able to explain how he had done so, and not shown himself, but rather scuttled away to avoid a confrontation. He did not think Saphira would appreciate his actions. Besides, he still wished to make his peace with Ann without letting Saphira know he was doing so. Once again, it crossed his mind he would prefer to enter into a battle skirmish without a shield and chain mail than come between two wronged women.

'Are you sure you are fully recovered, William?'

He saw that Saphira was looking into his eyes with some concern and realized he had drifted off for a moment.

'Hmmm. Perhaps I am not as well as I thought. Do you think you should nurse me a little longer?'

She put on a stern look and poked him in the chest.

'No. What you need is to immerse that fevered brain of yours in cold water and take a refreshing walk. Besides, I have other matters to attend to rather than look after a fool who swallows henbane for a hobby.'

She was wondering if she could trace Covele, the renegade rabbi turned amulet seller. She was sure he was up to no good in Oxford. Rising from the end of Falconer's bed, she straightened her dress, and tucked a stray red lock under her snood.

'I will go. Before you have ruined my reputation as well as Ann Segrim's.'

Falconer winced, but bowed before the reprimand. Saphira's comment, however, made him doubly determined to speak to Ann as soon as he could. If Saphira recommended a brisk walk, then he would obey. It was a fair distance to Botley and back.

The Jews' cemetery stood just outside the walls of Oxford at East Gate. The flat slabs were carved with the names of those interred within and other significant symbols. Covele sat on a slab that had a deer carved in it, denoting the deceased as belonging to the tribe of Naphthali. He passed a piece of bread to his son who sat at his feet. The gardens of the cemetery were a pleasant place to camp, with shady trees hiding them from the hot sun, and the gaze of anyone passing along over East Bridge and into the town. Neither he, nor his son, was disconcerted by the presence of the dead. Despite Covele's professing to be a rabbi, and practiser of ancient rituals banned by his more orthodox brethren, he cared little for appearances.

That morning he had even filled his water container from the small *mikveh* that stood at the end of the cemetery. This stone-built ritual bath was fed by the Crowell stream that ran on into the Cherwell, and was a bath three cubits by one cubit by one cubit for immersion and purification. To Covele it was a convenient reservoir. He passed the water jug to his son.

'Here, drink.'

The nameless boy took the jug and drank deeply. The morning was already bright and threatened to herald another hot, dry day.

'Do you remember, dad, when we were here last?'

Covele nodded.

'Indeed I do, son. It rained and rained, and we got stranded on the top of this very grave slab. It was like an island in a great sea that stretched for miles in every direction.'

The boy liked his father. He told tales that expanded on the mundane truth until he could believe his life was lived in a magical land. He listened with rapt attention as Covele continued.

'We might have starved to death, if I had not braved the elements and hunted for food. The fish were snapping at our heels where now all you can see is dry grass.' He waved his arms to encompass their surroundings. To the boy, their shabby, patched tent became a multicoloured caravanserai in a painted desert. His father's voice hardened. 'Then *they* came and spoiled our idyll.'

The boy knew who he meant. The tall, grizzle-haired man in the black robe, whose piercing blue eyes seemed to look into your very soul. And the pretty lady with red hair, who held on to his arm as though she was his wife, even though she was a Jew and he a Christian. After they had spoken to his father, they had been forced to flee. His father hadn't been accused of anything in the end, but Jews were guilty whether it could be proved or not. Since then, the boy and his father had been scraping a living selling talismans and amulets. It had been a surprise to the boy, therefore, to find his father leading them down the dusty road back to Oxford. And now he still wasn't sure why they had come.

'What are we doing here, dad?'

Covele looked down into the boy's innocent, brown eyes. 'Revenge.'

* * *

The black pudding had been particularly appreciated in Colcill Hall that dinner time. Thomas Symon now resided there temporarily while he sought a permanent living, or some other means of sustaining himself. He could no longer live at Aristotle's Hall, as he was now a master himself and Falconer kept hall for only students. Nevertheless, Thomas had not moved far. Colcill was a tiny hall tucked in between Aristotle's and Little Merton Hall. Five impoverished masters shared the cost of renting and putting food on the table. This Sunday, due to Thomas's involvement with Falconer's unseasonal slaughter of the pig that had become his teaching aid a week ago, Thomas had provided dinner. The blood and oatmeal mixture, spiced with cumin, savory and rue, and stuffed into a length of the pig's own intestines, had been delicious. Thomas wanted to thank Falconer again for his generosity. But at the same time he resolved to stop relying on his former master and to stand on his own two feet. He rose from the communal table and walked over to the narrow window looking out on the lane beyond. Just at that moment, he saw someone pass. The figure was distorted by the rough diamonds of glazing in the window, but it was unmistakably that of the regent master himself. Thomas hurried to the street door and swung it open. Stepping into the lane to call out for Falconer to wait, he bumped into another person also walking down the lane.

'Oh, excuse me, sir.'

Thomas grasped the man's arm as he stumbled sideways, seeking to prevent him from falling. The man cursed and wrenched his arm away from Thomas's grip.

'Let me go.'

Thomas flinched and stepped back from the violence of the reaction. Had he not merely bumped into the man by accident? Before he could repeat his apology, though, the man was hurrying off along the street in the same direction as William Falconer. Thomas stared after him, marvelling at his strange brown garb and broad-brimmed hat topped with a sort of spike. In the confusion, he utterly forgot his wish to speak to his mentor, who by now had turned the corner of the lane and disappeared.

Saphira thought she might spot Covele trading his wares at Carfax as he had done before. She spent a fruitless hour there, watching the crowds pass without seeing the talisman seller. Eventually, she started to make her way along the High Street, looking down each side alley for her quarry. She had not gone far before she saw him emerging from Shidyerd Street and on to the High Street. It was early afternoon and there were plenty of people thronging the wide thoroughfare. Most were making their way from the churches that were scattered around the town and back to their homes for dinner. A few students, more used to being in schools during daylight, were strolling along towards Smith Gate in the northern stretch of the town walls. Outside were open fields where they could disport themselves in the hot sun. Saphira had a more serious task.

She began to follow Covele, who seemed not to have learned that his hat gave him away. Even in the crowd, the straw hat with the horn on top meant she would not lose him. It was only when they both passed through North Gate and into the quiet of the lanes to the west, that she realized he was following someone also. A familiar figure strode at the head of their little procession. And as the afternoon beat down on them, she understood where William Falconer was bound. The long straight track led only to Botley, and Ann Segrim.

It was hot, and Falconer felt uncomfortable as he approached the yellowed stone manor house that was the home of Ann Segrim. But it was not only the weather that was causing his discomfort. He did not know how Ann would receive him. At least she was not alone in the house. He had heard that Sir Humphrey had arranged for his half-brother, Alexander Eddington, to look after the estate while he had gone crusading. Falconer could not picture Segrim as a warrior for God, nor could he see Ann Segrim taking too kindly to another man meddling with her domain. She ran the estate perfectly well whether her husband was there or not. Still, no one could accuse either himself or Ann of impropriety if Eddington was present when they met. He suddenly wondered how he might excuse his presence if the half-brother asked. Perhaps an enquiry about a borrowed book might suffice. He need not have worried. When he approached the front door of Segrim's dour manor, it flew open and Margery, Ann's servant and shadow flew out.

'Sir, can you help? The mistress is unwell and Master Eddington is . . . not available. I don't know what to do.'

Falconer had never seen the ugly, little servant so flustered. He wondered what it was that prevented Eddington from taking charge. Was he simply not at home? The way Margery had expressed it, it didn't seem so. He took the servant's arm firmly and led her inside.

'Show me where your mistress is.'

Margery's nut-brown face paled.

'She is in her bedchamber, sir.'

'Then you must take me there, and stay in my presence.'

Falconer knew that Margery would respond to firm decisions, and to the suggestion that no impropriety would take place due to his being in a married woman's bedroom. She nodded, regaining her composure, and led Falconer through the great hall and on up the staircase to the family's private rooms.

The bedchamber, when they entered it, smelled of vomit. On the crumpled bed-linen lay Ann Segrim dressed in one of her familiar blue dresses that complemented her flaxen hair. She had obviously dressed for the day, before succumbing to sickness, but her hair was uncovered. It lay tangled, wet and limp around her head. Her face was almost as pale as the linen she lay on, but she managed to sit up when she saw Falconer enter the room.

'William. What are you doing here?'

Her voice was low and shaky but she was still in possession of herself. And Falconer felt the same coolness that had characterized their recent meetings. He hesitated.

'I . . . thought to speak to you on a private matter. But that can wait in the circumstances.'

Ann rose shakily from her bed and began to arrange her hair.

'What circumstances? I have been a little sick, that is all. And somewhat hot. I shall soon recover.'

She turned to her servant, who hovered uncertainly in the doorway. Now that her mistress was apparently recovered, she was regretting allowing the Oxford master in the house. Her suspicious nature had returned and she was all for ushering Falconer out as soon as possible.

'Margery. You will go to Robert Bodin and fetch a remedy that he suggests for sickness.'

'Yes, mistress. I will go as soon as I have shown the master, here, out.'

Ann's voice, though weak, still had a touch of steel to it. 'You will go now.'

Margery gave her mistress a sulky look and backed unwillingly out of the room. Ann smiled, then clutched her head, which felt so delicate that it would shatter like crystal. She looked at Falconer, who stood uncertainly by the door. She patted the bed beside her.

'Come and sit, William. I have a few matters to discuss with you.'

A relieved smile filled Falconer's face, though Ann's reddened eyes worried him. He crossed the room and sat on the bed. He was glad that the awkwardness between them was broken, and they began to talk with candour, as they had once done. Then suddenly, a loud, male voice echoed through the chamber.

'I am glad you told me, Margery. What were you thinking, sister, allowing a man in your private room?'

Falconer observed the man who now entered Ann's bedchamber with the smug Margery in tow. This had to be Alexander Eddington, Sir Humphrey's half-brother. He now saw why Margery had said the man was unavailable during the crisis in Ann's health. His words were slurred and he was swaying as if in a high wind, despite there being no breeze in this comfortable part of the house. The half-brother was drunk, though the sun was still high in the sky. He thought to argue with Eddington, but saw the hollow look in Ann's eyes. With a nod, she indicated he should leave. Raising his hands in mock defeat, Falconer pushed past the drunken man, who clutched at the doorpost to support himself.

As Falconer left the house and started back down the dusty road to Oxford, he failed to notice Covele, who had concealed himself behind bushes close by the gates. The talisman seller had been close enough behind Falconer when he had first arrived to hear the words of the squat monkey-faced servant. He had followed the Oxford master to learn something that he might use against him. What he had immediately found out was that the mistress of this big house meant much to the man. He had looked most anxious on hearing the servant girl's words. And the fact that the mistress was sickening was doubly useful. He put on his extravagant hat, the *pileum cornutum* that Jews were made to wear in

the German principalities as a sign of their origins, and
strode up to the front door.

Falconer, meanwhile, was already crossing the causeway
leading over the water meadows and past Oseney Abbey. The
abbey sat low down in the meadow, but its twin towers soared
heavenwards pointing the direction of the monks' prayerful
observances. Falconer could only think how much money,
extracted in rents for properties in Oxford and its surroundings, it had taken to raise such a tribute to God. In the shade
of a wind-bent tree on the causeway, he was surprised to find
Saphira seated. He sat down beside her.

'You followed me, then?'

Saphira shook her head, and a lock of flame-red hair fell
out of her snood. Distracted, she poked it back.

'No. I was following someone else, who happened to be
following you.'

'Me? Why? Who was it?'

'You remember Covele?'

'Indeed I do. I have him to thank for meeting you again.'

Saphira laughed at Falconer's reference to the previous
encounter with the Jew.

'Hardly. I think we would have met anyway.'

Falconer was recalling that it was Covele's actions,
performing the forbidden ritual of *qorban*, that had sparked
off the riot aimed at the Jews. It was during that riot that
Falconer had nearly had his head split open. Saphira had
dragged him into her house for safety. The charged atmos-
phere of the moment had led to the consummation of their
relationship. Falconer now wondered if their new relationship
would survive his visiting Ann Segrim secretly. Warily, he
raised the matter of Ann's sickness.

'Ann is not well and I was concerned for her. She passed
it off as a mere inconvenience but I think it is more than that.'

Saphira frowned and looked closely at William.

'Tell me her symptoms. Exactly as you saw them.'

'She had been sick more than once and complained of hot
sweats. She looked pale and her eyes were red. I'm sorry but
I observed nothing more.'

Saphira rose and brushed the dust off her skirt.

'Come. I will prepare something that might help. You can
take it to her.'

Falconer understood she meant the last words as an indication of her trust in him, and he felt refreshed.

'What do you propose to give her?'

'Samson drummed into me the basic principle of treating any sickness where you are unsure of the cause. It is to treat a disease with materials from injurious agents causing similar signs to those you observe.'

'*Similia similibus curentur.*'

Saphira nodded in agreement with William's Latin quotation.

'Yes. Like cures like. I shall give you a tincture of opium, as opium itself causes vomiting.'

EIGHT

It took fully four days of hiding before Sir Humphrey Segrim plucked up the courage to emerge from his upper room in the Golden Ball Inn. Each day he sent out the innkeeper, Peter Halegod, to enquire if a Templar had been seen in Oxford. For his part, Halegod carried out his task with good will. After all, Segrim was paying good money to stay at the inn, when his own home was a few miles further down the road. And there were fewer travellers these days to occupy his room otherwise. Business was poor of late, which Halegod blamed on the drop in popularity of the relics held at St Frideswide's Priory and Oseney Abbey. Didn't those in charge realize that people wanted a new show every now and then? Even the strolling players avoided the place, preferring to go where the bones of new saints performed new miracles and drew large crowds. An innkeeper had a lot to complain about in the circumstances.

But Segrim's persistent enquiries were now becoming tiresome. So perhaps it was not surprising that, soon after he had taken too much to drink with a bunch of his cronies on Sunday, he had shot his mouth off about his only paying guest. The gossip must have spread quickly, for the following day Mistress Segrim arrived in his courtyard. She looked pale and sickly, and sat upon a mild-mannered rouncy. Being astride a horse was what drew Halegod's attention to the state of her health in the first place. Normally she was a strong and vital woman and would have walked into Oxford from Botley. He watched as his ostler held the horse's reins and Mistress Segrim descended to the ground. Her face had a grim look to it, as she approached the entrance to the inn.

'You've got trouble coming, Sir Humphrey,' muttered Halegod to himself. 'And it's far worse than some ferocious Templar.'

He hurried to the door in order to meet the angry wife of his only customer. And at that moment, Sir Humphrey came down the stairs. He must have seen her from his upper window, or heard her voice in the yard. Whatever it was, he showed no signs of embarrassment and embraced her as though nothing were amiss.

'My dearest Ann, I was just preparing to leave, when I saw you arrive. How sweet of you to meet me on the way home like this. Such a dutiful, loving wife.'

The show of affection did not convince Robert Halegod at all. If he hadn't known the loveless nature of Segrim's marriage, he would have deduced it from the lack of emotion in the display before him. No kisses were exchanged, and the embrace had been brief and one-sided. Ann stood stock-still and pale-faced, knowing now that her husband, who had been almost a year away from home, had delayed his return by four full days. For no obvious reason. But still Segrim babbled on, becoming more and more nervous by the moment. Sweat burst out on his brow, and he even cast a glance over Ann's shoulder at the people passing the entrance to the inn. Halegod speculated on how this Templar had scared the knight so. Maybe Segrim had refused him his bum at some time. Those Templars were renowned buggerers. Why else did their emblem show two of them astride a horse together?

'Halegod, fetch my bags. We are returning home. I just need to speak to my wife privately first.'

Grumbling at being ordered about, and wondering why, if Sir Humphrey was returning home, he needed this moment privately with his wife, Halegod went up the stairs. Segrim took his wife's arm and led her to the corner of the inn furthest from the door. There, they could sit without being seen or overheard. Once settled, Segrim leaned conspiratorially towards his wife.

'Ann, there is something I must tell you.'

Falconer would have taken the tincture of poppy essence the same day as he saw Ann in her bed chamber, but there was an unfortunate delay. Firstly, Saphira did not have the necessary ingredients and had to wait until Monday in order to visit Robert Bodin's shop. Though he sold herbs and spices for culinary purposes, he also stocked certain medicinal drugs. Unbeknownst to Saphira, indeed, Margery had also

gone to the spicer, as commanded by Ann. But, as the maidservant had only mentioned the sweats and headaches that
afflicted her mistress, as instructed by Eddington, the spicer
had simply given her a weak infusion of feverfew. Saphira's
needs were for something more powerful and she sought to
obtain them from Robert Bodin. However, even then she
had to reduce the poppy essence to a tincture, to which end
she resorted to Samson's kitchen. This took most of the rest
of the day. Samson did offer to help her but she insisted
she knew what she was doing. Besides it would be good
practice. He retired to his solar and left her to it. Once she
had finished what she intended to do, Saphira once again
hurried round to Aristotle's Hall. There, she gave the
precious pot, sealed with wax and parchment at the top, to
Falconer.

For his part, he resolved to take it to Botley first thing
in the morning. But fate was against him, as Peter Mithian
woke up with a fever of his own. This Falconer attributed
to the boy not drying out the old mattress properly before
lying on it. Several nights spent on its damp, mouldy surface,
aided by Mithian's poor diet and weak chest, gave the boy
a raging cough. He was barely able to breath, drawing each
lungful of air in with painful rasping noises. Falconer,
already feeling guilty over his neglect of the boy, moved
his truckle bed to beside the fire in the hall. And then he
hovered beside the bed until Peter breathed more easily.
Only then did he remember the pot from Saphira that stood
in the middle of his table. Fully two days had passed since
he had seen Ann last. He hoped her sickness had not
progressed in the meantime. Falconer rushed up the stairs
and, grabbing hold of the tincture, he hurried off to Botley
Manor. It was here his memory of the events of that day
began to deceive him.

He wasn't sure how he got there, but the next thing he knew
was that he was sitting on the cold, wet floor of a dark cell.
The only light was filtered through the bars set in the heavily
studded door of the cell. It cast a series of oblongs on the
slimy floor close to his feet. He knew this place. It was
Bocardo. But why was he here? He had had small memory
lapses in the past but had shrugged them off as part of growing
old. This was a chasm of darkness. He racked his brain to

piece some fragmentary memories together. And gradually the horror returned.

He remembered that when he reached the Segrims' house, he was surprised to find the place in turmoil. Servants were running hither and thither, and at first they all ignored the visitor. He stood in the hallway leading to the great hall of the old manor house, uncertain what to do. Then he saw Margery enter from outside and scurry past. He grabbed her by the arm.

'What on earth is going on, Margery? Why all the haste? And where may I find Mistress Ann? I have some medicine for her.'

Margery wrestled her arm free and stared coldly at the unwelcome arrival. This was the man she had been warned about by old Segrim, when she took over his duties as the mistress's protector. And she had erred badly by allowing him into Mistress Ann's presence once before. Now, here he stood boldly demanding to see her again. She spoke curtly though he was her better.

'I have just been attending to her. And I know the mistress would not wish to see you.'

'Why, is she worse?'

Falconer was filled with dread. If Ann's illness had progressed during his neglect of her, he would never forgive himself. Margery sneered, not wishing to give into the sort of fear she had felt last time Falconer had appeared. This time she would not resort to him for help.

'Not that it is any of your business, but the mistress is revived by the welcome return of our master.'

'Sir Humphrey is back?'

Falconer had not heard this and wondered how Segrim had turned up without announcing his arrival from his crusading duties to all and sundry. And why.

'Yes, he is. He arrived this very day. So you are not needed here.'

Margery turned on her heels and scuttled off towards the kitchens. Deflated, Falconer walked back out the door. He was still determined to deliver the pot of medicine to Ann, but didn't know where to find her. Then he recalled the monkey-faced Margery's first words to him. She had said she had been attending to Ann. If she had come in from outside, he knew where Ann was likely to be. He strode off towards the walled garden that was Ann's haven whenever she was troubled. She tended lovingly to the plants and trees and revelled in the protective warmth of the red-brick walls. It was her own world far away from Sir Humphrey, her husband. If he had indeed returned, then it was likely she would have already sought refuge in her garden.

Unfortunately, the darkness of his cell in Bocardo once again seemed to encroach, obscuring his recollection of the sequence of events. He squeezed his eyes with forefinger and thumb until red firecrackers sparked inside his eyes. The next image he had was of a blue bundle lying at his feet. He could see Ann's long blonde hair spread across the gravel – it must have broken free of her snood as she fell down. He collapsed to his knees.

She was lying face down and a bloody flux of vomit spread from her mouth. The pot of medicine lay close by. It had shattered on the path, spilling its contents. He was feeling for the pulse of life in her wrist, getting her blood all over his hands. He could feel none. In fact, her hand was quite limp and cold. He knew then that Ann Segrim was dead, and yet he spoke to her as if she were alive, begging forgiveness for his neglect. He was too late. It was as he was talking to her cold corpse that old Sekston happened upon him and called for help.

In his prison cell he remembered now. Ann was dead. The oblongs of light on the floor of the cell disappeared, obscured by a face that appeared at the grille. A voice called out to him. A familiar voice.

'Master Falconer . . . William . . . what has happened here? Will you tell me?'

He recalled the source of that voice. It was young Thomas Symon, one of his students. Why was he here? He tried to figure it all out, but couldn't. Then Thomas spoke again; this time to someone else outside the door.

'Who is it he is supposed to have killed anyway? You did not say.'

Killed? Why did they think he had killed someone?

Then he heard the sad, gravelly voice of Peter Bullock.

'It's . . . Mistress Segrim. Ann.'

The shock of what the constable said roused him from his

stupor for a moment. Why did they think he had killed Ann? By neglecting to take the potion Saphira had prepared? That thought led to another and dark ideas filled his head. He called out distractedly, his voice cracked with emotion.

'Thomas? Is that you? For God's sake, take care of Saphira.'

NINE

Thomas Bek, chancellor of the University of Oxford these past three years, was a nondescript sort of man in appearance. For a start, he was short and skinny. His sandy hair was receding rapidly towards the back of his head, and his eyes were small and pig-like. True, he had a sharp beak of a nose that cleft his features in twain. But it was an item more for derision than admiration, and some called him Chancellor Beak behind his back. And in the same way that his appearance failed to make him stand out from the crowd, his tenure as chancellor had not been spectacular either. He craved the fame of many of his predecessors, such as Henry de Cicestre and Nicholas Ewelme. But chiefly he wished for the notoriety and power of Thomas de Cantilupe. Cantilupe, while Chancellor of the University, had picked the wrong side in the Barons War, choosing to support the barons against King Henry. He had won and then lost his place as Chancellor of England because of that. But the word was, from Bek's own younger brother who was close to Prince Edward, that Cantilupe would soon rise to a high estate again. Thomas Bek felt a need to make his mark, and the opportunity had just presented itself.

'Tell me again, Roger, the case against Master Falconer.'

Roger Plumpton was large and fat where Bek was short and lean. His face was round and reddened, outlined by a loop of black hair round his bald pate, which was finished off with a trim black beard around one of his many chins. He was the proctor for the northern nation at the university and as such wielded great power. His counterpart, Henry de Godfree, proctor of the southern nation, was not present at the moment. Between them they supervised the conduct of the two groups at the university, which had grown up from internal strife within the ranks of the students in the past. The *boreales*, or northerners, came from north of the River Nene, and the *australes*, or southerners, from below it. Though this faction included so many Irishmen that sometimes they were all called

Irish. Roger eased his not inconsiderable frame forward in one of the uncomfortable chairs that adorned the chancellor's rooms.

'Well, as you know, Chancellor, Falconer has long been a thorn in our flesh. Prone to free-thinking, and challenging the authorized viewpoints that we all teach.' The proctors were masters as well as keepers of the peace. 'And he has all too often poked his nose into cases of murder that do not concern the university. Moreover he does not set a good example to the students. There was that matter of the firecracker thrown at Master Ralph Cornish recently. And he is known to associate quite freely with the Jews in the town.'

Bek leaned forward, waving a dismissive hand.

'Yes, yes. I know all this. Cornish has spoken to me *ad nauseam* about his behaviour. But it is this most recent event I wish to know more about. The wife of Sir Humphrey Segrim.'

Plumpton pursed his fat lips and shook his head.

'It has long been known that Falconer spends . . . spent . . . too much time in her company. And so it has been surmised, quite reasonably in my opinion, that he has broken his vows of celibacy with her. And she a married woman too. When he was found in the presence of her body with a tincture of opium in his possession, it was no great leap of imagination to assume he was responsible for her death.'

Bek smiled coldly.

'That is what I wanted to know. You think there is a clear case against him?'

Plumpton nodded eagerly, wishing to please the chancellor, who was rubbing his hands with glee.

'So the facts prove his guilt. Quite an irony, bearing in mind his own application of Aristotelean logic to murder cases. We shall use that to rid ourselves of this nuisance of a master, and soon.'

'How come so soon? The king's justices are not due in the county for a long while. It must be not until—'

Plumpton was not allowed to finish calculating the month in which the king's own justices were due to come to Oxford to dispense the law of the land. Bek's eyes sparkled and he spoke out firmly.

'I want you to call a meeting of the Black Congregation. We will try Falconer ourselves.'

Plumpton squirmed in his seat and stared at the chancellor in horror. It was true that over the last twenty years the office of chancellor had been granted greater and greater powers by the king. And almost fifteen years had passed since a vice-chancellor had successfully wrested from the custody of the town constable three scholars who had seriously injured a couple of local traders. Since then, the chancellor had concerned himself with most cases involving scholars of the university. But murder and mayhem had always remained an exception to the rule. Now Thomas Bek sought to challenge that and thereby exercise even greater power over the town.

'We will set a precedent that will not be overturned.'

The chancellor continued to stare Plumpton in the eye. The proctor gave in first.

'Yes, Chancellor. I will summon the Black Congregation.'

'Who is Saphira?'

Peter Bullock responded to Thomas Symon's question with a look of surprise. He knew that Falconer had been very careful about preserving the woman's reputation, but not to the extent that his ablest student was oblivious to the relationship. Falconer had not worried about his own reputation – many masters at the university paid only lip-service to the vow of celibacy. They were simply bound never to marry. But Falconer did care about Saphira Le Veske's situation, as a Jew in a Christian society and because of her own standing in Jewry. She was a widow with a son, who carried out the family business for her still in Canterbury, and she relied on her good name to preserve that business. Moreover, Bullock had heard she was learning medicinal skills from old Samson. People would not want to call on the curative skills of a woman with a bad reputation. It was a pity that Falconer hadn't had the same sensitivities concerning Ann Segrim. He could have preserved her reputation. Now it was too late.

'Saphira Le Veske. She lives in Jewry just up from St Aldates Church. A good-looking woman in her forties. Red hair.'

Thomas suddenly pictured the woman who had followed Ann Segrim out of the spicer's shop the other week. She had red hair under her head-dress of a snood, and a comely face. No wonder Master Falconer had avoided both women at the

time. It seems as if his new conquest must have met his former
one. He wondered if this Saphira was as proud and fierce as
he had found Ann Segrim. Well, he would find out soon
enough. He looked the constable in the eye.

'Could you take me to her? Master Falconer wishes me to
take care of her.'

Bullock eyed up the slightly built young man, who was
clearly more used to delving in books than handling a woman.
He grinned wryly in anticipation of what Saphira might say
about a boy taking care of her.

'Come on then. It's not far.'

As they walked down Northgate Street and across the bustle
of Carfax, Thomas began to question the constable about the
facts relating to Ann Segrim's death. He was trying hard to
emulate his mentor, whose guiding maxim as a *deductive* –
for that was the very word Falconer used about himself – was
taken from Aristotle himself. He even remembered the first
time he had heard Falconer utter the word. The imposing
master with the piercing blue eyes had been standing on a
raised platform in front of a new intake of eager students, one
of whom had been Symon himself. He scanned the faces
before him as he wandered off on a favourite digression of
his concerning a murder in the town. His voice was clear and
strong.

'It is the *Prior Analytics* of Aristotle that clearly show the
theory of deduction. Two general truths, not open to doubt,
often imply a third truth of more limited scope which was not
previously known.'

This was the world of the deductive – a world redolent with
truths and reason and logic. Thomas would now embark on
such a course himself. He would collect as many known truths
as he could, analyse them, compare them, list them, and hope
to find the greater truth hidden amidst the others. Breathlessly,
because Bullock's bandy legs seemed to eat up the ground,
Thomas drew out from him what was known about the death.
He listened carefully to Bullock's words.

'Mistress Segrim was found lying on the path between her
garden and the manor house, as though she was returning.
She had a bloody flux coming out of her nose and mouth,
which could not have been caused by her simply falling.'

'Why do you say that?'

'Because there was apparently no damage to her face and
nose. The sort that might have been sustained if she had tripped.
It was more like she had just . . . slipped to the ground and
expired.'

Bullock shook his head sadly at the thought.

'Who told you this?'

Thomas was desperately trying to think of all the questions
Falconer would have asked at this stage. He knew he would
forget something and it might prove crucial. But his teacher
had no one else to represent him, other than Peter Bullock
himself. And he was constrained by his duties as constable.

'Who told me? Well, I think it was old Sekston, when they
brought William to Bocardo. As I told you, it was Sekston
who found William kneeling over the body . . . over Ann.'

Bullock still could not bring himself to think of sweet Ann
Segrim as a dead body. Unlike his usual pragmatic approach
to a suspicious death, he wanted to keep referring to her by
her name and not as some inanimate object. Not the body,
the corpse, the victim, but Ann. Thomas snorted in derision.

'So, we only have the word of a half-blind old man, who
disliked William intensely, that Mistress Segrim did not trip
and bang her head. Indeed there could have been many other
causes not attributable to William. And his presence could
merely have been a coincidence. No, it *was* a coincidence, as
he is obviously innocent.'

Bullock stopped in his tracks, grabbed Thomas's arm and
pushed his weather-beaten face into that of the fresh-faced
master.

'Is that the sort of help you are going to give William. He
must be innocent so we won't bother collecting all the facts
that prove it? If that's what you are going to do, then you
might as well give up now and let me get on with it. Because,
when the royal justices arrive, they will want more than a kid,
who owes William everything, crying out his innocence.'

Thomas was about to protest at being called a kid, about
having his efforts so derided, but Bullock held up a warning
hand.

'No. You will let me finish. William deserves more than
protestations of innocence. He needs proof. Moreover he needs
us to find out who it was that killed Ann Segrim.' Bullock's
face was puffy and bright red with anger, his brows beetling

over his washed out, old man's eyes. He paused in his rant. 'And I can't do it by myself. I never could. William was . . . is cleverer than me, and so are you. So help me, and between us we will find out who did this foul deed.'

Despite the seriousness of the situation, Thomas grinned wolfishly at Bullock's words.

'Of course I will help. I want to do nothing less. So, let's get on with it.'

They were soon at Saphira's door and Thomas let Bullock knock. He was the official representative of the law, after all. The red-haired woman with the striking features, who he had seen leaving the spicer's, opened the door to them. Her friendly smile enveloped Thomas in its warmth. Of course, she didn't know what had happened yet. However, Bullock's awkwardness soon alerted her to the fact there was a problem. Anxiously, she looked over both their shoulders. A Jew soon developed a sixth-sense for trouble. Bullock tried to put her mind at rest.

'Don't worry, Mistress Le Veske. There is no trouble brewing. Not for you at least.'

'That's a very strange thing to say, Peter Bullock. You had better come in. And you too, young man.'

She led them through the main hall of the house and into the kitchen. Here, everything was much more comfortable than the bare, chilly hall at the front of the house. A fire burned in the hearth and two high-back chairs were set either side of it. A book and some clean parchment lay beside one chair on a simple table. Saphira clearly spent most of her time in this cosy room. She offered her two guests the chairs and Thomas sat down on one. Then was filled with embarrassment, when he realized that Bullock had remained standing. The constable insisted Saphira take the other chair and he perched on a chest on the other side of the room. Thomas wasn't sure whether he had done that out of courtesy, or deliberately, so that he was on the margins of the conversation, leaving Thomas to broach the awkward matter of their reason for being here. He coughed nervously and looked at the beautiful woman. For a time, he was so engaged by her emerald-green eyes he could not remember her name. It came as something of a surprise that he could recall his own.

'My name is Thomas Symon, mistress . . . errr . . .'

She smiled easily and offered what his brain could not supply.

'Le Veske. But please call me Saphira. I may be old enough to be your mother but please don't make it obvious.'

Thomas felt a hot blush travelling up from his neck and over his cheeks. He could only stammer meaninglessly. Fortunately, Bullock took pity on him and spoke out.

'Mistress, it is a hard business we are here about.'

Saphira stiffened slightly in her chair. She knew Bullock well enough by now to see from the tone of his voice that this was a serious matter.

'Then you must speak out plainly. I am no weak maiden, who cannot take the truth when it is presented to her.'

'It concerns William.'

'Ahhh.'

Saphira glanced at Thomas Symon, not sure if he knew, as Bullock did, that she and Falconer were intimates.

'Tell me.'

'He is arrested for the murder of Ann Segrim.'

The colour drained from Saphira's face. Her body seemed to lose all its vivacity and she slumped in her chair. She shook her head, looking from Bullock to the boy and back again.

'William? Taken for murdering Ann? How can that be?'

Bullock explained how Falconer was found at the side of Ann's body close to her walled garden at Botley.

'Her maid had only just left her and said she was fine when she departed.'

'Fine? How could she be fine when William told me that Ann had been very sick only a few days ago?'

Bullock frowned. This was news to him. He had assumed that the death had been sudden. Now it seemed that Ann Segrim had been unwell for some time. Did this mean anything, or was it unrelated? He realized he did not have a clue how Ann had died, merely assuming from the garbled story from Sekston and the serfs from Botley that she had been killed by a blow or a dagger. His embarrassment was spotted by Thomas, who ventured to make a suggestion.

'Master Bullock, is there any way that I could examine the body?'

The constable looked aghast. He knew exactly what Symon meant. He had been aware of Falconer's reliance on the little grey master called Richard Bonham. The inoffensive-looking man, now dead, had carried out quite illegal examinations of the bodies of people who had died in suspicious circumstances. Bullock didn't wish to contemplate the details, but he knew Bonham actually cut the bodies open in the belief that the entrails would tell him something about the murder. It sounded more like necromancy to him than science. But it produced results. And Bullock had turned a blind eye to the breaking of civil and canon law. Now it seemed that this young whipper-snapper was suggesting he carry out the same defiling of Ann Segrim's body. He was about to deny the request, when Thomas Symon explained.

'I would not have to cut open . . . the body. Besides, even if I did, I am not yet as expert at that as Master Bonham was. No, I merely wish to look at her features, the colour and state of her skin and so on. And I need to ask some questions of the servants. This maid of hers, perhaps.'

'Margery, yes.'

'Can you take me to Botley and do that?'

Bullock nodded, glad to be doing something positive at last. He didn't know how he would persuade Sir Humphrey to let an Oxford master see the body of his dead wife. But he would think of something. Having got a satisfactory answer to that part of his investigations, Thomas turned his attentions to the obviously distraught Saphira Le Veske. He put on a solemn air and explained his reason for coming to her house.

'Mistress Le Veske, I can see that you are distressed by all of this. And I have promised William that I will take care of you. Tell me, is there anything you need?'

Despite the desperate situation, Saphira was amused by Thomas's funereal face. She glanced over at Bullock, perched on her clothes chest, and winked.

'You are most courteous, Thomas Symon, but I find that I am not in any immediate need. Other than a report from you as soon as you find out what you think caused Ann Segrim's death.'

Thomas's face fell.

'I don't think that I should involve you in such a terrible matter. I am sure that was not what William intended, when he said to take care of you.'

Saphira leaned across to where Thomas sat and patted his arm.

'I am sure that is exactly what William intended. I am no

courtly lady lacking experience of the darker side of life. I have seen dead bodies and been in peril of my life. Believe me, I can help you the same way I helped William at times.'

Thomas, uncomfortably aware of the swell of Saphira's full bosom over the top of her dress and the heat of her hand on his arm, looked across at the constable for support. Bullock merely smiled crookedly.

'She's right, Master Symon. Mistress Le Veske has a wit as nimble as Falconer's.'

'Better, sometimes, Peter.'

Saphira rose and walked over to a small cask set on its side on the kitchen table. She picked up a pewter jug and held it to the tap, turning it on.

'Let us toast our success in proving William's innocence. We may have a hard road to travel over the next few days, or even weeks, but I am sure we will be successful.'

They raised their jugs of ale and saluted the solemn enterprise.

TEN

Thomas Bek was taking a chance by establishing himself as the arbiter in the case of William Falconer. But if his plan came off, he would wield considerably more power over the town as well as the university. Until now, he sat in the weekly Chancellor's Court deciding on tedious cases which were at the same time petty and convoluted. Two days ago, he had banished from Oxford a friar who had libelled two Bachelors of Theology, and made a vicar swear never again to make suspicious visits to a tailor's wife. At the same court he had become so intemperate that he had turned on a petitioner from the town. He had made the innkeeper of the Cardinal's Hat make good the value of a horse he had foolishly allowed two Welsh students to purloin. The innkeeper had left his court fuming but impotent. Now, he sought to try a man for murder. And in order to strengthen his position, he had decided to deal with it in the grand context of the Black Congregation.

This august body was made up of the Regent Masters of the Faculty of Arts, which held sway over the running of the university, much to the chagrin of the other faculties. By holding the trial in front of the Black Congregation, Bek reckoned to legitimize the whole affair. Besides, he knew there were many masters in its numbers who hated Falconer sufficiently to preordain the result. What Bek did not want was an acquittal. That would not suit his purpose one little bit.

Roger Plumpton bustled into his room and interrupted his musings. The fat man was sweating heavily. Whether from his hurried entrance up the stairs, or from the precarious nature of his mission, Bek could not tell. Plumpton did not have the adventurous nature that possessed Thomas Bek and was perturbed at stepping over the boundaries of existing rules. Bek would have to rely more on his counterpart, the proctor of the southern nation, Henry de Godfree. He was a much more pragmatic sort of man, who would see the possibilities of what Bek proposed. Godfree was due back in Oxford tomorrow. He had been on a visit to London on behalf of the Chancellor. It had been on a minor intrigue of Bek's that was now superseded by a much more important scheme.

Early on the morning after their agreeing to work together, three sombre people met at the small castle gate in the town walls of Oxford. The sun having barely peeped over the walls, the day was still chilly. So the constable had protected his old bones by donning a sheepskin coat over his tunic, as well as putting on thick leggings. The red-haired woman had also taken the precaution of wearing a dark-coloured cloak over her green gown. Besides keeping her warm, she thought it suitably sober for the task ahead. The young teaching master had ignored the morning chill and wore his usual long black robe. He shivered as he shook Peter Bullock's hand, but felt sure he would warm up as they walked towards Botley.

'I have sent a boy ahead with a message to ensure our arrival is not unexpected.'

Bullock's words were the only ones spoken before they passed through the narrow gate. The constable locked it behind them, and they set off. The morning chill was slowly being driven off the low-lying land and mist hung like tattered shrouds across the fields surrounding Oseney Abbey. The abbey itself seemed to float above the clouds, its towers reaching up to the heavens. The long straight road led directly to Botley, and as no one felt inclined to talk, the three plodded on in silence. As they reached the grounds of the manor house, Bullock spoke at last.

'Leave this to me. I will say that you . . .' He indicated Thomas Symon with a horny finger. '. . . you are here to represent the interests of the accused. Segrim might protest, but I will say that the King's Court requires it. And he will not know any better. You . . .' The finger pointed at Saphira Le Veske. '. . . are with me to ensure propriety when I look at the body.'

The others nodded their agreement with Bullock's plan. As they approached the door, it swung open and a man of middle years stood squarely in their way. He wore his hair long and curly but was otherwise shaved. Though the shaving had been patchy and areas of stubble were interspersed with nicks and red rashes. His face was puffy and showed all the signs of being that of a drunkard. Bullock guessed this was the half-brother who was supposed to have looked after the manor in Sir Humphrey's absence. The man confirmed this with his first words.

'I am Alexander Eddington, brother to Sir Humphrey Segrim. Whatever your business here, it can wait. My sister-in-law is dead and my brother does not wish to see anyone. So be gone.'

Bullock stood his ground, used to the bullying nature of minor nobility and landowners.

'I fear what I wish to do cannot wait. I am the town constable of Oxford, and as the death of your sister concerns a resident of Oxford, I have jurisdiction over the matter. I have come to see the body. Did you not receive my message?'

'Yes, but I sent the boy away. You cannot come in. We are in mourning.'

Bullock stepped forward so that his face was inches from Eddington's.

'I will come in, and I will do what I am here to do. I have with me Master Thomas Symon of the university and Mistress Le Veske, a widow of good repute in the town. They are here to see fair play in all matters, so you will let me pass.'

Eddington's eyes dropped to the floor, and grumbling under his breath, he stepped aside and let the three visitors in. At Bullock's request, he reluctantly led them up the staircase and into the bedroom where Ann Segrim's body lay. A heavy tapestry was drawn across the window and the room was icy cold. Ann lay on the bed still dressed in the clothes she had been found in. There were dark stains on the neck of the dress, which Bullock took for blood, and other marks around the skirt from where she had lain on the gravel path. Her face was serene but her skin was slack and pale as snow. Her arms had been folded across her chest in a prayerful attitude. Eddington stood in the doorway looking nervous; biting the nails on the fingers of his right hand. Bullock turned back to the door and closed it firmly in the brother's face. Then he placed a chair against the latch, making it difficult to reopen the door. He looked at Thomas Symon quizzically.

'Quickly now, what can you tell me?'

Uncertain, Symon stepped closer to the body and took a deep breath. This was very different from practising on a pig in Falconer's cellar. Looking closely at a dead body, and of a person he had known in life, made him quite ill. He had to swallow hard to prevent himself from retching. But then he took a decision and looked back at Bullock.

'Can you open the drape? It is hard to examine her in this poor light.'

Bullock did as requested and the morning light flooded into the room. Fortified, Symon once again bent over the body of Ann Segrim.

'Yes, look here. There is vomit still on her lips – greenish with smears of blood in it. Did you say, Mistress Le Veske, that she had been vomiting earlier?'

Saphira nodded.

'Correct. For a number of days apparently. That is why I prepared a tincture of opium for William to bring to her. She had been sweating too.'

'Really? I would like to know some of her other symptoms. Perhaps we can ask her husband that.'

Bullock interrupted the young man's musings.

'Yes, but that is for later. Please try and stick to the matter in hand. I don't suppose that Sir Humphrey or his brother will take too kindly to us being here alone for too long. What can you tell me from what you see?'

Thomas was a little put out by the constable's abruptness and was about to make a retort. But behind Bullock, he saw Saphira quietly shake her head, and gesture at the body. He contained his annoyance and looked more closely at Ann's face and arms, which were the only parts of her that were exposed. He thought for a moment about looking further, but didn't suppose it would have been seemly to examine any other part of the body. What he did see confirmed the suspicion of foul play, but it wasn't of a physically violent nature, as had been suggested.

'She has been poisoned. Look at her arms, where the skin is darker than normal, and here on her palms . . .' He turned the hands over so Bullock could see. '. . . there is scaly skin. And here . . .' He turned them back over again. 'Here there are white lines on her nails.'

Bullock squinted closely at Ann's hands, also seeing what Symon was pointing out.

'What does it mean?'

'It means that Ann Segrim was possibly poisoned with arsenic powder.'

This revelation was interrupted by a thunderous knocking on the door and jiggling of the jammed latch. This was followed by a call from outside.

'What are you doing in there?'

Alexander Eddington was back and, by the sound of it, was not prepared to allow them any more time. Bullock moved the chair causing the obstruction and pulled the door abruptly open. Eddington's face was, if anything, more suffused with a red flush. He had either let his anger build, or had been drinking some more. Bullock pushed him roughly back on to the gallery outside that overlooked the main hall of the manor house. The private room where Ann lay was located off this galleried area, and further along was a second door that Bullock presumed was that of Sir Humphrey. He knew from Falconer that he and his wife inhabited separate bed chambers. The second door was firmly shut and no sound came from within. Though Eddington had caused a great deal of noise, it seemed the grieving widower was not to be disturbed. Bullock had to try, however.

'I need to speak to Sir Humphrey, if you please.'

He made to pass Eddington, but this time the brother was having none of it. He stood up to the constable, bolstered by his extra intake of Segrim's best Rhenish.

'You will not disturb him now in his time of grief. It is enough that you have . . . desecrated his wife's rest with your pryings. Now take your crew and leave.'

Bullock knew that if he insisted now his investigations may be compromised by ill feeling. He may even be reported on to the sheriff and aldermen of Oxford, to whom he nominally answered. So he decided not to push further, thinking he had plenty of time before the King's justices arrived to try any case brought against William. He was not to know that in this instance he was mistaken. Time to prepare was rapidly running out for Falconer.

'Very well. We will leave for the time being. But bear in mind that I will need to interview everyone in the house. Including Sir Humphrey, and yourself.'

Eddington spluttered in anger.

'Are you suggesting I am involved in this unfortunate matter?'

Bullock gave him no reply, but simply smiled enigmati-
cally. Then he turned on his heels, leading Saphira and Thomas
back down the stairs and out the front door. It was only when
he returned to his quarters in the castle that he heard of the
chancellor's plans for Falconer's trial. Suddenly time had run
out and the matter was becoming very urgent.

Unaware that Falconer would face the Black Congregation
the very next day, Saphira Le Veske returned straight home
after the trip to Botley. She sat in her kitchen, where the maid
she employed had laid out a cold meal. She was hungry but
could only toy with the food. There was something on her
mind. At Botley, she had seen more than she was prepared to
admit to Bullock or Thomas Symon. When they had entered
the bedchamber where the body of Ann Segrim lay, she had
simply watched as Thomas examined it. Her knowledge of
the signs of death was limited. But when Bullock pulled the
drapery back to let in more light, she had spotted something
that the two men ignored. Lying on the table next to the bed
was a small silver box carved to look like filigree which was
fixed to the end of a chain for encircling the neck. Inside the
box, showing through the intricate carving, was a small piece
of parchment. Some may have thought it purely decorative,
but being a Jew, Saphira knew it immediately. It was a kimiyah
– a small amulet to protect against illness. The parchment was
an angel text. It would have the name of an angel inscribed
on it, and to some it would be a powerful talisman. Saphira
was prepared to bet that it had been bought recently from
Covele, the Jew she had seen in Oxford the other day. It made
her all the more determined to track him down and find out
why he had been at Botley. And if he had anything to do with
Ann Segrim's death.

Her reluctance to tell anyone else of her observation
stemmed from her deep understanding of what it meant to be
a Jew in Henry's England. Her race was no more than toler-
ated by most Englishmen. They were reviled for lending money
with interest, when that very practice had been forced on them
by the English king who effectively owned them – in body if
not soul. The Christian religion forbade profiting from lending
money, but noblemen needed to borrow money to sustain their
lifestyle. It was a simple step, then, to leave money-lending

as the only avenue for Jews to make a living. Saphira's own son ran the family business which was based in Canterbury and Bordeaux, and there they traded quietly in wine under cover of lending money. But if any hint of wrong-doing was attached to a Jew, the consequences could be dire, for the individual concerned and the community at large. So Saphira was reluctant to place Covele at the scene of the murder without investigating further. Pushing her bowl of untouched victuals aside, she picked up her cloak and went to search for the amulet seller.

While Saphira was embarking on her own secret investigations, Thomas Symon sat in Colcill Hall racking his brains as to how his mentor would have started his inquiry into Ann Segrim's murder. He knew he should have insisted on interviewing Sir Humphrey Segrim, but the half-brother's intimidating presence had scared him off. Many said, however, that you should look for a murderer in the bosom of the family of the victim first and foremost. Thomas knew he would have to talk to the husband eventually, despite Alexander Eddington's efforts to prevent him from doing so. In the meantime, Thomas knew he should be accumulating known facts in accordance with Falconer's tenet on being a deductive. Several smaller truths, when laid out together, would reveal a greater truth. He sighed and picked up a quill, a pot of black ink and a piece of old, scraped parchment. By the light of the afternoon sun streaming through the narrow, glazed window of the hall, he began to write down what he knew.

An hour later, the light was beginning to fade and Thomas had scratched out no more than a few words on the cleaned parchment. Below the name of Ann Segrim he had written the words 'poisoned' and 'arsenic?'. He had pondered long and hard over the question mark after arsenic but had finally added it. He was already unsure of his analysis of the signs on the victim's body. Beneath that expression of uncertainty he had added two more. Firstly, he had written down Sir Humphrey's name, to which he had added another question mark. Then after a longer pause, he had put down Alexander Eddington's name, also followed by a question mark, for the sole reason that the man had been present in Botley Manor. By the same reasoning, he could have put down all the servants' names, and had indeed sat with his pen hovering over the

parchment for some time. The silent witness to his indecision
was the large ink blot that completed his list of known facts.
It had dropped off the end of the quill as he hesitated, and
had caused him to finally lay down the pen. Now the ink had
dried on the quill tip and his mind had emptied of ideas. It
was not a lot to show for his first day investigating the death
of Ann Segrim.

Suddenly a shadow fell across the parchment, and he heard
a tapping sound. Looking up at the window, he could see a face
behind the small panes of glass. Somewhat distorted, it was
still recognizable as Peter Bullock's. The constable gesticulated
through the glass, indicating that Thomas should let him in the
hall. Hurrying to the door, Thomas wondered what had happened
now. Had Falconer been freed before he could even begin his
investigations? He sincerely hoped so, as he felt inadequate to
press his mentor's cause. But the news wasn't good.

Flinging the door open, he saw the expression of horror on
Bullock's face.

'What has happened?'

'Chancellor Bek means to try William himself before the
Black Congregation. And the trial starts tomorrow.'

PART TWO
THE TRIAL

ELEVEN

A t terce on that Thursday morning in April, a rare sight was seen in Oxford. Solemn men in black robes appeared from all corners of the town, and began converging on St Mildred's Church in the northern quarter of Oxford. To the many onlookers, it would seem as though a dark mass of water flowed down the narrow lanes, pulled by gravity into an unseen deep pit situated somewhere below the church. The Congregation of Regent Masters of Oxford University's Faculty of Arts met periodically to consider matters of relevance to the workings of the university. The seventy or so Masters of Arts jealously guarded their status and pre-eminence over all other masters, and they were familiarly known as the Black Congregation. But the issues coming before the Congregation were often tedious and not everyone attended. However, it was rumoured that today was to be an unusual occurrence. They had all been summoned by the chancellor for a most serious purpose and were required to attend at the ninth hour of the morning without fail. Rumours of their attending a murder trial had ensured that no one stayed away under any pretext, and had also made certain of their promptness. Soon, the church was filled with the black sea and the doors were closed on the curious outsiders.

Three chairs had been set up just below the altar, one slightly raised above the other two, which flanked it either side. A group of senior masters placed themselves close before them to establish their precedence, though still not sure what was to take place. Others nodded to this pre-eminent group as they moved around, seeking a suitable place to sit. Amongst the senior group was the tall, angular figure of Master Gerald Halle, and the coarse features of one of the few foreign Masters, Heinrich Koenig. Ralph Cornish briefly spoke to both of these men before retiring to the side aisle of the church. He was still smarting from the humiliation meted out to him by Falconer and preferred to lurk on the fringes for the time being. He himself was not surprised that he could not find Falconer's

face in the crowd. Bek had already spoken to him privately
and could guess what was about to develop. A deep-seated
sense of revenge was bubbling within him.

After an initial period of subdued conversation, when questions were bandied around from master to master but no answers
supplied, the congregation began to arrange itself in the seats
either side of the nave. All the masters wore a black tabard,
over the top of which was arranged a black sleeveless cope,
or a cloak with a hood bordered with fur. All knew how cold
the interior of St Mildred's could get, even in summer, and
had ensured they wore something warm. It was likely to be a
lengthy business they were summoned to sit through. No one
knew at the time just how lengthy. Headgear saw a mixture of
square birettas and simple round pileums. A few had already
pulled up their hoods to keep warm, and no doubt in order to
doze off beneath them should matters become tedious. The
assembled crowd were not kept in uncertainty for long.

As the conversation in the church lulled, Thomas Bek, with
a deep sense of theatre, strode from the gloom of the side
aisle towards the chairs arranged below the altar. He wore a
scarlet cope trimmed with black over his robe and a scarlet
biretta on his head. The two proctors scurried along either
side of him and arranged themselves in the lower chairs
flanking the chancellor's chair. Bek sat regally on his raised
throne and smoothed his cope over his rather lanky limbs. His
entrance had ensured complete silence and he finally broke it
with a sombre pronouncement. With Robert Plumpton looking
embarrassed and Henry de Godfree grinning in clear satisfaction, Chancellor Bek explained why the Black Congregation
had been summoned.

'We are here today to deal with a most serious matter. One
that has not been brought before this court before, but which
it is my firm belief we are competent to examine.'

His announcement caused a buzz of interest in the assembled masters. All wondered what was to follow except for
Ralph Cornish. Would this outdo the case of Master Swallowe
who had attached a new document to an old seal in order to
ensure a living? Or had another student drawn a dagger on
one of the proctors like young Hoghwel de Balsham? The
chancellor allowed the murmur of curiosity to subside before
continuing.

'This very day, I bring before you for trial for murder, Regent Master William Falconer.'

Amidst the cries of disbelief and shock, Bek detected a few satisfied sighs. He also saw Ralph Cornish lean forward eagerly in his seat. Bek had plans for the regent master, relying on Cornish's hatred for Falconer to get him on his side. He waved an imperious arm into the shadows on the left of the church. The reluctant figure of the constable, Peter Bullock, emerged from the gloom leading a disconsolate Falconer by the arm. He led his friend to a small chair to the left of the chancellor and sat him down, ashamed of his part in this charade. But the chancellor wielded great power in the town and Bullock could not prevent Falconer from being tried by the university. He could only hope that any judgement, if it were against Falconer, would be found invalid in time to save his friend's life. He looked down at the seated figure, worried that William appeared to be paying no attention to what was going on around him. In fact, he seemed as withdrawn as he had been since being incarcerated in the Bocardo. When the constable had the most need of Falconer's skills to solve this extraordinary murder case, they weren't available. It looked as though the regent master could not even help himself.

The morning was proving to be just as anxious a time for Saphira as it was for Bullock. She was awoken by the sound of someone knocking urgently on her door. Wrapping a fur-lined cloak around her, she descended to the door and cautiously pulled it ajar. A boy stood there saying he had a message from the constable. Peter Bullock had told the boy to tell Mistress Le Veske that the chancellor of the university meant to try a certain person for murder that very day. The boy then ran off down the street, the richer by a small coin given him by Saphira.

Once Saphira had been advised of this perilous state that Falconer found himself in, she hurriedly dressed. She immediately knew what she had to do, as a result of the information she had culled the previous evening. At that time, she had hoped to easily track Covele and his boy down. Upon enquiring around the Jewish community, she had discovered that someone resembling the talisman seller was camped out in the Jewish cemetery. She cursed herself for forgetting that was exactly where Covele had been the last time he came to Oxford. It should have been no surprise to her that he would use the same spot again. Having wasted a few hours finding out what she should have known already, she hurried across town and through East Gate. Though she had no real plan in her head other than confronting Covele, she sensed that speed was of the essence. Peter Pady at the gate warned her that, with dusk approaching, he would be closing the gate shortly.

'If you wish to avoid being locked out, Mistress Le Veske, you will need to return soon.'

'I hope I will not be long about my business, Peter.'

'Very well. You can always try the wicket-gate, if the main gate is shut.'

Saphira thanked the watchman, knowing that Pady appreciated the sight of a well-turned ankle when a lady lifted her skirt to step through the small gate set in the larger one. He would keep the wicket-gate open as long as he could. Even so, her business was briefer than she had expected. When she got to the cemetery there was no one there. Covele and his son had fled.

She retraced her steps to East Gate, which was now closed. Stepping through the wicket-gate, she smiled at old Pady. He was seated in his usual spot on a low stool by the entrance, where he had a better view of female legs.

'Peter, have you seen the talisman seller recently? He wears a big conical-shaped hat with a spike on top and has a boy with him.'

Pady nodded happily.

'I don't know about the boy, but . . .'

So saying, he thrust a hand down inside the front of his tunic. From below the greasy collar he produced a stone on the end of a leather cord that encircled his neck. He held it between a grubby finger and thumb, showing the marks on its surface.

'I bought this from him this very morning. It is protection against the joint pains I have been suffering from. It's so hard getting out of bed these days, I'm so stiff. He told me this would stop all that.'

Saphira doubted very much that the old man would be any better tomorrow for the wearing of a pebble. Except for his own mind telling him he was. But there was no point in disappointing him now. Covele relied on the credulous to buy his amulets and then wait for their effects to appear. In the meantime he moved on before they could complain of their failure. It looked as though that was what had happened now. Unless Covele was truly guilty of the murder of Ann Segrim and had fled the consequences. She had another question for Pady.

'Where did you see him when you bought your talisman?'

'Well that was a bit of luck, really. You see, my knees were aching something awful and I was thinking of seeing Old Mother Gertrude over in Beaumont. She has some wonderful recipes for pains. Though she charges the earth for them too . . .'

Saphira almost broke into the old man's ramblings to hurry him up. But she knew he might clam up on her if she did, so she contained her impatience. He would get to the point eventually.

'. . . Anyway, I was just passing Robert Bodin's shop, when I saw the Jew coming out. He wore that hat, just like you said, and had talismans and amulets hanging off his cloak. All sorts of silver cases and big stones with coloured lines running through them. But I could not afford anything like that. So I stopped him, and told him my neighbour had bought one of his smaller stones. Did he have another like it? He said, yes, and produced this from a pocket inside his cloak.'

He held up the pebble again. The marks on it were not natural grains in the stone, but had been painted on. Saphira could see it was the Hebrew letter aleph. At least wearing it would do Pady no harm. Which is more than she could say for some of the preparations Gertrude concocted. Pady had saved himself from a bad stomach ache at the expense of a few pennies for a pebble with a hole in it. But what he had said about Covele intrigued her.

'Coming out of the spicer's shop, you say?'

'That's right.'

Saphira thanked the gatekeeper by planting a kiss on his bald pate and rushed off along the High Street. Unfortunately, she had been too late. The spicer's shop, along with many others, was already closed with the shutters up. She would have to wait till the morning to investigate further what Covele's business had been in the shop.

Now the morning had come, and the new urgency of the

situation had driven Saphira round to the spicer's shop a little
too early. She was standing outside Robert's door but the shop
was not open. She waited impatiently, watching as the other
shops around opened up. Shutters were lowered and goods
laid out on display. The town was gradually waking up.
However, there was no sign of the spice shop opening. Finally,
she decided to knock on the door. In fact, she hammered on
it ceaselessly before getting any response. Robert Bodin's head
popped out of an upstairs window and looked down. He seemed
to be quite fearful of all the commotion.

'What do you want, woman?'

Saphira looked up, wondering why Robert had not opened
his doors as usual, and why he looked so worried.

'I just wanted to ask a question about one of your customers.
A Jew – the talisman seller. He was here yesterday.'

'Yes. What about him?'

Robert looked very pale and his voice quavered. Others in
the street were looking at the strange interchange with curiosity.

'What was his business in your shop? Can you tell me what
you sold him?'

'I don't think that it is any of your business. But I can see
you won't leave me in peace until I tell you. The Jew bought
arsenic.'

Bodin's head then disappeared and his shutters slammed
shut.

In St Mildred's Church the trial ground on. After establishing
that the death of Ann Segrim had been by poisoning, with
which Peter Bullock was made to reluctantly agree, Bek was
now calling his first witness.

'I begin the case by taking evidence of Regent Master
William Falconer's . . . relationship with Mistress Ann Segrim.'

Thomas Bek deliberately hesitated in his sentence to suggest
he knew more about the relationship than he really did.
However, Falconer had annoyed so many of his fellows over
the years that it had not been hard to find someone who would
testify against him on the subject. And who would turn rumour
into truth with pleasure. In fact, Master John Samon had
responded with alacrity to the approaches of the Southern
Proctor, Henry de Godfree. Bek had suggested him as a
witness, as Samon still carried with him the burden of his

reputation as a student troublemaker. He would therefore do anything to ingratiate himself with the hierarchy of the university. His disreputable past was largely centred on a hot-headed incident in 1264, when he and two other clerks had broken down Smith Gate in protest at its being locked against the students. Since becoming a regent master he had worked hard to change that perception, deliberately turning himself into the most conservative of teachers. This mantle had set him in opposition to Falconer on many an occasion. Bek knew Samon would happily slander Falconer, if he thought it would improve his standing with the chancellor.

'I summon Regent Master John Samon to testify against the accused concerning his and Mistress Segrim's behaviour.'

John Samon rose from his place halfway down the nave and moved towards the altar. He was a sturdy man running a little to seed, as his healthy appetite now outdid his levels of physical exertion. The Smith Gate incident had come about because the locked gate had prevented Samon and his friends from exiting the town to desport themselves on the fields beyond. These days, his most strenuous labour was to climb the stairs to his solar in Vulp Hall. He was relishing his place as the centre of attention, under the approving gaze of the chancellor. He stood before the assembled congregation, tree-trunk legs spread wide, his hands nestled over his generous belly.

'Chancellor, fellow regent masters, I know it for a truth that William Falconer . . .' Here he cast a sidelong glance at the accused to emphasize his point. '. . . has on many an occasion met with the late Ann Segrim – God rest her soul – and touched her intimately.'

There was a gasp of shock and disapproval from the other masters that Peter Bullock found hypocritical, and almost laughable. He could swear that he had seen most of those present in one or other of the bawdy houses down Grope Lane at one time or another. Even the stately Master Halle, sitting on the front row of seats with his face a picture of sour disgust, had recently been seen by one of his watchmen coming out of Agnes's brothel, his patrician grey hair in disarray. To criticize improper conduct in William was ridiculous. But he was in no position to stop the vilification. All he could do was listen as Samon quoted chapter and verse concerning times he had observed William and Ann in compromising situations. It amounted to nothing more than a touching of hands together, or the friendly patting of a shoulder. But it was enough in the circumstances. Though no proof was offered of a more intimate relationship, Bullock knew what people would infer. He had long cautioned Falconer about how his dalliance with Ann might have seemed like to others. Now, the chickens were coming home to roost, and all Falconer could do was sit impassively and listen to it all. Samon rounded off his accusations with a final sally.

'This man has corrupted the wife of an important local landowner and must be brought to book for his misdeeds.'

A ripple of agreement ran through the black-robed masters and Samon stomped back to his seat. All eyes turned to the chancellor, wondering where this evidence might lead next. Bek did not keep them waiting.

'I wish to call before you Alexander Eddington, half-brother to Sir Humphrey Segrim, and master of Botley Manor while Sir Humphrey was following the Cross in the Holy Land.'

Bullock grimaced at the pronouncement. The chancellor was making every effort to paint a picture of the whole Segrim family being as pure as the driven snow. Speculative murmurs echoed through the church, as the masters waited for Eddington to be brought forward. As an outsider, he had had to wait outside the church until this moment. When the half-brother strode up the centre aisle, well-scrubbed and dressed in a sombre purple tunic, he looked very unlike the drunken wretch the constable had seen two days ago. With a deferential tone, Bek invited him to offer his testimony.

'Sir, when did you last see Falconer and your sister-in-law together?'

Eddington took a deep breath and turned to address the rows of eager faces that confronted him. They were agog with expectation.

'Last Sunday. I was called to my sister's bedchamber because that man . . .' He pointed an accusing finger at the impassive, almost bowed figure of Falconer. '. . . that man had forced his way in. It did not take me long to eject the coward, however.'

The muttering that had broken out at the mention of Ann Segrim's bedchamber now turned into a hubbub of protestations.

Eddington threw a sly look at Falconer, triumph etched into his features as he carried on.

'I did not see him the second time he came, or he would not have had the chance to murder my dear sister.'

Amidst the crescendo of noise, Bullock wondered if there was more to Alexander Eddington's outrage than first appeared. Was he a little too eager to throw accusations of murder at William? The constable made a mental note to look closer into Eddington's behaviour whilst at Botley. For now though, the damage was done. But the damning evidence didn't stop with the half-brother. Bek banged the flat of his hand on the ornately carved arm of his chair until silence was restored in the church.

'I now call to witness the maidservant of Ann Segrim. She is called . . .' He leaned over to Henry de Godfree, who supplied the forgotten name. '. . . Margery of Botley.'

Eddington stepped away from the chancellor and walked back down the nave. When he came back, he was dragging a scared Margery by the arm. He positioned her where he had stood. She cast a fearful look around the assembled throng of black-robed masters. Their eyes seemed to bore deep into her soul, and she trembled. Bek attempted to reassure her with words but his tones were still imperious.

'There is no need to be afraid, child. Tell us the truth and all will be well.'

Margery nodded and wrapped her arms around her ample waist as if to comfort herself.

'He came that day, just like the master's brother said, and made me take him to the mistress, God rest her soul. Even though I told him she was in her private bedchamber.'

Bek intervened for the benefit of clarity. He did not want any error made here.

'*He* is Master William Falconer.'

Margery looked scornfully at the chancellor as though he were a dim child in her care.

'Yes. *Him.*'

She pointed at Falconer, who still sat impassively on his small chair, his eyes fixed on some point in the roof of the church.

'He pushed his way in and badgered the mistress when she was sick. He said he would cure her, but it was days before he came back. That shows how much he cared for her.'

Bullock thought he heard a quiet groan from Falconer's lips. But when he looked at his friend, his eyes were once again empty and unfocussed. Margery carried on telling her story about how she went to the spicer's shop to get a preparation of feverfew.

'That is what made my mistress better, not what he brought that day.'

Bek leaned forward in his chair, his eyes sparkling.

'Master Falconer brought a preparation that fateful day. The day your mistress died?'

'Yessir. He had a small pot in his hand and said he had brought this for the mistress. I said she was much better, but he still went to her with it.'

Bek was triumphant.

'And after he had taken this . . . unknown substance for her to drink, Ann Segrim died.'

Margery gulped and looked as though she was about to vomit on the floor of the church. She coughed out her words though.

'Yessir. That's true. He gave her the stuff and she died.'

TWELVE

The Black Congregation adjourned in the early afternoon, in order for the masters to eat their dinner. Thomas Bek admonished them to return in two hours when further evidence would be heard. He need not have laid such a burden on them. Every man there was sure to return to the church for this unique opportunity to take part in the uncovering of a murderer in the heart of the university. The black-robed masters were gossips and rumour-mongers one and all – crows picking over the carrion of a dead body.

Peter Bullock took William back to the Bocardo, and on the way asked him about the medicine that he had given to Ann.

'What was it, William? Did it contain something poisonous?'

Falconer cast a sidelong glance at his friend and now gaoler. He did not speak, but Bullock knew what the sad look in Falconer's eyes meant. Was Bullock also suspicious of Falconer's actions? He knew he had not explained himself properly.

'By mistake, I mean. Maybe you gave her something accidentally. Did you prepare the potion?'

Falconer looked away and Bullock sensed there was something that his friend was hiding from him.

'Did someone else make it up? Someone who you think might have harboured malice towards Ann?'

It was no good. Falconer was clearly not going to say anything. When they reached the jail, Bullock tried to tempt William with a pork stew that Agnes the whore-mistress had prepared. She and Bullock were fine friends, just as long as she kept her house orderly, which she usually did with a ferocious will. But sometimes she had rowdy customers, so she was willing to feed Bullock's prisoner, knowing that put him in her debt. A debt that could be stored up for any future problems at the bawdy house. The stew was finely spiced, but Falconer sat on the three-legged stool in the corner of the cell, spooning it into his mouth as if it were ashes. He looked as

though he cared not whether he lived or died, and it was
worrying the constable. He needed to get Falconer to snap
out of this mood quickly, or he would find himself proven
guilty of murder by default. William needed to defend himself,
because it looked like Bullock had damned little to go on
so far.

Walking back to his own rooms inside the castle keep, he
was glad to see Thomas Symon waiting for him. But the young
man had no fresh news himself. He was calling on the constable
to see how matters were progressing in the chancellor's court.
When he asked, Bullock glumly shook his head.

'It looks bad for William. Both Alexander Eddington and
the maid Margery say that he was in Ann's chamber when
she took ill. And later, he took her some preparation on the
very day she died. They say she drank it and collapsed.'

Thomas frowned.

'But didn't William go to her bedside that first time because
she was ill already? How could he have made her ill? What
are they suggesting?'

'I can't say for sure that she was ill already the first time
he went. You know he was used to meeting with her whenever he could. Maybe he had just taken it into his head to go
and see her on that day because Sir Humphrey was far away.'

'But Segrim had been away in the Holy Lands for almost
a year by then. Why go then but not before?'

As soon as the question was posed, both men looked in
embarrassment at each other. Both by now had learned that
Falconer's friendship with Ann Segrim had broken down for
some reason. And that the Jew Saphira had replaced her in
his affections. Neither was prepared to admit, however, that
there was a strand to these events that had led to murder.
Others might kill for love, but not Falconer. It was Thomas
who quickly moved to another subject.

'What is this preparation they are talking of? The one Master
Falconer is supposed to have given her? And where did it come
from?'

Bullock waved his arms in the air in a gesture of despair.

'Who knows? You are well aware of the nostrums and vile
mixtures in his room. You've seen them. It could have been
any one of them. You would do well to ask William. Except
he seems in no mood to answer any question put to him.

They might as well hang him now and be done with it. It does seem that that is what he wants.'

Thomas patted the bowed old man on his hunched shoulders, surprised to find himself the stronger of the two for once.

'We won't let that happen, Constable. I will go to Aristotle's Hall and see what I can find out there. Where is Saphira, by the way?'

Bullock raised his shaggy-haired old head and shook it gloomily. He looked to Thomas like an ancient lion, which had just been toppled from its position by a younger beast. Defeat was etched into every line on his wrinkled face.

'I don't know where she is. And we should not rely on her to solve this for us.'

Thomas nodded sagely, not wishing to argue with Bullock. But privately, he was not prepared to discount Saphira Le Veske just yet. She struck him as a very determined woman, who would stop at nothing to achieve her goal. If she could find evidence of Falconer's innocence, she would do so. In the meantime, he would have to gather all the truths he could himself. Starting with the evidence already presented at the Black Congregation. He wanted to test for himself the truth of what Eddington and Margery had been saying. That required another trip to Botley, and perhaps this time he could get Sir Humphrey to talk to him.

Saphira was now ready to tell Peter Bullock about Covele and his purchase of arsenic. She could no longer hide such information in the light of the commencement of Falconer's trial. Especially as the young master, Thomas Symon, had been of the opinion that Ann Segrim had died of arsenic poisoning. What she could not work out was the reason for Covele's possible actions. True, he had purchased arsenic and, true, she had seen him at Botley Manor. In fact, the presence of the talisman in Ann's bedchamber appeared to confirm that he had even been in the house. And his disappearance, along with his son, argued for guilt. But what reason did he have to kill Ann Segrim? As the afternoon drew on into dusk, she brooded on this, watching the fire in her kitchen die down to embers. She thought back to her previous encounter with Covele and the events that had taken place in Oxford at that time.

A forbidden ritual had been enacted in a house at the back of St Aldate's Church. It was perpetrated by Covele, whose guise at the time was that of a rabbi. Deudone, one of the hot-heads in the Jewish community in Oxford, was present and had later told her about it. A small band of men had assembled in the back room on the ground floor of the house. They were all nervous, as if only too well aware of the awful nature of what was to pass, for the men's purpose was sacrifice. In the grubby yard at the back of the narrow tenement building, a child played in the straw of the animal pen.

Deudone had been uneasy about what was intended and spoke up.

'I still think we should not do this. I was taught that a *qorban* – a sacrifice – could only be performed in the Temple. And as the Temple is destroyed . . .'

His question was cut off by the stranger in their midst. He was an older man whose dark locks hung down the sides of his head, mingling with his thick black beard. His pate was completely bald and his skin shone richly, like honey in the light of the guttering lamp. Covele had sneered at the waverer.

'It is only the weak-willed who say that. The tradition has been carried on in secret for centuries, and your rabbi probably knows it. You have all sinned and can expiate your wrongs by offering this sacrifice. You asked me to come here in the month of Elul – the month for forgiveness – and you knew what I would do. If the Temple cannot be used, then another place will suffice. Now, does anyone else want to join this . . . boy and run off?'

Each of the other men dropped their eyes in turn as the stranger stared them down. Even Deudone bit his tongue and acquiesced to the power evident in the man. Covele grunted, as if scornful of their weakness, lauding in his power. He brandished the sharp-edged knife in his right hand.

'Then let us proceed.'

Unfortunately, the curate of the church, an illiterate and ignorant man, had seen something of the ritual. Enough, together with his prejudices, to accuse the Jews of slaughtering a Christian child. Of course, the child in the yard had been Covele's own son and the sacrifice a goat. But the ensuing riot had endangered several lives, including those of both Saphira and William. Afterwards, they had exposed him as a fraud and even suspected him of being involved in a murder. Covele had fled then, too.

Saphira now wondered if that was cause for seeking revenge. Maybe he held his discomfiture against William. But how did Ann Segrim fit in with that possibility? Saphira decided she would tell the others who were trying to save William and see if it made any sense to them. She would be meeting Thomas Symon and Peter Bullock again in the morning. Time enough, then.

Bek returned to St Mildred's Church after filling himself with a well-seethed mutton dish. He liked to dine on rarities, and sheep was so valuable for its fleece that its flesh was not often served at the table. Except at the chancellor's board. His entrance down the central aisle of the church caused the hubbub to cease and he was pleased to see the same crowded pews. Everyone had returned to witness his triumph. His two proctors were already at the left and right hand of his throne, Plumpton still with a sour face which disapproved of the proceedings. But Henry de Godfree looked positively gleeful. Bek would remember that at the end of the year, when the proctors stood again for election. He eased into his chair, gazed around, then tapped de Godfree on the arm to indicate he was ready for the next witness. The proctor of the south stood up and spoke in a loud, clear voice.

'Summon Peter Mithian.'

The youth who appeared was pale-faced and petrified. To be surrounded by well-nigh seventy regent masters was any clerk's greatest nightmare. For the reluctant scholar that Mithian was, and scared of losing the only thing that stood between him and abject poverty – his place at the university – this was worse than a nightmare. It was living hell. Standing before the chancellor, who pinned him down with his severest gaze, Mithian felt his legs giving way beneath him. But he managed to stay upright, though he felt like vomiting his pitiful dinner on to the stone flags underneath his feet.

'Tell me what you have witnessed in Master Falconer's solar, boy.'

The chancellor's question did not make sense to him. He knew he had been summoned to say something about his tutor, and expected to be asked if he was a good teacher or not.

What on earth was it that the chancellor thought he had seen in Master Falconer's room? Did he mean some fell deed he had witnessed that would condemn Falconer? His mouth opened and closed, but he didn't know what words to form. Thomas Bek hissed in annoyance. De Godfree had been sent to Aristotle's Hall especially to select from Falconer's students one who might be intimidated into revealing incriminating evidence. The proctor had chosen Peter Mithian as the weakest vessel. However, it looked as though he was too stupid to be of use. But this was the material with which the chancellor would have to work. Bek decided he would have to lead the youth down the road he wished him to go.

'What books does he have? What texts and tables does he secrete away? What prophecies and incantations did you see written down? Are there amulets and panaceas, or other signs of alchemy in Aristotle's Hall?'

Peter bowed his head, not wishing to displease the chancellor, but not sure which, of all the wondrous things he had seen in Falconer's solar, held any significance.

'Please sir, concerning books I did borrow *Sophistici Elenchi* from the master. Does that count?'

At the mention of such a basic work by Aristotle in the context referred to by Bek, some in the congregation sniggered. The chancellor's features darkened, not sure whether the boy in front of him was stupid, or if he was mocking him. Mithian, however, was eager to continue.

'And I saw *Historia Scholastica* and *De Sphaera Mundi*, and works by the Arab Al-Khowarizmi. Then on the table in the master's room there were all sorts of marvellous things. Bones and skulls, and dried plants and stones with strange shapes carved on their surfaces.'

'Arab texts and relics of the dead. Sure signs of necromancy,' stated de Godfree smugly, making sure all in the assembly had heard.

'I don't know about that, sir. But there were two scrolls lying open on the table. Master Falconer said they were in Hebrew, but they could have been spells and incantations for all I know. And he had lots of pots with potions in them. They smelled strange, sir, and the master said I was to take care because they would be deadly if swallowed.'

With this revelation, the hubbub in the church broke out

again. Bek sat back in satisfaction. The boy had come up trumps after all. He let the talk rumble on this time, as each master built a greater speculation of misdeeds with his neighbour. On his little chair, Falconer strived to remain unconcerned, but his hands were clasped tightly together, the knuckles showing white.

THIRTEEN

By the time Thomas Symon reached Botley Manor, he had decided to use the servants' entrance. He didn't want to confront Alexander Eddington again. Rather, he wanted to speak to the servant, Margery, alone. Fortunately, the layout of the building made this an easy task. Segrim's manor house was constructed of a yellowed stone that had grown dull over the years, and now contrived to look merely drab. It was of the old style, being a simple oblong grange with a sloping roof and narrow windows, designed more for keeping invaders out than letting light in. A flight of stone steps led to the main door, which was on the upper level of the house, leaving a vaulted cellar below. Once through the heavy front door, again built for defence, a visitor gained access to the great hall, where the main business of daily life was conducted. It would be difficult to enter that way without someone in the family being aware of his presence. But various additions had been made to this basic structure over the years. One extension had been built to create solars for the family and a guest room, where Thomas assumed Eddington now lodged. The solars were separate bedchambers and private quarters for the Segrims, and one was where Ann Segrim's body had lain the last time Thomas had been to the manor. The kitchen and servants' quarters were in a stone and timber addition tacked on to the eastern end of the house. It had its own external door and this was where Thomas was bound.

The door was open to allow the heat of the kitchen to dissipate, as the kitchen fire was kept burning day and night. Thomas stepped unobtrusively over the threshold to find a household in disarray. Botley was clearly lacking a controlling hand now the mistress was dead. The fire was burning low and the remains of a meal lay scattered around. Over the fire, hanging from a chimney crane, was a copper pot with its contents burning on to the base. Thomas could smell it from the door. Yet no one was paying it any attention. On the large plank table in the centre of the room lay scattered bean pods and onion skins, discarded cabbage leaves and an array of utensils. There were various knives, a hatchet, a pestle, a meat hook and a gravy-soaked trencher. An old woman lay dozing in the corner, sitting on the rushes that were strewn across the floor. Another woman had her head inside the cook's cupboard, where would have been stored the precious aromatic spices. Sensing his presence, the woman turned round. Thomas recognized her by her hairy face as Margery. She scowled at the intruder.

'What do you want?'

She had obviously been in the act of removing something tasty or valuable from the spice store, for she abruptly slammed the door closed behind her. Dusting her fingers off on her apron, she strode over to Thomas.

'This is a house of mourning. No one will see you today.'

Thomas found his voice, trying to pitch it harshly like Falconer did when confronting a guilty-looking individual.

'I know that, and it is you I am seeking, Margery.'

She blushed deeply and Thomas relished the fact he had managed to wrong-foot her. He pressed his advantage.

'I want to hear what really happened here when your mistress died. And I want the truth, girl.'

In reality, the servant was probably ten years his senior, but there was no harm in placing himself on the high moral ground. Margery wrung her spice-stained hands and looked at the floor, examining the cracks in the stone flags.

'I'm sure I don't know what you mean, sir. I told you everything I know.'

Thomas realized she thought he had been in the Black Congregation, before which she had testified. He decided not to disabuse her of that misconception, though he could only rely on what Bullock told him about Margery's evidence.

'Yes. That you showed Master Falconer into your mistress's presence some days before she died.'

'Yessir.'

'And that was after she had taken ill.'

Margery screwed up her hairy face, making it look even more monkey-like. She had to think about that one.

'Yessir, she was already ill. And he taxed her with all sorts of questions.'

'What about?'

'I don't rightly know, sir. The mistress told him she had been to Godstow Nunnery recently and had spoken to Mother Gwladys about a private matter.'

This was probably nothing but knowing Falconer's propensity for seemingly irrelevant details, Thomas felt he had to find out more.

'A private matter? What was it? Did Mistress Segrim say?' Margery shook her head.

'No, sir, I was sent for a potion for the mistress, but I fetched Master Eddington first. He went to her solar and he made Master Falconer leave.'

'No matter. Now I want you to tell me clearly about the day Mistress Segrim died. You say Master Falconer went to her with a preparation.'

'He did, sir. I saw it in his hand. A small earthenware pot – so big.' She made a circle with the thumb and forefinger of both hands. 'He was here at the house just as I came back from attending to the mistress. I took her something to eat – to tempt her appetite – and she was alive then. He took her the poison. She drank it and she died.'

Thomas frowned, thinking this was bad for Falconer, even if the contents of the pot were accidentally poisonous. He had to have this clear in his own head.

'So, did she fall immediately to the ground, or some time later?'

'Oh, I don't know that. I wasn't there, was I?'

'You weren't . . . So, you didn't actually see her drink from the pot?'

Margery waved her hand dismissively. Why were these Oxford masters so slow on the uptake?

'Of course I didn't see her actually drink it. But she must have done. She died, didn't she?'

Sir Humphrey spent long hours staring out of the solar window, fearing the arrival of the night. He imagined that, should the Templar come for him, he would arrive under cover of darkness. He was that sort of man – capable of bold and extreme violence, but always in the dark. He recalled the black ship that had sailed up the Thames past

Shadwell and Wapping. In his mind's eye, he now saw it sailing under a shroud of darkness, casting its own gloomy shadows. The evening was now drawing on and the shadows on the forecourt of his house were lengthening. He shivered with cold. Out of the corner of his eye, he saw a darkly clad figure and gasped. It was him! Then the figure resolved itself by stepping into a shaft of late sunlight. It was a young man in a clerk's robe – a student or a master at the university. In fact, when the figure looked up at the window where Sir Humphrey stood, he recognized him as the young master who had accompanied Peter Bullock and the red-haired woman the other day. He had seen them arrive from this very window and had expected them to speak to him. He had sat for a long time in his room awaiting them. All he had heard was a muffled altercation on the gallery beyond his door. Alexander blustering again. And then the visitors had gone. It was said by the servants afterwards that the young man had looked at Ann and told immediately what had caused her death. The servant who related this to him had super-stitiously made a sign against the evil eye. But Sir Humphrey did not care whether he used necromancy or plain common sense. If he could see the hand of the Templar in the murder, then he was a man to talk to. He waved his hand out of the window, calling down to the man to wait. Then he hurried out of his solar and across the gallery to the front door.

Thomas Symon felt frustrated by his interview with Margery. He had learned that she hadn't witnessed Ann Segrim taking the potion brought by Falconer. She had convinced herself her mistress had swallowed it, merely because Ann had taken something that killed her. But equally, he had no proof that Ann hadn't swallowed it. He needed to find out from William what had actually happened, even though his evidence would be useless before the Black Congregation. It would be the word of an accused murderer against that of an apparently ingenuous serving maid. But he would believe Falconer and it would eliminate another possible suspect – whoever had prepared the potion.

He was walking around the front of Botley Manor, deep in

thought, when he cast a glance up at one of the narrow windows to the left of the main door. He saw a pale face hovering in the darkness of the room. Was it Sir Humphrey? Thomas stood and stared, wondering if he dare try to speak to the man. Suddenly, the matter was resolved for him – the figure leaned out of the window, holding on to the central pillar, raised an arm and beckoned to him. He walked towards the steps up to the front door.

Peter Bullock decided he could not wait any longer on Thomas Symon. The youth had left earlier in the day, saying he would search Falconer's room. It was now early evening and Symon had not returned. He pushed himself up from his comfortable chair by the fire that burned in his castle sanctuary and, grumbling at the inconvenience, set off for Aristotle's Hall. The town streets were unusually quiet, as though the murder trial had preoccupied everyone, and kept them from their normal night-time revelries. Any students he passed were very subdued and not a single drunk was in sight. He exchanged a few words with one of his watchmen, Samuel Burewald, who confirmed that the town was dead.

'And a good thing too, constable. That's the way I like it – nice and peaceful.'

Bullock simply nodded in agreement and made his way down St John's Street to Aristotle's Hall. If the town was dead, then the hall was truly a rotting corpse. When he entered through the door, there was no sign of life. Even the hearth was devoid of heat, now merely a pile of ashes blown across the floor by the gust of wind that blew in after Bullock. He stood, hearing a distant sigh from the cubicles that made up the students' sleeping quarters at the far end of the hall. He guessed it was Peter Mithian churning over and over in his mind the devastating statement he made about his master before the chancellor. The boy had been outwitted by a man who could twist any simple statement into a confession of guilt. That was the trouble with these scholars, as far as Bullock was concerned. Even his old friend William could misconstrue any simple fact and turn it into something it wasn't. Well, he was not going to fall into that trap. Facts were facts, and he would lay them out simply before the chancellor and prove Falconer's innocence. Avoiding disturbing the student, he mounted the rickety wooden stairs to Falconer's private room and pushed open the door.

For a moment, he thought he saw a ghost – a white figure high up in the corner of the room. Then the shape hopped to the windowsill. With a whispery beat of its wings, Balthazar the barn owl flew into the darkness. The bird had such a cold stare, and so impassive a manner, that Bullock often imagined him as William's familiar. He thrust the thought from his mind, however. It was not wise to even think about Falconer in terms of witchcraft in the present circumstances. He fixed his mind on his recent resolve to stick to facts and began to examine Falconer's room.

His search proved to be just as frustrating as waiting for Thomas Symon had been. He knew the room very well, having sat in it with Falconer a hundred times before. He simply could not see anything that would offer him a clue as to Falconer's guilt or innocence. The cot still stood in one corner, its coverings neatly folded. Falconer kept tidy quarters for the same reason Bullock did. Both had been soldiers, and you had to keep your possessions orderly when on campaign, or you would lose them if there was an urgent call to arms or a quick retreat. A pile of books and scrolls were stacked to one side of the chimney piece. It was no use Bullock examining them. He knew he would not be able to understand a word. If he was to find anything, it would not be amongst the books. A single chair stood close by the hearth, which was swept of ashes – probably by Peter Mithian on the very morning he had ended up betraying his master. A stool, the only other seat, was set close by the long table that dominated the room.

Bullock cast a despairing glance over the contents of the table. They always bewildered him in their variety and apparent uselessness. Stones and bones, and more scrolls. He did spot some pots set on top of an opened scroll and wondered if they were the ones Mithian had referred to. The so-called poisonous preparations. He cautiously sniffed at one and recoiled in horror. The stench was terrible. If you didn't die by swallowing it, you could expire inhaling it. He spotted a piece of parchment lying next to the pots, in a bold hand he knew wasn't Falconer's. He picked it up and slowly read the words out loud.

'Take care! This preparation is dangerous. I should know, because I now have learned how to poison someone!'

The short message was signed with a flourish of a letter. It looked to Bullock like a capital S.

FOURTEEN

It was the second day of Falconer's trial and, as agreed, Bullock met with Saphira Le Veske and Thomas Symon at the castle. When Saphira entered the spartan room that Bullock used as his office, however, he was alone. And she noticed the constable was strangely reticent. He seemed unable to look her in the eye, but she chose to ignore this. Falconer's dire situation was more important than puzzling out Bullock's mood. So, without waiting for Thomas Symon, who was late, Saphira began to tell the constable about Covele, the talisman seller, and his connection with Ann Segrim. How he must have been at Botley because an angel text had been in Ann's solar. How he probably had a grudge against Falconer. And how he had purchased arsenic from Robert Bodin. But she admitted that was where the facts began to fail her.

'I can only connect Ann Segrim's death to him, if he somehow assumed she was William's . . .' She coughed in embarrassment, but finally spat the awkward word out. 'If she was his lover. And Covele thought killing her would hurt him. That is all I have so far.'

Bullock had been deep in thought while she spoke. Now he stood up and pushed a clean sheet of parchment over the table to her.

'Can you write all this down. My hand is poor and you would scribe more quickly than me.'

Saphira was a little surprised but agreed to write down what she had discovered. As she wrote, Bullock leaned over her shoulder, apparently engrossed in the formation of each letter. Suddenly, Thomas burst into the room, a broad grin on his face. He slapped a startled Bullock on the back.

'I have it. Proof that Falconer is innocent.'

Bullock stared at the young man in astonishment. Saphira laid down her quill and asked the obvious question.

'You do? What is this proof?'

'Yes. Well, if not actual proof, a definite reason for Ann Segrim being murdered.'

Bullock snorted. He would have bet the boy hadn't any proof. Still, he would hear him out.

'Go on.'

Thomas's eyes were wide with excitement.

'You will not believe what I am about to tell you.'

'Let us be the judge of that. Spit it out.'

Bullock was sceptical, but the story that emerged was indeed astonishing.

At Botley yesterday, Sir Humphrey had hustled Thomas into the manor house and slammed the door behind him. He threw the bolt on the door, checking it was in place twice, before he ushered Thomas up to his solar. At no point en route would he speak. In fact, he held a finger to his lips when Thomas tried to ask a question. Only when they were both in the private solar did Sir Humphrey say anything. And even then he paced around in a most agitated way.

'I am telling you this because you need to know. But I must warn you that your life will be in danger, if I do speak. Do you want me to go on?'

Thomas was all agog at this overture, and even the threat of his imminent demise did not prevent him from urging Segrim to continue.

'Please go on. If it affects the matter of Master Falconer's trial and your wife's unfortunate death, then I must hear you out.'

Sir Humphrey clasped his hands as if in prayer and put them to his lips. After a brief moment of silence, he began the most extraordinary tale. It was all to do with a Templar and a plot to murder King Henry's family.

Bullock's eyes widened and he held up his hand to stop Thomas Symon in full flow.

'Wait just a moment. Are you seriously suggesting that Ann Segrim's death has to do with a treasonable act by this . . . Templar?'

Thomas nodded eagerly.

'Just hear me out and you will be convinced. It apparently all began when Segrim fell in with a Templar on the crossing to France last year.'

Thomas recounted Segrim's tale as he had been told it. How the Templar, a tall, well-built man with black hair and a full beard, had borne the choppy crossing without turning a hair.

His green eyes were for ever on the horizon and the approaching coastline. Segrim had engaged him in conversation, which had been mostly one-sided, as the man hardly spoke. He didn't at that stage give away even his name. After listening to Segrim's prattle, he had reluctantly agreed to share the costs of his journey with him. And all had been well until they reached Viterbo. When Sir Humphrey had heard that Henry, son of Richard King of Germany, and nephew to the King of England, was also in Viterbo, he was determined to see the man. He always had an eye for possible royal contacts and advancement. He suggested to the Templar that they attend the service at the Church of San Silvestro on the morrow of St Gregory, as Henry would be there. The Templar was unimpressed and said he did not wish to be there, suggesting Sir Humphrey would do well to stay away too. Segrim chose otherwise and lived to wish he hadn't.

On the day, Sir Humphrey found himself at the back of a packed church, as it turned out that many noblemen were also seeking to speak to Henry, who was on his way home from Africa. All Segrim got to see was the back of a distant figure, kneeling before the altar. Then all hell broke loose. A group of armed men stormed up the aisle, swords in hand. They hacked Henry, son of Richard, to pieces. Three of the men were later identified as Simon and Guy de Montfort and Count Rosso, father-in-law to Guy. It was assumed then that the deed was revenge for the death of the de Monforts' relative, Simon de Montfort, at the battle of Evesham, seven years before. But as the murderers left the church, running out the way they had come, one of them turned to briefly stare at Sir Humphrey. A pair of cold, green eyes shone from behind the full-face helm. Segrim was convinced it was the Templar. But when he next saw the man, nothing was said. Sir Humphrey had told Thomas Symon he was too scared.

'He told me they journeyed on together, but that he didn't join the Templar when the man left for Outremer from Cyprus. Segrim expected almost daily to hear of the death of Prince Edward, who was in Acre at the time. But it never happened. The next time he saw the Templar was back in Famagusta in late August. The news had just arrived of the death of Edward's eldest son, John, back in England. The Templar was one of a group of men-at-arms who seemed to be toasting the news, rather than lamenting it. That was when Segrim decided abruptly to return to England without ever having reached the Holy Lands.'

Bullock's face was clouded, as he tried to comprehend what Thomas was telling them.

'Are you telling us that Segrim has supposed a grand conspiracy, based on the possible involvement of this Templar in a revenge killing.'

'And his celebration of another death in the king's family.'

Bullock was transfixed, not sure what to believe. Saphira, however, pointed out the problem with Thomas's thesis.

'Even so. There is no proof here of any connection to Ann Segrim's murder. Merely a fantasy existing only in Sir Humphrey's mind.'

'Would it convince you, if I told you that, on the return journey, the Templar pursued Sir Humphrey by sea and land for months on end, until Segrim thought he had eluded him at Honfleur. Then, after crossing the Channel, Sir Humphrey next saw the Templar in Berkhamsted the very day Richard, King of Germany, died. And the Templar saw *him*. That is why he went into hiding in Oxford town before daring to return home. And why I think Ann was murdered by the Templar because he was afraid she had been told of the conspiracy by her husband.'

Bullock nodded as if finally convinced, so it was left to Saphira to speak again.

'How can we prove any of this? It makes a good tale but it doesn't save William.'

Thomas looked at the constable.

'Sir, Master Falconer told me you were once a Templar sergeant. Do you know anyone you can speak to who could help us?'

Bullock had a grim look about him, but he knew he was their only lifeline at the moment. He pulled himself up out of his chair and began to pace the room.

'I may be able to help. What was the name of this Templar? Did Segrim find it out?'

'Eventually, yes. He says the man's name is Odo de Reppes.'

'Then, after I have delivered William to St Mildred's Church today, I will go to the Temple at Cowley. There is a man there who owes Falconer a debt.'

'Good. Then I will go now to Aristotle's Hall and see if there are any clues there to this sorry business.'

As Thomas rose to leave, Bullock took his arm.

'I have already been to William's solar and looked around.'

Thomas frowned, thinking the constable had not seemed able to trust him with the task. But Bullock reassured him it was just a misunderstanding.

'I thought you were going to do it yesterday, but when you didn't come back to me with your findings, I decided to do it myself. I had no other clues to follow.' He patted Thomas's shoulder reassuringly. 'It was good that you followed up the possibilities you did. You found out far more than I did at Aristotle's.'

'What did you find?'

Bullock cast a furtive glance at Saphira.

'Nothing at all, I'm afraid.'

'And you, Saphira? Did you uncover any truths?'

Thomas smiled at Saphira, unaware of the constable's cold-ness towards their companion. He felt he had started them off on a new track which would lead eventually to Falconer's vindication. But he was still curious to find out if Saphira knew anything that would be of use. She told him about Covele, the talisman seller, being at Botley, and his purchase of arsenic.

'He may have resented both William's and my actions some months ago, when we thought he might have been involved in a murder. But we will need more facts before we can decide if this leads anywhere. And Covele has disappeared. I was setting down what I know for Peter when you arrived.'

She pointed at the parchment on the table and saw that Thomas barely gave it a glance. He was too interested in his own discovery to think about any other possibility. But Saphira knew that at this stage they should cast their net wide and not rely on one theory. Falconer's own methods had taught her that. She resolved to pursue her own enquiry, even if the two men were seduced by what Thomas had uncovered. She got up from the table to leave, with the first excuse that came into her head.

'I must go and make some purchases in the market or my maid will have nothing to prepare for dinner.'

Neither man saw that she intended the words ironically. They merely smiled and allowed her to go about her womanly duties. She smiled ruefully, having fallen into the trap of playing the homely wife. Well, she would show them, as she had shown Falconer once before when she was doubted.

After she had left, Bullock sighed with relief. Then he turned to Thomas, not certain how to proceed. He picked up the half-completed statement that Saphira had drafted and gave it to Thomas Symon.

'Tell me what you think of this.'

Thomas looked scornfully at the document.

'You don't think this Covele has any significance, do you? The Templar is . . .'

'No, no. Not what she has written. Just look at the script and compare it with this.'

He gave Thomas the scrap of parchment from Falconer's room. Puzzled, Thomas took it from Bullock's hand and compared the writing.

'It looks the same. And this one is signed with an S. It has to be written by Saphira. What does she mean – she knows how to poison someone?'

'Isn't it obvious? It means just what it says. And look at the first two words. "Take care". The very words Falconer used to you. He said, "Take care of Saphira." We both thought he meant comfort her and look after her. What if he meant "Beware of Saphira"?'

Thomas was aghast and stared at Bullock in astonishment.

'You don't think *she* killed Ann Segrim?'

Bullock held his gaze.

'I don't know. But while we pursue your Templar, let us not ignore the possible snake in our midst. Just in case. Jealousy is a powerful force.'

FIFTEEN

At the start of a new morning, Falconer sat alone on his hard wooden seat, apparently not at all discomfited by the evidence against him so far. Close by him sat Alexander Eddington who, after giving witness the previous day, had insisted on being present as a representative of the murder victim. Bullock had excused himself from the proceedings and Thomas Bek assumed perhaps he had either given up on his friend, or was dashing around seeking fresh evidence. The chancellor didn't care one way or the other. Until last night he had harboured doubts himself about the strength of the case against Falconer. If the regent master was a fornicator and had lain with Ann Segrim, why had he then killed her? It was enough to presage a sleepless night for Bek. Then someone had approached him with new information – a man of irreproachable probity, even though he might have had personal reasons for attacking Falconer. Bek waited for the Black Congregation to settle, then called his next witness.

'I call before this court Regent Master Ralph Cornish.'

A murmur of curiosity rippled through the church, mixed with a not inconsiderable strain of repressed laughter. Many still recalled how Falconer's juvenile prank at Inception had embarrassed the man who now rose to give evidence before them. A little red in the face, but with a determined look, Ralph Cornish strode to his place in front of the chancellor. Taking a deep breath, he began.

'After yesterday's evidence many of you may have already made up your mind about William Falconer. I know I have. But some may still harbour doubts about his motive for killing Ann Segrim. I will tell you why I am convinced of his guilt. I am in possession of information that has not yet been revealed, but will sway the minds of those doubters.'

There was tension in the air, and even Falconer himself leaned forward to hear Ralph Cornish's revelation. For a while longer, the truculent master played the moment.

'You are asking yourselves, why did he kill a woman who

willingly allowed herself to be used by him? Their dalliance
was carried out over a long period of time. Why now did he
kill her?' Once again he paused, milking the moment. 'I can
tell you . . . It was because he had found another woman to
fornicate with. And moreover she is a Jew.'

Ralph stared accusingly at Falconer, inordinately pleased to
see his enemy's face turn white with shock. His triumph was
that he had known something Falconer thought a secret, and
was able to use it against him so devastatingly. Over the hubbub
of noise in the normally sepulchral church, he developed his
theme.

As he spoke, Alexander Eddington listened with interest
for the first time during these proceedings. He had found the
trial unexpectedly dull until this moment. Now, he had a juicy
morsel of information to use to his advantage. He had insisted
on being present in case any evidence was brought forward
that implied he was involved in his sister-in-law's death. The
constable – Bullock – had intimated as such when he had
been examining Ann's dead body. And God knows what his
half-brother had said to that young clerk yesterday. He had
seen from his window as Humphrey had grabbed the youth
by the arm and dragged him into the house. He had heard the
slamming of his half-brother's solar door and the dropping of
the bolt. He had been powerless to intervene. And if the clerk
had been talking to Margery about her trip to the spicer's shop
for Ann's remedy, then he would be in trouble. But now he
could divert attention from himself and on to this Jew. Ralph
was concluding his vitriolic attack.

'Yes, not content with besmirching the reputation of the
wife of a local nobleman and breaking his holy vows of
celibacy, he wallowed in filth with a Jew.'

Suddenly, Cornish saw a movement out of the corner of
his eye. He felt his head explode in stars, as if a hammer blow
had come from nowhere and hit his left ear. He fell to the
ground, his head ringing and his senses stunned. He thought
maybe another firecracker had exploded next to him. It hadn't.
Unrestrained by any gaoler, Falconer had angrily surged from
his seat and landed a powerful blow on the side of Ralph
Cornish's head. If Roger Plumpton had not leapt from his
chair beside the chancellor and held Falconer back, Cornish
would have suffered further blows. The Black Congregation

descended into chaos, and in the cries of outrage Bek was left unheard calling for the trial to be adjourned for the day.

When the worried Saphira returned to her house on Fish Street, she found her maid kneeling on the floor in the kitchen poking at a crack in the stonework of the wall.

'What are you doing, Rebekkah?'

The girl was startled and jumped to her feet.

'Oh, you surprised me, mistress. I didn't expect you back so soon. It's just that I thought I heard a scraping sound from somewhere down there. Like rats.' She shuddered. 'And there have been scraps of food missing from the larder recently, too.'

Now it was Saphira's turn to shudder. Rats were an everyday part of life, but she hated the thought of them in her larder.

'We must lay some poison, Rebekkah.'

'Yes, mistress.'

'I shall see to that. Now, I do not need you for the rest of the day, as I will be out. I won't be having dinner, either, so there's no need to return until tomorrow morning.'

The girl beamed with pleasure, thanked her mistress and positively skipped out of the house. In truth, Saphira did not know what she would be doing today. But whatever it was she did, she preferred not to have her maid hanging around. Rebekkah was a little busybody, who revelled in knowing more than was good for her. With her out of the way, Saphira knew she should hunt for Covele, but was uncertain where to begin. Despite Thomas's conviction that Ann's death was related somehow to the Templar persecuting her husband, and Peter Bullock's determination to assist in that line of enquiry, she was mindful that William often advocated against having all your eggs in one basket. His principle of two small truths, taken together, often revealing a greater one, meant digging out many little facts, even ones which often seemed unrelated. No, she would continue to follow up on Covele, and saw that she had two routes to follow. She had already decided that Robert Bodin could tell her more about the talisman seller's purchase of arsenic. She should speak to him more. And now her dismissal of Rebekkah had inadvertently given her another course to follow. Servants were a good source of gossip. Ann's own maid, Margery, probably knew more than she was admitting to about the events surrounding her mistress's death. Margery might even have seen Covele at Botley. She reckoned she would have a busy day ahead of her.

The Templar commandery outside Oxford was small by the standards of the Order, but Laurence de Bernere loved the old grey stone building that was its main hall. Over the doorway that led into the hall was a semi-circular tympanum, and carved on it was an ancient image. Worn smooth by time, it was a carving of a soldier on horseback in a pointed helmet with a nose guard and a chain mail hauberk of old design. In his hand the warrior held a spear. The point of the spear was thrust into the mouth of a snake-like beast and the horse's hooves were trampling its coils. Like many fighting Templars, Laurence venerated George, the warrior saint. Early that morning, he had again gazed on it as he did almost every day on his way to the Temple chapel. It was a circular building that copied the layout of the Church of the Holy Sepulchre.

Three young knights were to be admitted to the Order that morning, the ceremony starting as it always did at dawn. The chapel was cold and gloomy, lit only by tall candles, but the ceremony never failed to move him. Now, the three men were coming to their final vows and the chaplain asked them the ritual questions.

'Are you willing to renounce the world?'

All three replied in clear and strong voices.

'I am willing.'

'Are you willing to profess obedience according to canonical institution and according to the precept of the Lord Pope?'

'I am willing.'

'Are you willing to take upon yourself the way of life of our brothers?'

'I . . .' Each gave their own name at this point. '. . . am willing and I promise to serve the Rule of the Knights of Christ, so that from this day I shall not be allowed to shake my neck free of the yoke of the Rule. And, henceforth, I promise obedience to God and this house, and to live without property, and to maintain chastity according to the precept of the Lord Pope, and firmly to keep the way of life of the brothers of the house of the Knights of Christ.'

As the three young knights then prostrated themselves on

the cold stone flags before the altar, de Bernere was aware of a shadowy figure slipping on to the stone bench beside him. Irritated by this interruption, he nevertheless did not look to see who it was, but concentrated on the ceremony's conclusion. All three men on the ground intoned their final prayer.

'Receive me, Lord, in accordance with your word and let me live. And may you not confound me in my hope. The Lord is my light. The Lord is the protector of my life.'

'As will be a strong, right arm.'

That cynical comment came from the man who had just sat next to him and he was annoyed enough to turn and remonstrate with him. He recognized the old, grey-haired man immediately, his bent back obvious even when he was seated.

'Sergeant Bullock. I might have known it was you, spoiling the mood of the ceremony.'

He cast a mournful glance at the three young men prostrate on the stone floor. They were just beginning their service to the Order that had dominated his life for over twenty years now. And the life of the old man next to him, until he left its ranks due to doubts about his calling. Bullock had been a sergeant in the Order, and as such he had served the needs of the true knights of the Poor Fellow-Soldiers of the Temple of Solomon, as the Templars were once called. Bullock would have worn a brown robe instead of white and had one horse instead of three. A sergeant was after all not a nobleman. Laurence de Bernere, however, respected the sergeant brothers. They were the backbone of the Order, often saving the life of the knight they served, when he allowed a sense of chivalry to overcome common sense. Bullock was no different from all the rough and ready sergeants of the Order. And if he was at the Temple so early in the morning, then something was afoot. And de Bernere owed Bullock and his friend, William Falconer, a debt of gratitude over the recovery of a precious relic, now stored safely in the Temple once again.

'Come, I have seen enough. Tell me what is on your mind.'

He rose, and led Peter Bullock out of the Temple and into the light and warmth of an English morning.

It was not long before the rumours of what had happened in St Mildred's Church spread around the students at the university. They would normally have been occupied with studies.

But as the Black Congregation consisted of around seventy of the regent masters teaching at Oxford, few classes were taking place. Therefore, many of the students were at a loose end, bored, and open to the gossip coming out of the trial of William Falconer. Those few classes that were taking place, were soon disrupted by clerks breaking in on the studies of others to pass on the news. Thomas Symon was in charge of one such class, when a wild-eyed youth clattered through the door at the back of the school room. All heads turned towards the intruder.

'Have you heard? Master Falconer has punched Master Cornish in the face, beaten him to a pulp, he has.'

There was a communal gasp from the assembled students and then a buzz of chatter that Thomas knew he was not equal to stopping. The trial had everyone distracted anyway, and now this incident was the final straw. He might as well give up for the day. Besides, he wanted to find out the truth for himself.

'Lessons are suspended. Learn your Priscian for tomorrow.'

His instructions were hardly heard as the students scrambled for the exit from the small, stuffy room. Thomas waited for the scrum to disperse, and then hurried off towards St Mildred's Church along the narrow alley that was called Cheyney Lane. He was in time to see the last of the regent masters leaving, and spotted the German, Heinrich Koenig. The man had been generous with his tuition when Falconer had been preoccupied by murder cases, and Thomas knew him to be unbiased and truthful.

'Regent Master Koenig, may I speak with you.'

The German stopped and looked back to see who had called him. When he recognized his former student, he smiled and stroked his luxuriant moustache.

'Ahh. Thomas Symon, I suppose you want the gossip, eh?'

His guttural, Bohemian accent was difficult for some to understand, and when an unwary student called him a German, he bristled and proceeded to give the poor youth a geography and history lesson. The King of Bohemia was one of seven German Electors of the Holy Roman Emperor. But Bohemia was not German to a proud Bohemian. However, beneath his prickly exterior, Koenig was a generous man, and a bit of a gossip.

'You want to know what happened in the Black Congregation today. Whether the rumours are true.' He chuckled, his moustache wobbling from side to side. 'What do the rumours say? That Falconer has now murdered Ralph Cornish with his bare hands?'

Thomas Symon gasped.

'He hasn't, has he?'

'No, no. It's just that I saw what really happened, and I know how the tales that circulate do tend to exaggerate as they pass from lips to lips. Don't look so worried. There was only one blow landed, though it was a mighty one that floored the unfortunate Cornish.' He smacked one fist into his palm as if to emphasize the impact. 'Oh dear, there I go, embroidering the story myself now.'

'But what made Master Falconer lash out like that?'

'Oh, it was Cornish's fault. He cast a slur on a lady friend of Falconer's. He called her a Jew, in a most derogatory way.'

'He knows of Saphira?'

A broad grin filled Koenig's face.

'Ach. So, it is true, then, that Falconer has been bedding a pretty, Jewish widow? Oh, dear, that will not play well with some in the congregation. If Cornish were merely stirring up trouble with unfounded rumours, it would not have mattered so much. But if he has spoken the truth, it will not go well with Falconer.'

Koenig bowed his head and strode off with his hands clasped behind his back, deep in thought. Thomas cursed his loose tongue and went off to see if Bullock had returned from his trip to the Templar commandery.

In fact, the constable was on his way back from the Temple, but was in no hurry. He let his old nag amble along the track that led back to Oxford, nibbling grass when it could, while he pondered what he had learned from Laurence de Bernere. It had all been a little inconclusive for Bullock, who liked his facts simple and straightforward. The first step had been identifying the Templar.

'Odo de Reppes? Why, yes, he is staying at this commandery at the moment. Why do you ask?'

De Bernere was curious about Bullock's enquiry, especially as it concerned de Reppes. The man had a fine reputation as

a warrior, but he also carried along with him some unsub-
stantiated, dark rumours. De Bernere had never delved far
enough into them to know what they were about, but now it
seemed he had a chance. Except the Oxford town constable
was reticent to divulge the reasons for his question.

'I would rather not pass on false rumours at this stage. I
merely wish to know if this de Reppes has returned from
Outremer recently.'

The Templar played along with Bullock, hoping to learn
more from him later.

'Indeed he has – no more than a week ago, I would say.
Unfortunately, the situation out there does not demand the
services of a warrior. Both Tripoli and Acre have worked out
truces with the Saracens. Even Prince Edward could do no
more than help fortify Acre. De Reppes came back frustrated
at what was going on.'

'Frustrated, you say? About what?'

'About the lack of action. And the disputes over who was
rightly King of Jerusalem.'

Bullock grimaced. Once again, high politics was getting in
the way, and he could not see where all this led. He would
have to talk to Thomas Symon later. In the meantime, he could
at least find out about Odo de Reppes's whereabouts.

'Can you say if he has been into Oxford since he came
back? Or elsewhere locally?'

De Bernere frowned.

'You will know, as a former sergeant of the Order, that any
knight must ask permission of the master before leaving the
commandery.' When Bullock nodded, de Bernere sighed. 'And
you know I am temporarily the master of this commandery.
So I can tell you what you wish to know.' Another nod. 'And
you also know the rule on rumour – *ne sis criminator et
susurro in populo* – do not malign the people of God.'

'I said before that I am not interested in rumour. If there
is any slur made against de Reppes, I know you will deal with
it according to the rules of the Order.'

It was Laurence de Bernere's turn to nod. The rule said a
brother who had sinned should be chastised privately by a
fellow brother, and only if he refused to accept that chastise-
ment from two brothers would he have to confess in public.

'Then I can tell you that Odo de Reppes was granted

permission to go to Oxford on private business last Saturday. As the rule demands, he went with a companion – his sergeant, Gilles Bergier.'

Bullock now sat on his nameless nag, which had stopped to graze on the far edge of Cowley Marsh, trying to get his facts straight. He needed to find out what business de Reppes had in Oxford that day. But he didn't want to confront the man at this stage and risk him fleeing before all the facts were known. That would not help William. He had thought of finding this Sergeant Gilles and finding out from him who his master had visited. But subtlety was not part of Bullock's armoury, and he would no doubt have still given the game away by doing so. So he had been relieved when de Bernere offered to dig a little himself. The only problem was, knowing the secrecy of the Order of Poor Knights at first hand, Bullock could not be sure that de Bernere would share with him anything he discovered. Especially if it incriminated a fellow knight in murder. As it might well do, for by now Bullock had put the days in order. If he was remembering it correctly, it was the day after de Reppes visited Oxford that Ann had taken sick and soon after had died of arsenic poisoning.

SIXTEEN

By the end of the day, Saphira had only achieved half of the goals she had set herself. Her interview with Robert Bodin had been frustrating and inconclusive. She had arrived at the shop on the north side of the High Street late in the morning, but though the shutters were open, the shop seemed empty. No wares stood outside, as they normally did, and inside, the rear of the shop was in darkness. It was unlike the spicer not to be keeping a sharp eye on his valuable wares. She wandered uncertainly around the bags and barrels of sweet and pungent-smelling spices. After some time had elapsed with no sign of Robert, she took a pinch of cinnamon in her thumb and forefinger and touched it to her tongue.

'What are you doing? I shall report you to the constable for stealing.'

From the door at the back of the shop, hidden in shadows, loomed the bulky figure of the spicer. As he emerged into the shaft of sunlight that illuminated the front of the shop, Saphira could see his face had lost some of its roundness, and his normally red complexion seemed almost yellow. He looked scared.

'I was merely sampling your goods. The cinnamon is excellent.'

'It was more than a sample you took. I would say that was a pennyworth.'

Saphira resolved to stay sweet. She needed to extract some information from this man, after all.

'Then I shall pay you a penny. Do you by any chance have any arsenic powder, too?'

Bodin's jaws wobbled as he shook his head.

'I recognize you now. You are the woman who asked me about the talisman seller. You wanted to know if he bought arsenic. Now here you are asking about it yourself. What are you up to, eh?'

'I have rats in my house. I wanted to kill them before they ate all the food in my larder. Is that not reasonable?'

Robert squinted at her suspiciously.

'No, there's something more on your mind. What have people been saying about me? The talisman seller said he just wanted the arsenic for killing flies. Now you want it to kill rats. Are you trying to trap me?'

Saphira was shocked by the man's onslaught, and backed off as he strode towards her, intimidating her with his large frame.

'Get out of my shop.'

She hurried out on to the street, only looking back when she realized that Bodin had not come further than the doorway of the shop. As she stared at him, he turned on his heels and disappeared inside once again. She decided to stay in the street for a while to see who else went into the spicer's. Someone had frightened him and she wanted to see if whoever it was would return. In the hours before Robert Bodin closed his shop for the day, though, she saw few people go in. She did not know what she expected anyway. It was not as if a heavily disguised man in a black cloak would sneak through the door and murder Robert Bodin while she stood there. She laughed at her own fool-ishness. But she did persist with her watchfulness, and besides a beggar boy, who was shooed away before he could set foot in the shop, she saw only three customers. There were two sturdy women who looked like serving maids coming and going, and a black-garbed master of the university. He had a burgeoning bruise on his cheek and must have gone in for a remedy. With her new knowledge from Samson, she would have recommended oil of immortelle or everlast flower. After he had emerged, no one else went in, and by the time she had given up, it was too late to walk to Botley to speak to Margery. She made her way home thinking of rats and arsenic, knowing she needed someone other than Peter Bullock or Thomas Symon to share her ideas with.

Thomas had to wait for Peter Bullock and he paced around the courtyard of the old castle at the western end of town. The castle was in a ruinous state, and what buildings were left standing were used for a prison. But the old St George's Tower still stood tall, close to the bulwark walls, its massive

stone façade both forbidding and awesome. The constable
had his quarters in this tower and Bullock insisted that the
little lane close by was named for him. Thomas knew that
Bullock Lane, however, was really Bulwark Lane, though he
would not tell Peter so. With time to think, he was reminding
himself of Falconer's tenets when investigating murders. He
knew he should not ignore other possibilities, just because
one in particular seemed promising. But then, if he was to
consider Saphira's suggestion that the talisman seller was
involved, should he not also include Saphira herself on the
list of suspects? Bullock seemed to think so, even if that
created a dilemma for them. How were they to discuss the
case with her and suspect her at the same time? He even
thought he should add Ralph Cornish to the list after talking
to Master Koenig. Cornish's evidence against Falconer, though
true in a way, could have been aimed at diverting attention
from himself. But when he had spoken earlier in the day to
one of Ralph's students, he had learned that Cornish had
apparently been occupied when Ann died. He had a living
outside Oxford, and divided his time between teaching and
pastoral care. Thomas had to assume he could not have been
anywhere near Botley at a suitable time to administer poisons
to Ann Segrim. No, the main suspect had to be this mysterious Templar. When he heard the ringing of horse's hooves
on the cobbles of the castle courtyard, he was glad. With
Bullock back, he would learn what the constable had discovered about Odo de Reppes. All other concerns could be
put out of his mind.

Laurence de Bernere was perturbed. After Peter Bullock's
visit, he had sought out Odo, and found him sweating away
in the courtyard, swinging his blade at a wooden post. At his
shoulder stood his sergeant, Gilles Bergier, clutching Odo's
shield and helm. The look on Bergier's face was one of pure
admiration. The knight was rhythmically gouging chunks out
of each side of the post as he exercised his strong, right arm.
The regular thud of the sharp sword hitting the post went on
ceaselessly, and Laurence marvelled at Odo's stamina. The
man was truly a tireless fighter, who any brother would be
pleased to have by his side in battle. But Laurence could see
something in his face that worried him. Odo's eyes were blank,

almost glazed, yet seemingly fixed on the post in front of him. Sweat poured down into the bush of his black beard, and still he did not cease his assault on the post. De Bernere had seen a similar look on visages in the Holy Land – those of Saracen fanatics, especially those strange warriors called assassins. It was said they took drugs before carrying out their deeds. It scared him.

He called for Odo to stop.

The man carried on slashing expertly at the post as though making a point, before finally turning to de Bernere.

'Yes, master.'

The tone of his voice was low, and Laurence detected a mockery in the two simple words. But he did not let the man rile him into a confrontation and phrased his question carefully.

'When you were in Oxford last week, were you aware of any undercurrents that might reflect on the Order? Only I have been subjected to a strange interrogation by the town constable. He wouldn't say what it was about, so I thought you might have heard something yourself.'

Odo exchanged a glance with his sergeant, who retreated to the far end of the courtyard at the unspoken command.

'I am afraid I cannot help you, master. I passed quickly through Oxford on my way to Godstow, where I was to deal with a family matter. The town seemed its normal, hedonistic self with drunken clerks and excessive amounts of cheap goods for sale. It was a joy to return to the discipline of the Temple.'

Once again Laurence detected that mocking tone. He grunted noncommittally in response, thanked Odo, and turned away. He was about to ask to speak to Gilles Bergier, but when he scanned the courtyard, the sergeant had disappeared.

As darkness fell on the town, a woman clad in a black cloak with the hood pulled up, slipped out of her house in Fish Street. She kept discreetly to the shadows of the now closed up shops, making for Carfax. There, she waited in a doorway while a rowdy bunch of clerks ran past, punching each other playfully on the arm and shouting friendly abuse. When the din had died down, she swiftly crossed Carfax northwards, up Northgate Street, then left into Bocardo Lane. Saphira Le

Veske had decided it was time to rouse William Falconer from his apparent lethargy. Standing at the grille in the prison door, she called urgently to the man incarcerated within. At first there was no sound, but then she heard a rustling sound that put her in mind of the rats Rebekkah said lurked in her larder. A pale face appeared on the other side of the grille.

'Saphira! This is not safe for you.'

Saphira smiled. It seemed that William was not entirely lost to the world.

'Why? It is after curfew and the gates are locked against robbers and whores. Save for those inside the walls, of course. Here, I have brought you an apple stored in my cellar last autumn.'

She pushed the sweet fruit through the bars and Falconer took it gratefully. He bit into the slightly soft flesh with relish and there was silence between them for a few moments. Saphira broached the subject on her mind.

'William, why are you not defending yourself at the Black Congregation. Peter Bullock says you are silent while others blacken your name.'

Falconer kept silent, chewing slowly on his apple, so Saphira pressed on.

'Thomas Symon and Peter are doing their best to discover who really killed Ann Segrim. But they are no match for you. I too have some ideas but we all need you to guide us.'

Again, there was an ominous silence from the other side of the grille. Then Saphira heard Falconer sigh. His reply, when it came, was brief.

'I cannot speak.'

Suddenly, she saw the quandary he was in. He was keeping silent because of her.

'You think if you tell the truth, then they will discover that you took a tincture that was prepared by me. That I had usurped Ann Segrim in your affections, and that it would look like I killed her deliberately. But they would have no proof of that.'

'They would not need proof. The Black Congregation thrives on rumour and innuendo, and you are a . . .'

'Jew?'

'Yes. For some no further proof is needed. You should not worry about me. The King's Court will soon be here and will reverse any decision made by this illegitimate assembly of fools.'

Saphira grasped the bars of the grille and pulled her face as close as she could to William's.

'I am not so sure of that. Peter Bullock thinks the chancellor is in a strong position. And though the right of the congregation to try a member of the university for murder has never been tested before, the verdict may hold. You must help us to save you.'

William's face looked grey in the gloom of his cell. He wrapped his fingers round Saphira's.

'Then tell me what you and the others have learned so far.'

Sister Margaret was scared. The arrival of Odo de Reppes at the nunnery had brought back all the horrors of the last few days. And though he had been turned away, she feared for her life. She lay back on her narrow and uncomfortable bed staring through the darkness of her cell at the ceiling. She could not rid her mind of the images of her sister nun in the cell next to hers that now stood empty. She had first heard the voice of her neighbour praying fervently. She had tried to shut her ears, pressing her hands hard against either side of her head. But the voice chattered on, getting louder then softer, but always at a great speed. Finally Margaret had slipped off her bed and entered the next cell. For a moment she thought the sister was flying, only to realize that she was just leaping from the end of her bed with her arms wide open. Her eyes were wide and staring, her voice coming in great gales of prayerful Latin, but so fast Margaret could not understand it. The nun could not stand still, her arms fluttering around her head as if warding off invisible creatures. She once again climbed on her bed and leaped off it with her arms wide apart. Margaret grabbed her as she fell and held her companion tight. After what seemed like hours she calmed down, but Margaret was scared to see the life drain out of the young woman's eyes right before her. She dropped her on the floor, cleared up and ran away. But every night since then it seemed as though she was being watched by those dead, fish eyes. She closed her own quite tight shut now, and prayed.

*   *   *

Robert Bodin also could not sleep. When he had seen the Jew woman in his shop, and she asked about the purchase of arsenic again, his heart almost stopped. He wished he had not got involved in the sale of the powder. He had got rid of the woman and tried to reassure himself that no one would listen to her gossip. But now he was scared and lay in his bed staring at the roof beams above his head. Beside him, his wife Maggie lay on her back snoring peacefully as though she had not a care in the world. He was annoyed by her serenity as much as her snores, and thought about digging her in the ribs. If he was going to spend a sleepless night of worry, then she could share it with him. He was about to poke her with his elbow, when he heard a noise. It sounded like the cracking of a piece of timber. He started up in his bed, pulling the wool blanket off his wife. She merely snuffled and turned her back to him. All his senses alert, he waited for another sound. There was nothing to break the silence and he sighed in relief. Then he heard it. A scuffling noise was coming up through the timbers of the bedroom floor. The shop was directly below and it sounded like someone was moving around. Bodin had dealt with robbers before – his goods were valuable and only small quantities were required to make a good profit for a thief. He had a large wooden club beside his bed, carved from a single tree bough. Groping for it in the dark, he knocked over the candlestick that stood by the bed. It clattered across the floor. Maggie moaned and turned towards hm. He put a finger to his lips and hushed her, though in fact she was barely awake. She rolled back over and was soon snoring again. Swinging his legs out of the bed, he found the club and crept across the floor to the landing and stairs that led down to the shop. At the bottom of the stairs, he stopped and listened again. There was no sound, and he wondered if the thief had been scared off by the noise of his candlestick rolling across the floor above. He grasped his club firmly and moved into the back of the shop.

He was hardly aware of the shadow that flitted across the edge of his sight, before a heavy sack landed on his head. He tumbled to the floor, the sack on top of him, covering his face. He tried to push the sack away, but someone sat astride him, pinning him down. The sack pressed firmly against his face, smothering him and he could smell cinnamon. He drummed his bare heels on the floor, but felt weaker and weaker as his chest tightened. He couldn't breath, and he drowned in the scent of cinnamon.

SEVENTEEN

F alconer had much to think about thanks to Saphira. She had laid out in detail not only her own concerns about Covele, but also Thomas's revelations about the Templar, Odo de Reppes. He settled back on to the damp straw on the floor of his cell, tucking his legs up and circling them with his arms to keep warm. With his chin on his knees, he reviewed the known facts. Humphrey Segrim had told a convincing tale of a Templar who had slain King Henry's nephew in Viterbo, his ailing brother in Berkhamsted, and had revelled in the news of the death of his grandson. It all spoke strongly of a conspiracy against the family of Henry, and Falconer had an inkling why Thomas was so convinced.

Seven years ago, when Thomas Symon had first arrived in Oxford as a raw, country boy he had stepped unwittingly into a series of murders perpetrated in the name of revenge. A single man had been consumed with so much hatred for the de Montforts that he had embarked on a series of killings that had culminated in an attempt on the life of Simon de Montfort, the Earl of Leicester. It was during the Barons War and had been foiled by Falconer. Though it had mattered little to Earl Simon, who a year later lay dead at the Battle of Evesham. Thomas Symon was therefore perhaps inclined to see parallels with the present situation. Falconer had to admit it was curious that the murder in Viterbo, witnessed by Segrim, contained an echo of that terrible time in England. The sons of Simon de Montfort had been guilty of the murder of Henry, nephew to the King, but it seems that among the other unidentified murderers had also been Odo de Reppes. What worried Falconer was why de Reppes, knowing Segrim had seen him, hadn't disposed of Sir Humphrey on their journey to the Holy Land. Maybe he thought the old man was no danger until he saw him again in Berkhamsted. If he had started to track him down then, how had he lost sight of him so close to home? And had de Reppes really killed

Ann because he thought she had learned too much from her husband? There was so much still to know, and Falconer was locked away. It was frustrating for him, and he jumped to his feet and began to pace his tiny prison.

The talk at the Golden Ball Inn was all about the murder trial. The regular bunch of drinkers sat around the fire had already consumed three jugs of Peter Halegod's best ale, but as the speculation grew Harold Pennyverthing decided to call for another. Tom Peckwether, Saul Griffin and Peter Inge acceded to his generous offer. They knew Pennyverthing had been paid for a carpentry job that week and could afford to splash out. The jug was passed around, and when each man's mug had been refilled, and the ale tasted to ensure Halegod had not watered it down, opinions on the murder of Ann Segrim were proffered. The trouble was that the killer was a university man, and the damned chancellor had taken it upon himself to try the case. This meant no town man was involved, and all they had to rely on was rumour and gossip. Of which there was plenty.

'It's said that this Falconer was a regular visitor to Botley while Segrim was in the Holy Land.'

Griffin offering to the debate was accompanied by a pointed wink of the eye. The others guffawed at the innuendo. Inge came in with a rejoinder.

'Aye, and that he had a whole gaggle of women at his beck and call. And he made one of them sneak into Mistress Segrim's house and stab her in the dead of night.'

'I heard they acted together and tied her down first, so she was awake when they did the foul deed.'

The shock created by this assertion from Peckwether caused a clicking of tongues and a shaking of wise and disapproving heads. More ale was sucked while each thought of a scandalous titbit to top this last remark. From the shadows in the corner of the ale-house, far away from the warmth and red glow of the fire, came another voice.

'For all I know Falconer had many whores, but I can tell you for a fact that Mistress Segrim was poisoned by his own hand with a preparation concocted by a certain Jewess who lives in fine style in Fish Street.'

The four gossips peered into the gloom of the far corner,

but could only clearly discern the legs and feet of the speaker stretched out in front of him. He was well shod and his tunic was that of a gentleman. The mention of a rich Jewess struck a chord with all four men. They were all hard-working Englishmen and that race did precious little but lend money at extortionate interest rates, feeding off others' need. Harold Pennyverthing spoke up for all of them.

'A Jewess, you say, sir?' He was not sure of the man's station in life, but it did no harm to be polite to someone who could set them straight about the murder. 'And she is lording it over us in all her finery, thinking she has got away with murder, you say?'

'Oh, yes. The house is number eight – the one with the steps and opposite the end of Jewry Lane.'

The four outraged men, fired up with beer, threw the last of their drinks down their throats, and vowed to teach the Jewess a lesson right away. As they tumbled out of the inn door, Alexander Eddington leaned towards the light of the fire at last, and grinned evilly.

When Saphira returned to her house after talking to Falconer, she felt more optimistic than before. She was sure that William would now pay attention to what was happening around him, and come up with some sort of solution. Even from his prison cell. Her new cheerfulness was probably what prevented her from seeing the four men who were lurking under the eaves of the house opposite. As she slid the large key into the lock on the front door, there was a cry of triumph.

'That's her, the Jew tart.'

'Yes. The murdering bitch.'

She turned in horror to see four sturdy men with clubs in their hands hurrying across the street, leaping the filthy drainage channel that ran down the centre. The key seemed to turn terribly slowly, and she jiggled it to get it to undo the lock. Finally it gave, and the door pushed open from the pressure of her leaning on it. The men were already at the bottom of the short flight of steps that led to the door. Their faces were contorted with rage. The few people who were passing looked away in horror and hurried on. There would be no help for Saphira from them. It was already dark, and the doors of the houses opposite were closed and probably barred. Jews lived a circumspect life after dark. She pushed through her own door and tried to swing it closed. In the fleeting seconds before the red face of the leading assailant appeared in the gap between door and lintel, she thought she saw a light flickering in Samson's house on the other side of the road. A flicker of hope soon extinguished by her attackers, as she tried to force the door closed against the pressure of their bodies. She could smell the beery breath of the leading man, who was snarling like a beast. She spat in his face and he recoiled briefly. Enough time for her to slam the door and try to drop the bolt. But it was too late, and the bolt caught only halfway down. The thunder of the ensuing assault on her door convinced her that the bolt would not hold long.

She fled into the kitchen at the back of the house, swinging the door closed behind her. With a strength multi-plied by fear, she dragged the heavy kitchen table across the door, knowing it would not stop the men for long. She hunted for a weapon and found a knife beside the hearth that must have been discarded by Rebekkah. Her chest heaving, she listened in horror as the front door splintered and the men rushed in. Soon they were pummelling on the kitchen door.

She was preparing herself for the worst, when the world seemed to tilt. She imagined the fear had made her dizzy, as the floor lurched beneath her. She stepped to one side and watched in amazement as one of the heavy stone flags tipped upwards. A pale face framed by grey locks appeared in the opening like some demon out of Hell. Except she suddenly recognized Samson's anxious look. He beckoned with his free hand, the other barely managing to hold up the heavy slab.

'Come quickly, before they break in.'

Stunned, she gathered her skirts around her ankles and slid down into the opening. With a groan of relief, Samson let the slab fall back into place. In the gloom, he held a bony finger to his lips. Saphira sat on the steps that were under her feet, trying to hold her breath. Above, they could hear the kitchen door creak and the table being forced over the floor. Then the men were in her kitchen, and must have been amazed at her disappearance. She suppressed a giggle. Perhaps they would think she was a witch now. Their muffled cries of frustration gave her great pleasure, but the sound of smashing pots soon stifled it. Then she felt Samson grasp her arm and he began to lead her away into a subterranean world.

For the first time, she looked about her. The walls either side were built solidly of good ashlar, and arched over their heads. It could have been a simple cellar, but this was more than that. Samson led her through this first arched room, and on into another, and then into a low tunnel at a junction of arches. He held a small lamp in his hand to give them light. She stopped and looked around her in amazement. The air down here was cool and she could hear the sound of water dripping further off. Their voices echoed slightly.

'Where is this?'

Samson's brown eyes sparkled in the lamplight.

'Right now you are underneath Fish Street. Many of the cellars in the houses on either side of the road are linked together, and joined by this tunnel. Rabbi Jacob even has a *mikveh* down here.'

Samson was referring to the ritual bath used by his faith for cleansing purposes. Saphira thought the only one in Oxford was by the river in the Jewish cemetery. Bodies, as well as women, needed ritual cleansing. It now seemed there was one in the heart of Jewry. And a convenient chain of escape routes in times of trouble. She grasped Samson by the arm, pulling him to her and hugging him.

'Thank you for saving my life. I am sure those men would have beaten me to death if you hadn't seen what was going on.'

In the lamplight, Samson blushed.

'I heard them plotting to attack you from where they were hiding. Right under the eaves of my house. They seemed to think you were guilty of the murder of Mistress Segrim. Something to do with poisoning her for Falconer. Of course, I knew it was nonsense, but before I could think how to warn you, there you were at your door. All I could do was to come down these tunnels.'

'It was enough. I don't know why they got it into their heads that I was involved. I suppose I will have to be careful for the next few days.'

'Come. You can stay with me for the time being. And I will

talk to Peter Bullock tomorrow. He may be able to sort this out. He is a good man.'

Saphira wondered if Peter would be as amenable as Samson imagined. He had appeared to be uncommunicative with her lately, and she didn't know why. Unless he too thought she was guilty of murder. The idea made her shiver. Samson took it simply as her feeling the cold down in the tunnel, and took her into his cellar, which led to the way out on the other side of Fish Street.

Falconer was unaware of the danger that Saphira had found herself in. Though he heard distant noises and shouting, he assumed it was no more than the normal disorderly behaviour of townsfolk and students after dark. After they had taken too much ale. He hoped none of his students lodged at Aristotle's Hall were involved. Without his presence to keep them under control, they might be straying from the straight and narrow path. With Thomas Symon preoccupied by the Templar conspiracy, they had no one to stop them getting into trouble. Still, he was sure that Peter Bullock would keep any fracas well under control with a few swipes of the flat of his sword blade. He chuckled at the comfortable thought and squatted down on the straw bedding that Bullock had now thoughtfully supplied. He would apply his brain logically to the task in front of him, and enjoy the fact that he was not being pulled hither and thither by conflicting responsibilities.

There was something to be said for a spell of incarceration to concentrate the mind. His old mentor and friend, the Franciscan friar, Roger Bacon, had been locked away by his order in a convent in Paris for several years. He spent his time completing three treatises – *Opus Majus*, *Opus Minus* and *Opus Tertium*. Amazingly, despite their vast scope, they had been nothing more than an introduction to what Bacon saw as a comprehensive work on the whole of human knowledge. Pope Clement had approved them, but then had died before Roger could progress the project. Despite now being free, he had had impediments put in his way, and could not carry on with his life's work. Imprisonment had worked for him in a way his order had not imagined. And if that was the case, then Falconer reckoned it could work for him. He began arranging the known truths in his mind, mentally lining them up in a way that was much neater than he could have put down on parchment. And it was not long before he saw a problem that had to do with chronology.

EIGHTEEN

Maggie Bodin woke to find her husband's side of the bed empty and cold. She eased her legs over the side of the bed, grumbling about Robert.

'What's the silly bugger been and done now?'

She sat scratching the itchy thatch of her frizzy, brown hair, trying to remember what had happened the night before. She was sure they had gone to bed together. Yes, she recalled that all right, because he had moaned about her cold feet. And come to think of it, she had a vague idea that he had been moving about in the middle of the night. She knew it irritated Robert that she slept so soundly, and she could swear that he deliberately crashed around when he couldn't sleep. Last night had been no exception. She was sure he had got up and knocked something over. Peering across the bed to her husband's side, she saw that a candle lay on the floor by the wall. It must have rolled there after he had knocked it. But where was he now? It was not like him to have got up so early. It was still quite dark, after all. She yawned and pushed herself up. Swaying a little on her heavy legs, she stretched, and decided she urgently needed a piss. The bucket was full and had to be emptied in the midden in the street. So, with a sigh, she pulled on a threadbare cloak and hefted the bucket in her fist. She hobbled down the stairs and started to cross the floor of the shop. She stumbled against something that had been left right across the way to the front door, spilling some of the bucket's contents on the floor.

'Bodin, what have you been doing?'

Normally she could negotiate her way through the shop in the dark with ease. Every sack and barrel had its place in the shop, and Robert was most meticulous about his precious goods. She put the slop-bucket down and groped out in front of her until she encountered the obstruction. It felt like a leg. She dropped to her hands and knees and peered closely as her eyes began to adjust to the dark. Slowly she made out two sturdy, hairy legs and a patched linen nightshirt sticking out from under a brown sack. The legs were unmistakably those of her husband. She screamed.

Peter Bullock stood in the house in Fish Street and felt somewhat abashed. The attack on Saphira had been brought about by some scurrilous rumour bandied about at the Golden Ball Inn. This he already knew thanks to Samson's clear recollection of the ringleader of the four men who broke in. The Jew knew most of the folks in Oxford, some of whom secretly came to him at one time or another for remedies. He had identified Harold Pennyverthing from his window last night, and early this morning had told the constable what had happened. Bullock now turned round to the grey-haired old man, who stood at his shoulder surveying the damage.

'I have already spoken to Harold Pennyverthing, and he says a man he does not know told them about Saphira being guilty of helping Falconer kill Ann Segrim. But I have a description and will follow the matter up with Peter Halegod. The rumour was a vile and evil slur to cast out.'

In truth, that was why Bullock felt some shame himself. He had shared a similar suspicion of Saphira's behaviour with Thomas Symon, guessing without substance that she might have poisoned Ann Segrim. He himself could have passed that suspicion on to another, who then could have acted like Pennyverthing. So this mess might have been his fault in other circumstances. And though he still could not rid his mind of Saphira's possible involvement in Ann's death, to pass on a suspicion without recourse to the facts that Falconer so loved was dangerous in the extreme. With Samson, he looked at the results of the drunken rampage.

'Pennyverthing will repair any damage caused. He is a carpenter and can repair the door and this table.' He indicated the table that lay upside down on the kitchen floor, its legs broken and splintered. 'As for the rest of the damage, they will all replace pots and pans with money from their own pockets.'

The kitchen was an unholy mess, brought about by the four drunken men in their rage of frustration. Broken pans and utensils lay scattered across the floor, and the stench of beery piss hung over the blackened hearth. They had obviously found their own way of putting out the fire. All four culprits now knew that they were lucky not to have found Saphira Le Veske, or they might have been waking from their hangovers to face charges as serious as Falconer's. Their penitence would ensure their good behaviour for months to come. Bullock rubbed his hands through what hair remained on his head. How easy it was for this town to get out of hand. Behind him, Samson gave a little cough.

When Bullock turned round, he saw Saphira had crossed the street from the safety of Samson's house, and now stood in the doorway of her kitchen. He felt like a fractious pupil brought before his dominy.

'I will ensure that everything is restored, and that the men will be on their best behaviour in future. You have nothing to fear from them.'

Saphira smiled easily. The horror of the previous night had fled, and though she had experienced a momentary pang of fear when she stepped out beyond Samson's safe and solid oak front door, she soon conquered it. She had experienced worse threats in Bordeaux when her husband had still been alive, and their son a vulnerable child. Now she was a widow with a grown son travelling between France and Canterbury, and could face up to whatever the world threw at her.

'No matter, Peter. Broken pots can be replaced and doors mended. Nothing worse happened. Thanks to Samson.'

Bullock frowned.

'That is what I cannot understand. How he got you out of the house and across to his home without the idiots knowing.'

Saphira and Samson exchanged glances, and she realized that the tunnels and cellars were Jewry's secret. She waved a dismissive hand.

'Oh, they were drunk and easily fooled. And it was dark.'

'Hmm.'

Bullock knew he was not being given the whole truth, but felt he couldn't press the matter further in the circumstances. His personal sense of guilt still hung heavily on his shoulders like a chain mail coat. But he would find out how the escape had been engineered at some other time. He hated a mystery as much as Falconer did.

Saphira began to clear up the mess in the kitchen, and Bullock was about to help, when a cry came from the front door.

'Constable. You are needed elsewhere. A hue and cry.'

Bullock recognized the voice of his watchman, Peter Pady. He normally stood night watch over East Gate, and should have been in bed by now after his latest shift. Instead, it seems he was searching for Bullock, and in an agitated state, to boot, over a call to hunt out a criminal. He stomped out of the kitchen and saw Pady hovering in the street doorway. His wild eyes were running around the damage caused to the front door.

'What on earth has happened here?'

'Never mind that. It is being dealt with. Who has called a hue and cry?'

'Maggie Bodin, the spicer's wife. She has found her husband dead in his shop.'

Saphira, who had followed Bullock to her door, heard what the watchman said. She was suddenly interested in this matter, because she had wanted to talk further with Robert Bodin about his sale of arsenic and other possible poisons. Now it looked as though someone had prevented her from doing that. Someone who could be the real killer of Ann Segrim. She grabbed the cloak she had left by the shattered front door, and started after Bullock and the watchman. She called out.

'Peter, I am coming with you.'

Bullock, without breaking his bandy-legged, rolling gait, waved an arm over his head in weary acknowledgement. He knew nothing would stop her, if she was determined to come too. Soon, they were both having to push their way through a knot of people, who had gathered outside the front of the spicer's shop close by All Saint's Church. The shutters were still up, and the shop in darkness, but everyone could hear the wailing that emanated from within. The newly-made widow was in full flow. Bullock waded through the crowd like a sturdy little ship cutting through waves in the English Channel. Pady and Saphira followed swiftly in his wake. Inside the shop, Maggie Bodin's caterwauling was deafening. She was kneeling before the body of her husband, half hidden under a burst sack of reddish powder.

'Cinnamon,' murmured Saphira, recognizing the aroma of the spice.

Bullock hefted the sack aside and sneezed as the exotic spice flew up around him, irritating his nose. He wanted to be sure Bodin was not still alive – a possibility that Maggie seemed to have ignored. But, when he looked at the spicer's face, he could tell there was no hope. Bodin's eyes were wide open, and as dull as stale fish on a market stall. There were red spots in the whites of the eyes that Bullock had seen before too. Smears of red powder were evident around his mouth and nose, where he had tried unsuccessfully to breathe air into his chest. He had suffocated on a sack of spices. Bullock leaned over to Maggie Bodin, grasping her arm firmly and turning her to face him. Slowly her sobbing ceased.

'I suppose there is no chance that this was a tragic accident. That the sack fell on him when he was lifting it, and he couldn't crawl out from under.'

Maggie snorted in derision, wiping the snot from her reddened nose.

'Robert was strong. He could lift two of these sacks and carry them across the shop. No. Someone has killed him.'

Saphira squatted beside the distraught woman.

'Can you think of a reason why anyone would want to do that?'

'No, I do not. But why are you asking me that? Don't you believe me?'

'I didn't mean that. But it would help the constable if you could tell us about anything suspicious that happened recently. Anything out of the normal.'

Maggie eyed this strange woman asking questions that were the province of the constable with curiosity. Then she looked at Bullock questioningly. He nodded in encouragement, and then made sure he stood between Maggie and the body of her husband. He didn't want her caterwauling to start afresh.

'Please answer Mistress Le Veske. It would help me.'

Maggie Bodin rocked back on her heels and gazed up to the ceiling. She recalled how Robert seemed to have been on edge recently. Always looking over his shoulder nervously, and looking scared every time he heard the door of the shop open. Previously, he had been such a strong man, even over-powering at times if the truth were told. But lately he had lost his confidence and she didn't really know why. Though it might have had something to do with one of his sales. There had been a couple of customers with whom he had dealt rather secretively. Once, she had come down into the shop, only to

be told abruptly to get back upstairs by her husband. She had
retreated to the landing, but had peered down to see who else
was in the shop. It had been a figure dressed in dark clothes
– brown or black, she couldn't tell – and that was all she saw.
Their head had been cut off by the angle of the stairs. She
began to tell her inquisitors this.

'I couldn't see his face as he was standing in the shadows
at the rear of the shop. In fact, it might have been a woman,
come to think of it. Like a nun or suchlike.'

She began to cry and her mouth hung open, though no
sound came out. To see her like that was more frightening
than hearing her original cries of horror. Bullock looked away
in embarrassment, as Saphira took the woman's arm and
guided her back upstairs to her solar. The constable beckoned
to Peter Pady, who stood in the doorway of the shop, preventing
the curious from peering in.

'Call off the hue and cry. There is no need to go hunting
for a killer now. He must have died in the early hours of the
morning by the feel of him. He is stiff and icy cold. Arrange
for the body to be dealt with properly. The widow is in no fit
state to know what to do herself.'

Pady nodded solemnly, and left the shop, pushing his way
through the crowd, to carry out his task. Bullock stood on the
step and closed the door behind him. He glared at the mob
of onlookers, until they began to take the hint and disperse.
He did call out to one portly, old woman, though.

'Mistress Stockwell, Maggie Bodin will need a kind soul
to help her through the next few days.'

The old woman nodded sadly.

'Aye, you are right, there, Peter Bullock. If you will let me
in, I shall sit with her.'

She shuffled past him, as he opened the door. And a few
moments later, Saphira joined him at the threshold.

'There is much to follow up here, Peter.'

Bullock groaned.

'But we do not know if this murder has anything to do with
Ann Segrim's death.'

'But it's too much of a coincidence. Here we have a man
murdered who dealt in poisons, if only to kill beasts. We know
for sure that he sold arsenic to Covele, the talisman seller,
who was later at Botley. He could easily have sold some to

other people we don't know about. Mistress Bodin said the person she saw was wearing brown or black. That is a start.'

Bullock gave a mocking laugh.

'You might be decked out in colourful clothes, mistress. But look around you now. Poor people, working people, are mostly garbed in simple cheap brown cloth. And most of the masters at this university of ours wear black.'

It was true. As Saphira looked at the people passing by, she did see the occasional young buck dressed in purple or parti-coloured clothes. But this was the exception, rather than the rule. Most were clad in rough, dark cloth. But she was sure the description of the mysterious person whom Robert Bodin wished to hide from his wife would help in the end, when all the facts were assembled. And she couldn't but remember two particular facts. Firstly, Covele was last seen clad in a brown robe, and, secondly, she couldn't get out of her mind the beggar boy she had once seen at the door of the spicer's shop. She didn't think of it at the time, but she was convinced it had been the talisman seller's son. And that meant that he was still lurking around Oxford somewhere.

For his part, Peter Bullock was uncertain of his own dismissal of the brown or black clad figure. It came to mind that, like himself in his Templar days, Odo de Reppes's sergeant, Gilles Bergier, would be dressed in brown.

NINETEEN

C hancellor Thomas Bek was a worried man. He was afraid that Falconer was slipping through his hands. For most of Saturday, he sat brooding on the problem. He had thought his case against the troublesome man conclusive, but now he was hearing rumours of another possible murderer. Roger Plumpton, an indecisive and wavering reed at the best of times, had gone behind his back. He had been talking to some of the regent masters, and had learned that Sir Humphrey Segrim was hinting of wider implications to his wife's murder. When Plumpton had smugly communicated this to Bek, the chancellor had been doubly annoyed. Not only did it mean that the thorn in his side in the form of Falconer might escape, it also implied that he, Bek, had got it wrong from the beginning. That was an impossible pill to swallow. Moreover, the tale Segrim told was of a grand conspiracy against the crown of England. A conspiracy that Bek was completely unaware of. If, as he desired, he was to follow in the steps of his predecessor at Oxford, Thomas de Cantilupe, and become Chancellor of England, he should have had his finger on the pulse of such a traitorous movement in the midst of Oxford life.

Angrily, he rang the bell on his table to summon his servant. He needed fresh wine to help him think. With the trial not proceeding until Monday, he had a day and a half to come up with incontrovertible proof of Falconer's guilt. Even if he had to concoct it himself. When his servant poked his bald head nervously into his master's private room, Bek snapped out his commands.

'More wine, Peckwether. And summon Master de Godfree.'

He eased back in his ornate throne of a chair. Henry de Godfree was a slippery customer, but that's just what Bek needed now. He would do anything to please his master and ingratiate himself into his good books. De Godfree would work something out, he was sure, or he wouldn't be Proctor of the Southern Nation next year. He was drinking deeply of his second goblet of Rhenish, when Henry de Godfree entered the room. Bek, flushed with wine, greeted him imperiously.

'De Godfree, my dear man, thank you for coming.'

The proctor squirmed a little before the chancellor. He knew Bek was at his most dangerous when drunk and genial. His mood could change in a flash, and the heavens could fall on the unlucky victim of his displeasure. But he had nailed his colours to the mast of Thomas Bek, and hoped to go all the way with him to the heart of government. He modestly inclined his narrow head, testing an obsequious smile on his lips.

'I am your servant, sir.'

Bek, ignoring the fact de Godfree was left standing, began to explain his dilemma. Once he had heard him out, de Godfree eagerly responded. He knew exactly what was needed.

'If we are to nail down Falconer, we must do it without decrying this possible conspiracy.'

Bek angrily broke into de Godfree's exposition, tapping on the table for emphasis.

'No, no. Surely we must scotch this rumour and concentrate on what we have already got. His sexual peccadilloes. Can't we embroider that a little more?'

De Godfree was warming to his thesis and took the risk of contradicting the chancellor.

'On the contrary, sir. If we deny the conspiracy exists, and then it later proves to be true, you . . . we . . . will be seen as gullible fools. No. Whether it is true or not, we must weave a tapestry that shows Falconer is probably involved in it too. Then, whatever the masters believe is the cause of the murder – high politics or base sexual wrongs – Falconer will be damned.'

Bek grinned broadly, forgetting de Godfree had contradicted him. This sounded a most intriguing proposition. He pushed a goblet towards the proctor and poured the Rhenish, albeit sparingly, into it.

'Sit down, man. And tell me how you plan to make this work.'

The day was hot, and Bullock had sent a message to Colcill Hall asking Thomas Symon to meet him at Grandpont. The long bridge spanned the meandering Thames south of the town

walls, and cool breezes blew along the river valley. The loca-
tion also reminded Peter Bullock of more innocent times,
when as a child, he had dipped a fishing pole in the waters
of the Thames at this very point. Thomas found him sitting
on the grassy bank of the river, his boots off and his bare feet
plunged in the flowing waters. He stood beside the constable,
but didn't dip his own feet in. Once a farm boy himself, he
now was very conscious of his new solemnity as a master of
the University of Oxford. Maybe a little too self-conscious.
Sometimes he yearned to be the carefree boy he had once
been. With a moment's indecision, he sat down on the bank
next to Bullock.

'The rumour is there has been another murder.'

'Yes. Robert Bodin, the spicer. And Mistress Le Veske is
certain that his death is linked to Ann Segrim's somehow.'

Symon detected the cool tone in Bullock's voice when he
spoke Saphira's name. Surely the constable did not still think
that she was responsible for Ann Segrim's death?

'And you? Do you think it is?'

Bullock gave a deep sigh and kicked his feet in the river,
creating ripples. Both men watched as they swelled out from
the bank and disappeared in the general maelstrom of the
rushing waters.

'I was trying to think like Falconer. And I can hear his
voice as clear as if he was standing here. He would say there
was no coincidence in death. And it is true what she said.
The death of a dealer in poisons as well as herbs and spices,
killed so soon after someone was herself poisoned, demands
an answer. But what if Mistress le Veske was deliberately
leading me in that direction to move suspicion away from
herself? What then? God's breath, I need William's advice
now.'

Thomas knew he was a poor second best to Falconer, but
felt he had to aid the constable as best he could.

'William would tell you to use every resource you had, and
collect as many facts as possible until they begin to make
sense.'

Bullock groaned and began drying his wet feet on the long
grass.

'I feel as though I am drowning in facts. There's Chancellor
Bek who is convinced that Falconer is the killer, and points

to the pot he had with him when Ann died. And his switch of allegiance from Ann to Saphira Le Veske. He blames Falconer's grosser feelings. The half-brother, Eddington, looks in that direction too. Though I have my suspicions that he was jealous of the attention his sister-in-law paid to Falconer. I would not be surprised to discover he attempted a seduction of Ann Segrim himself. And then we have Sir Humphrey's testimony of a murderous plot to kill the entire royal family, implicating the Templar, Odo de Reppes. And he killed Ann because her husband had spilled the beans about the plot. Why he has not yet killed Sir Humphrey, I don't know. Mistress Le Veske, however, would have us believe that some Jewish talisman seller killed her to get back at Falconer for some perceived slight last year. If she didn't kill Ann herself out of envy. Have I missed anyone out?'

Thomas could not suppress a laugh at Bullock's exasperated listing of the possible murderers. Nor could he resist adding to the list, just to see the constable's face.

'Well, I could add one man more. I did think Master Ralph Cornish might have borne witness against Falconer for a greater reason than mere vindictiveness. If he had killed Ann, then accusing Falconer would throw us off the scent. But then, why would he kill Ann in the first place? And I learned he could not have been at Botley at the time of the poisoning, or have had an opportunity to doctor any of Ann's food. So we can remove him from the list, you will be pleased to hear.'

'Thank God.'

'What we now need to consider is, if Bodin's murder is connected, are there any signs that would point to any one of our suspects? If the poison that killed Ann was obtained from Bodin, then presumably the spicer was killed to ensure his silence. Was anyone seen entering his shop before he was killed?'

Bullock sighed in exasperation.

'Of course people were seen entering his shop. He sold expensive but popular spices and herbs. Half of the servants of the rich merchants in Oxford were seen entering his shop at some time.'

He had his boots back on now and began to walk along the river bank past the Blackfriars' house. Thomas followed him.

'When was he killed?'

'In the dead of night, so no one would have seen the killer entering or leaving. In fact, the front door was still locked in the morning. Whoever killed him must have broken in the back of the building.'

It irked Bullock that he had not even established this at the scene of the crime. He had not thought of it till now. He would have to go back and investigate further. He wondered if he was he getting too old for this game. At his heels, the black-clad Thomas persisted with his enquiry, ignoring Bullock's bad temper.

'Then maybe the killer spoke to Bodin yesterday some time, and Bodin said something that gave him reason to think the spicer was about to reveal the truth.'

'Hmmm. Saphira did say she thought Bodin had seemed nervous when she last spoke to him. And I will tell you something else . . .' He stopped and faced the intense young man by his side. He would show this scholar he could put facts together. 'The wife saw a man in the shop who her husband didn't want her to see. And he was dressed in brown, like a Templar sergeant.'

'Then we must follow this up. Can you get to speak to the sergeant? In the meantime, I will try and talk again to Segrim, or his half-brother. Perhaps the Templar has been spotted lurking around Botley. He must still be intent on killing Sir Humphrey if his plan is to suppress any knowledge of the conspiracy.'

Bullock shook the young man's hand firmly, pleased that he was taken heed of. He was so used to Falconer tossing his ideas aside, that it was heartening to be taken seriously by a scholar for once. Even if it was only young and impression-able Thomas Symon.

The flagstone rocked under Saphira's feet as she crossed the kitchen, and Rebekkah cried out a warning.

'Take care, mistress. I nearly tripped over that on Friday. Nearly measured my whole length across the floor.'

Saphira recalled how the magical appearance of Samson from under the slab resulted in her salvation yesterday. She was not surprised it was not seated properly now. But her maidservant had just said it had been loose the day before

Saphira's rescue. She stood and rocked backwards and forwards on the secret trapdoor thoughtfully. Rebekkah continued to prattle on as she finished preparing dinner on the newly repaired table. Harold Pennyverthing had done a good job, and had shamefacedly promised to come back the following day and finish the work on her front door. For now the bolt and frame were fixed temporarily. Saphira tipped the slab once more with her foot.

'It's very odd, Rebekkah, but I don't recall this flagstone rocking before. How long has it been like this?'

'Oh, a good few days, mistress.' She laughed. 'If it wasn't a foolish idea, I would blame those rats for it. They started eating your food from the larder about the same time.'

Saphira smiled and tapped her foot on the flagstone.

'When you have served my dinner, Rebekkah, you can go home. I won't need you any more today.'

Rebekkah smiled broadly. Mistress Le Veske was a most generous employer. And she was hoping to meet her boyfriend in the afternoon without her parents knowing. She prepared and served the repast with great alacrity. Saphira, for her part, was glad for her maid's speed. She had an idea concerning the access to the tunnel and what might lie within. After the dishes had been cleared away, and Rebekkah had slammed the front door behind her, Saphira poked around the kitchen until she found a sturdy iron trivet with a long handle. It was perfect for inserting in the inconspicuous slot at one end of the flagstone. She levered the stone up and pushed it to one side. Cool air rushed up into the kitchen from the underground tunnels and cellars below. She lifted her skirts and slowly descended the steps which she had almost slid down on the previous occasion. She held a candle in her hand to light the area below. The flame guttered a few times as draughts from other parts of the tunnel blew through. Once more, she admired the neat ashlar stonework of the walls and curved arches. She retraced her steps from the previous occasion as far as she remembered them, until she came to the intersection of tunnels. She knew that, if she turned right, she would come out where she had before, in Samson's cellar. So turning left should bring her out higher up Fish Street, under Rabbi Jacob's house. She recalled that Samson had told her there was a *mikveh* under his house.

And if she was right in her supposition, she would find what she was looking for near running water. She turned to her left.

Bullock took the right fork just outside Oxford and rode towards Temple Cowley again. He was not sure what he would be asking Gilles Bergier, but he knew he couldn't expect the sergeant to admit to murder. Or betray his master, Odo de Reppes. He would have to rely on that sense of comradeship that permeated the squires and sergeants in the lower ranks. And the Templar knights' feeling of superiority that some-times set them apart from the rank and file. It was Saturday and the Rule decreed that on that day the knights benefited from three meals of vegetables, where the squires and sergeants got one alone. It had always annoyed him as a sergeant, and he was sure the mood persisted even now. So, instead of announcing himself to the commander – Laurence de Bernere – this time Bullock just aimed his old nag towards the dormi-tory where the sergeants bunked. It was late afternoon and their masters would have dined, and would now be in the Temple to hear the divine offices. The sergeants would be making the most of the time off, and shooting the breeze with each other.

He was in luck. Wandering round behind the dormitory, he found a bunch of sergeants rolling the dice on the dusty ground. Gilles Bergier was one of them. He squatted down awkwardly, his stiff old legs protesting at the abuse. A couple of the sergeants gave him a sidelong glance, but then went back to their gambling. Bullock observed for a while, and noted that Bergier was on a roll and winning the small coins that were being wagered. The knights may have taken a vow of poverty but their sergeants surely hadn't. Eventually, Bergier scooped up his winnings and, amidst protests from those who he had taken money from, rose and walked away. Bullock followed him down to the fish ponds that helped support the commandery. Bergier stopped and stood looking over the flat and murky waters.

'You wanted to talk to me.'

Bullock realized any subterfuge he had planned was pointless.

'Yes. It's concerning Odo de Reppes. I have heard stories

about his journey to Outremer, and extraordinary events that seem to dog his heels.'

'And you are wondering if they are true. Well, you know the words of the Rule as well as I do. "Do not accuse or malign the people of God."'

Bullock realized that word had got around he was an old soldier, and former sergeant of the Order of Poor Knights. Well, he could quote the ancient Rule laid down by their founder, Hugues de Payens, too.

'It also says, "Remove the wicked from among you."'

'Hmmm. I still cannot help you. You see, I have only been appointed his sergeant since he came through France. A matter of a few weeks ago.'

Bullock felt disappointed. Perhaps this man could not help him nail down the truth of the conspiracy tale after all. Though it was still possible that he had acted for de Reppes in the murder of Robert Bodin. He had to try and winkle the truth out.

'Then you were with him in Berkhamsted when Richard of Germany died.'

Bergier turned and stared hard at him. He looked as though he was assessing the old man who stood before him. Whether he could trust him, and whether he was someone who could keep a secret. Bullock held his right hand behind his back and crossed his fingers. The sergeant took a deep breath and continued.

'Yes. The old man. He was suffering from the half-dead disease. His face all pulled down at one side, and dribbling from the side of his mouth. If that had been me, I would have wanted to die. He was hanging on to a life not worth living, so maybe it was a mercy he died when Odo was there.'

Bergier's slow and deliberate delivery told Bullock all he needed to know about what had happened in Berkhamsted. But it did not help him with either Ann's or Bodin's death. He risked another question, as the man had been as co-operative as he could be so far.

'And Odo, has he got any reason to be in Oxford? Has he asked you to aid him with anything in the town?'

Bergier's eyes narrowed.

'Like what?'

'A matter concerning a local knight of Botley, and his wife who is now dead.'

'Botley?' The sergeant looked puzzled. 'No, if that is what you are seeking to sort out, you have the wrong man. Odo de Reppes is here on family business in Oxford, and that is all I can say. We went nowhere near Botley.'

Bergier turned and walked back to his comrades, leaving Bullock as puzzled as before.

TWENTY

The cool air led Saphira to the ritual bath. At the northern end of the tunnel under Jewry stood a vaulted chamber with a flight of stone steps leading down into a cistern. Cool, clear water filled the cistern to halfway up the steps. Her candlelight reflected off the smooth surface of the water as off a mirror. She paused and listened, but could hear nothing save the steady drip of water somewhere. She turned, and heard a faint scrabbling sound. Perhaps it was just rats, and she was wrong. But she didn't think so. In the compacted earth at her feet she saw something odd. Bending down she picked up a small stone, which might have otherwise gone unnoticed. But this one had a hole carved in it where a cord might be threaded, and a Hebrew letter painted on its surface. She called out in a hushed tone, which echoed back to her.

'Covele, where are you?'

Silence. She tossed the talisman in the air and caught it.

'Boy, I know you and your father are there.'

The scrabbling began again, and Covele appeared from round one of the pillars at the end of the chamber, his boy shielded protectively by one arm. They stood a little way off from her, cautiously assessing her.

'What do you want? We are doing no harm.'

'None, I am sure. Except for robbing my food store.'

'Would you begrudge your own kind sustenance?'

'Not at all. If you had asked for it. But you sneaked up out of the earth and took it like . . . rats.'

Covele sneered at the insult and stood his ground. It was the boy who eventually broke the deadlock. He walked up to Saphira and spoke.

'Will you feed us, please? I am hungry and tired of hiding down here.'

In the kitchen, as the boy was tucking into the remains of the fish cooked by Rebekkah for her, Saphira began to question Covele. At first he sat defiantly straight with his brown robe pulled around him, a satchel full of talismans and amulets at his feet. He refused the food offered by Saphira and evaded her questions. But then the boy pushed a piece of bread towards him which was soaked in fish oil. He gave his son a fleeting smile and took the offering.

'You ask me why I followed the university master to that manor house. It was to find a way of exacting revenge on him. And you. Last year you drove me from this very town. And me a fellow Jew.'

Saphira knew that she and Falconer had only questioned Covele because he had been responsible for carrying out a forbidden ritual. If he had fled, it was of his own free will.

'We were only asking questions, as I am now. If you were innocent, there was no need to run away.'

Covele snorted with laughter, some crumbs of bread spewing from his mouth.

'Innocent? You are a Jew, too. You know what it's like. Where does presumption of innocence come into it?' He hooked a stained thumb at the lad, whose eyelids were beginning to droop despite the tension in the room. 'I had to flee with my boy for our safety. So then I set myself up as a talisman seller, and in the guise of a German Jew I thought I was safe to come back to this place. When I saw you staring at me in the street, though, I knew you had recognized me. We went back to where we were camped in the cemetery, and began to pack once again. Then I had second thoughts and stayed around, not wishing to be pushed out again. Later, I saw that man of yours and followed him. I thought I could maybe learn something about him that I could use against him. And I did.'

'What do you mean?'

'I followed him to that manor house and waited. After he had come back out, I went round to the kitchen block. You can always get gossip out of servants. I spoke to this monkey-faced girl, who had plenty of spleen in her. She told me the fellow in black had been in the lady's chamber on his own. And the master all the way in the Holy Lands at the time. She reckoned he was her lover.'

He wasn't looking at Saphira by now, but staring into the embers of the fire. She, for her part, was blushing at his revelation, even though she knew how things had stood between William and Ann Segrim. Covele continued, his hands clasped tight together as though he were squeezing the life out of Falconer.

'I gave her an amulet in reward for the information she gave me. And that was as far as I got.'

The amulet, no doubt, that Saphira had later seen in Ann Segrim's solar, which had set off her suspicions of Covele in the first place. It appears he had never even got as far as Ann herself. Margery had probably put it in her mistress's room hoping to cure her.

'But the arsenic you bought from the spicer?'

'Arsenic? What's that got to do with revenging myself on this man? I bought it to mix with milk to kill the flies in our tent. The weather is hot and the flies are prodigious in numbers. But then I heard tales of murder and mayhem being bandied around town, and found a better place to stay. Those tunnels are cool and safe. I told the boy to take the arsenic back and see if the spicer would return our money. But he chased him off. Ask him.'

She looked at the boy, who was now asleep. She was sure he was the beggar-boy she had seen on the doorstep of Bodin's shop that day. Covele's story was plausible. The talisman seller leaned back in the chair and yawned.

'Now my revenge will have to wait.'

Saphira didn't tell him that Falconer was already in a worse fix than merely having rumours of adultery being spread about him. She left the pair to sleep in her kitchen and retired to her solar, aware she had not spoken to Falconer all day.

Thomas had also spent the whole day without speaking a word with Falconer. Which was unfortunate as William had some precise opinions about the Templar conspiracy and its impact on the death of Ann Segrim. But Thomas was still determined to uncover the threads of Odo de Reppes's misdeeds from his end, whilst Bullock tried to talk to his sergeant. In the end, he had no need to go to Botley, for in the afternoon he encountered Margery in La Boucherie – the end of High Street where all the butchers traded. He saw her coming out of a shop and called her name. The maidservant cast a wary eye over towards him and for a moment looked as though she was going to flee. Then, when she saw who it was had called, she sighed, and waited for him to cross the street.

'What do you want now?'

Thomas ignored her sullen demeanour and smiled sweetly.

'I was just wondering how your master was. I was planning to go over to Botley and ask him about . . .' He realized Margery would know nothing of the high politics of Sir Humphrey's situation, being a lowly servant. '. . . the state of his health.'

Margery took a defiant stance in the middle of the street as people flowed by them on both sides.

'The master is still very unwell, as you might expect. He has not set foot outside the house for days. In fact, he has told us to tell anyone who calls that he is not at home. That he never came back from the Holy Lands.' She put on a cute face, which was at odds with her sour look and dark hairs on her upper lip. 'So, there is no point in coming to Botley. The master is not at home. Now, if you will excuse me, sir, I must buy a potion from Bodin the spicer.'

Thomas realized that no one at Botley could know of the spicer's murder, that had taken place only that morning. He warned Margery of the situation.

'You will not be able to carry out your task, I fear. Robert Bodin was murdered this morning.'

Margery went very pale and swayed a little. Thomas reached out an arm in case she collapsed, but she recovered her composure quickly.

'Who did it, sir?'

'That we don't know yet. But we shall find out, and it might throw light on your mistress's death too.' He paused, a thought jumping into his head. 'Constable Bullock told me that when you gave evidence at the Black Congregation, you said you had gone to Bodin for a medicine for your mistress.'

Margery's jaw clenched tight and she cast her eyes down to the dusty ground. Thomas wasn't sure if it was because of him reminding her of the scare she had got bearing witness in front of the Black Congregation, or for some other reason. He decided not to pass over the errant idea, however. Here was a tenuous link between the spicer and various people at Botley, after all.

'What did you fetch, Margery?'

Margery ground the toe of her shoe in the dust.

'It didn't matter. The mistress never took it anyway.'

'What didn't matter, girl?'

'I was supposed to get the mistress a preparation of feverfew for her sweats. But when I told Master Alexander where I was going, he said not to bother. The mistress was not all that ill. He said go to the spicer and get something harmless that tasted bitter but would do nothing. So I did. And I gave it to the master when I got back.'

'You gave it to Alexander Eddington?'

'Yes, but he could not have passed it on. The Oxford master killed her before she could take it, didn't he? Either that or she got some murrain from that nunnery she went to almost every day.' She shuddered. 'Dangerous places, those nunneries.'

William Falconer was frustrated by a lack of knowledge. He didn't think he would ever think that, but being locked away in a cell had kept him from knowledge. The accumulation of knowledge about Ann's murder. Why had no one come to him today, and kept him informed about what had developed? Where was Saphira? He was bursting with questions to ask. But then, he supposed he only had himself to blame. Ann's death had overwhelmed him, and for a few days he could not even think clearly. Then, when they told him that the chancellor was to try him, he had been scared. Not for himself, but for Saphira, whom he would have incriminated if he had said anything. It had been her potion he was bringing to Ann, and no would believe a Jew was an innocent. Especially one who, it seemed, was now known to have replaced Ann in his affections. Even though he knew the real situation, Ralph Cornish had twisted it to suit the chancellor's view of the facts. And where did he learn about his relationship with Saphira anyway? Falconer was sure he had been very careful, for Saphira's sake if not his own.

In fact, he had kept silent about so many matters that it was no surprise now that he was not being consulted. But Saphira had told him last night about some of the threads of truths that had been uncovered. He had spent a sleepless night thinking about them, rearranging the facts and events as he knew them. He had seen a flaw in one set of facts, and needed to find out more before he could tell Bullock what needed doing. It was all to do with the timing of Humphrey Segrim's arrival in Oxford, and the presumption that the Templar could have murdered Ann to silence her.

He had spent quiet hours in the night recalling what he knew about the sequence of events. Finally, he had convinced himself he was right. Whenever Segrim had arrived in Oxford – and apparently he had closeted himself in the Golden Ball Inn for quite a while – Ann had not encountered him or spoken to him until after she had fallen ill. He was sure of this because, when he had visited her on her sickbed, she had made no mention of Humphrey's return. If Bullock thought the Templar had killed her because he feared Humphrey could have told her his secret, he was wrong. There might have been other reasons, but that is what he needed to talk to Bullock about. And he had a bee buzzing in his bonnet about Godstow nunnery. That is what Ann had spoken to him about before Alexander Eddington had thrown him out of Botley Manor. And Falconer had some important information for Bullock or Saphira to follow up in connection with that. He didn't know where it might lead, but it needed investigation. And time was running short. Tomorrow was Sunday, and he didn't think the Black Congregation would convene until Monday. So there was a whole day to set matters in train. If someone would only visit his cell.

TWENTY-ONE

As the bells rang out over the town, the constable of Oxford, Peter Bullock, was called upon by someone unexpected. The commander of Temple Cowley, Laurence de Bernere, had made a rare visit to the town. And he was incognito. He did not wear the white robe of a Knight of the Temple, but a nondescript brown tunic that must have been borrowed from one of his sergeants. The fine black hooded cloak rather gave him away though as a nobleman. That, and his bearing. The Rule of the Order said that brothers should always visit towns in pairs, but Laurence de Bernere was alone. Bullock had heard the clatter of horse's hooves on the cobbles in the courtyard of Oxford Castle. Full of curiosity as to who would be calling on him so early on Sunday, he descended the spiral staircase inside St George's Tower and stepped into the watery sunshine of morning. The hooded figure had already dismounted and was pacing the yard. At that moment, Bullock did not recognize the man as his face was hidden. He touched a hand to the dagger at his belt with the instinct of an old fighting man and called out.

'Hello, good sir. Can I do something for you?'

The man looked over his shoulder and then threw the hood off. The constable recognized the sharp features and big bushy beard of de Bernere immediately.

'Brother de Bernere, have you any news for me?'

The Frenchman strode over to him and took his arm firmly.

'May we go inside, Sergeant Bullock?'

Having slipped into the old, Templar ways of addressing each other, the two men felt an intimacy that might otherwise have been lacking between a noble knight and a humble town constable. Bullock smiled more easily.

'Of course, brother. Come this way.'

He led de Bernere back up the spiral stairs and into his spartan living quarters. He invited his visitor to sit, but de Bernere stayed on his feet, looking around the tidy chamber. He appeared nervous despite their intimacy.

'I see you haven't altogether given up on your Templar vows of poverty and humility.'

'Nor of chastity, brother. Though I confess that is more down to my age now.'

De Bernere laughed gently at Bullock's self-deprecating jest. Pulling at his beard, he began to explain his mission.

'What I am about to say I would tell no one but a Templar. And I expect utter discretion in return for my confiding in you.'

Bullock inclined his head in acquiescence to the request. He was intrigued. What was it that the commander was going to tell him? Was it about Odo de Reppes, and would what he say exonerate Falconer? If it did, he hoped he could use it without breaking the confidence of de Bernere.

'Go on.'

'When we last spoke together, you were asking about Odo de Reppes. What his business was in Oxford. At the time I was not clear myself and have made it my business to find out. The man himself is incommunicative to the extent he is contemptuous of his duty of obedience to me. But I have spoken to Sergeant Bergier.'

Bullock hoped the Templar had got further with the tight-lipped sergeant than he had done. He listened with interest as de Bernere continued.

'Odo de Reppes has a sister – a nun of the Benedictine Order – called Marie. She was locked away in that nunnery the other side of town. At Godstow.'

'Was? Where is she now?'

Laurence de Bernere sighed and cast his eyes to Heaven.

'I should not have said he *has* a sister, rather that he *had* a sister. She died in the nunnery. Quite recently.'

'And that is why de Reppes came here?'

'Well, apparently he decided to come here while she was still alive. Whatever it was he wished to communicate to her, he was unable to pass on. She died before he reached Temple Cowley. Now he is intent on unearthing the facts of her death. I feel sorry for the prioress of Godstow.'

Bullock smiled wryly, thinking of the formidable Mother Gwladys.

'Don't. Rather feel sorry for Odo de Reppes. If he thinks he can browbeat her, he will soon learn a salutary lesson.'

De Bernere frowned, sure that no woman could be a match for the hot-tempered de Reppes.

'Does this help in any way with your murder investigation?'

Bullock was immediately suspicious of de Bernere's motives. When he had spoken to the man before, he had made no mention of murder in connection with Odo de Reppes. De Bernere saw the look on his face and apologized.

'Sergeant Bergier told me you were investigating a murder over at Botley. He was very defensive about his master, saying he was with de Reppes at all times in Oxford. And that neither of them had ever been to Botley, and only once to Godstow, when the doorkeeper told them of Sister Marie's death. Odo is now very disturbed and wishes to know more. I have forbidden him from leaving the Temple.'

Bullock could hear his empty stomach groaning from lack of food. De Bernere had prevented him from taking his usual breakfast of bread and ale. Now, the man still dallied in his chamber, as though he had more to say but couldn't work out how to start. The constable thrust himself up from the chair he had slumped in as the Templar paced the room.

'Well, if there is no more, brother, I have business to attend to.'

De Bernere looked surprised at Bullock's abrupt move.

'Yes, yes of course. I must go and attend the divine offices anyway. Today is the Feast of St George.'

The two men returned to where the Templar's horse had stood patiently in the courtyard. De Bernere swung up on the saddle, pulled on the reins, and as if having an afterthought, asked Bullock a question.

'Have there been any rumours about de Reppes?'

'Concerning the murder?'

'That, and any motive he might have had for committing it.'

Bullock wondered how far he dare go, bearing in mind the Rule's proscription on false rumour.

'There has been . . . talk . . . of attacks on the family of King Henry. But it is all speculation and nonsense. Why do you ask?'

'No reason other than trying to make sense of all this. As you say, nonsense, indeed.'

De Bernere swung his horse's head round and he cantered out of the courtyard. Bullock would have dearly loved to know what was going through the Templar's mind. For Laurence de Bernere had other reasons for locking de Reppes in the

Temple than merely stopping him from bothering the prioress at Godstow. Yesterday, he had received a curious letter from none other than the Templar Preceptor in the County of Tripoli. Guillaume de Beaujeu was a man known to Bullock and his friend William Falconer as a quiet but determined righter of wrongs. But he was also an ambitious man who some said would be, after the death of Thomas Bérard, the next Grand Master of the Templar Order. And his ambition had caused him to ask questions about a faction within the Templars who had supported the Lusignan, King Hugh of Cyprus, in his bid to be King of Jerusalem. De Beaujeu supported Charles of Anjou, and so did the King of England. Laurence de Bernere had been asked by the Preceptor to find out the truth about Odo de Reppes. And he already had his doubts about the man's loyalty. As he raised a hand in farewell to the old man at the gates of Oxford Castle, he turned his mind to ways of dealing with de Reppes.

Saphira carried some good Rhenish wine she had decanted from the barrel into a stone flagon across Carfax and up to North Gate, where the Bocardo jail stood. It was both a treat for William and a peace offering for not having visited him the night before, as she had promised. She was glad he was now taking an interest in the murder of Ann Segrim, and didn't want him lapsing into the morose state he had descended into immediately after her death. She need not have worried. As she turned the corner into Bocardo Lane, she heard peals of female laughter coming from the direction of the prison cell. A short, middle-aged woman with an overlarge and overexposed bosom was leaning against the bars of the cell-door window. She was the source of the loud laughter, and she turned her cheerful face towards Saphira as she approached. Her face showed signs of age, and Saphira wished she could describe her as ugly. But she wasn't. On the contrary, she was really something of a beauty, despite her years. Falconer's face was pressed to the bars on the inside and he wore a wide grin.

'Ah, Saphira. There you are at last.' He was quite unashamed at having been discovered with this woman. 'Say hello to Agnes. She is the owner of the best bawdy house in Grope Lane, and an excellent cook too. If it wasn't for her, I would have starved in here.'

Saphira was embarrassed that she had not thought to bring
him some food, and that it had been left to some brothel-
keeper to supply Falconer. However, she smiled sweetly at
Agnes, thanking her for her kindness. Then she turned a severe
look on William.

'I hope you don't describe it as the best bawdy house from
personal experience.'

Agnes's infectious laughter pealed out again and Saphira
found herself laughing too. She passed the flagon through the
bars to Falconer.

'I did remember to bring you some good wine.'

Agnes saw the look that passed between the two and
coughed gently.

'I think it is time for me to go, Master Falconer. There is
enough in the pot I gave you for dinner today and to break
your fast tomorrow. After that, I have no doubt you will be
released.'

'Perhaps, Agnes, perhaps.'

The brothel-keeper swayed seductively off down the lane,
leaving Saphira to talk freely to Falconer. Saphira had already
decided she would say nothing about the attack on her. Nothing
had come of it, after all. In fact, it had helped her to discover
Covele's hiding place. Her rescue, by way of the tunnels under
Fish Street and through the cellars of Jewry, had pointed the
way to the talisman seller. She began her presentation of the
facts for Falconer by explaining why she thought Covele innocent of Ann's murder.

'He was never in her chamber, nor in any position to poison
her food. And no matter how vindictive I think he can be, I
don't believe he is a murderer.'

'I believe the same can be said of Odo de Reppes too.'

Saphira was startled by William's assertion. How could he
deduce that from his prison cell? She asked him, and William
explained.

'Ann did not know of her husband's fears and opinion of
the Templar. Not even after she had found him hiding in the
Golden Ball. He could not have killed her to shut her mouth.'

'But what if he killed her to frighten Sir Humphrey into
silence? He couldn't trace Segrim, so his wife was the next
best target.'

Through the bars, she could see Falconer shaking his head.

'If he wanted to scare Segrim, why poison her slowly? It is not the way of the Templars – they are fighting men. He would have scared Segrim more if he simply cut her head off. Besides, the Rule of the Templars makes it difficult for knights to work alone. They do not have a private life, and much of what they do is open and visible to their brothers. Unless there is another reason for de Reppes to have killed Ann, I would discount him.'

Saphira felt downhearted. With Covele no longer suspected, she had put her hopes on the Templar, and Thomas's and Bullock's investigations.

'Then where do we go from here?'

Falconer smiled in the gloom of his cell.

'I want you to go to a nunnery for me.'

The ashes in the grate of Colcill Hall were as grey and life-less as Thomas Symon's theory about the Templar conspiracy being the cause of Ann's death. Peter Bullock sat next to Thomas having described his conversation with Laurence de Bernere. Thomas, who had heard rumours that Chancellor Bek was to produce a final witness to Falconer's guilt the next day, had hung all his hopes on Sir Humphrey Segrim's story. Now it appeared to be a threadbare cobweb of half-truths at best. He still wanted to be clear about the Templar's motives though.

'Odo is here because his sister died in Godstow?'

Bullock shrugged.

'Not precisely. He came because she was alive at the time and he wished to see her. He is still here now because she died.'

'But she cannot have died in suspicious circumstances, or you would have known surely. She must have died a natural death.'

The constable shook his head.

'Not necessarily. Mother Gwladys is a dragon of a woman and fiercely protective of the nunnery's reputation. I recall a long while ago there was a murder at Godstow. She would not let me in to investigate. It took me ages to persuade her to even let Ann carry out an inquiry on my behalf. Which just as well. The unpleasant business was soon resolved, and Gwladys was grateful to Ann that she could get on with the smooth running of the place.'

Thomas nodded, poking the cold ashes with the toe of his boot.

'That is probably why Mistress Segrim was still welcome there.'

'Ann still called there? How do you know that?'

'Margery, her maidservant told me. She said her mistress was a regular visitor there right up to before she died.' Thomas paused, stirred by Bullock's interest in his chance remark. 'You don't think there is any connection there, do you?'

Bullock leaned forward, his mind once more working hard.

'What? Think about it. Ann Segrim is a regular visitor to Godstow nunnery, even perhaps confiding in the prioress or the nuns. One of those nuns is the sister to Odo de Reppes, who has reason to keep a secret he thinks Ann's husband knows. The sister dies. Ann dies. No connection? You know what Falconer would say. We may not be sure of Segrim's claims about the Templar, but there is a link there that demands investigation.'

Both men were now reinvigorated by the idea of continuing their quest. But Thomas had a question for his senior partner.

'Should we not tell Master Falconer all of this?'

Bullock shook his head vigorously.

'Not yet. Let us not get his hopes up before we know more for a fact. I will go to Godstow tomorrow.' He raised a hand to stop Thomas's protest and grinned. 'You are too young. Gwladys will refuse you entry for fear you will inflame the passions of her sister nuns. This is work for an old and ugly man long past the carnal urges of youth.'

TWENTY-TWO

St Mildred's Church was once again filling with black crows, eager to feast off the carrion that was William Falconer. It was Monday morning, and Chancellor Thomas Bek was content with his preparations for what he imagined would be the final day. And the final nail in the regent master's coffin. A guilty verdict would seal his power as chancellor of the university, and lead to greater power in the realm. He deliberately waited until all the regent masters had seated themselves in the main body of the church, before making a triumphant entrance from the side chapel, flanked by his two proctors. Henry de Godfree had carried out his task well, and swore he had schooled the next and final witness to perfection. Roger Plumpton was still dragging his heels, and Bek resolved to see him ousted at the next annual election of officers of the university. There was no place in Bek's world for antagonism to his way of doing things.

He settled in the throne-like chair, front and centre below the altar, and cast a glance at the humbled figure of Falconer. After his attack on Ralph Cornish he was closely guarded by one of Bullock's watchmen, though Bek noted that the constable himself was not present. That pleased Bek, as the rumours of treason that he was going to build on today had apparently begun with Bullock. He did not want the man around to claim prior knowledge. The regent master was seated as usual on a low, small chair below Bek's eye level. It was a chair Bek had deliberately selected to make the tall and normally imposing figure of Falconer seem small and uncomfortable. However, this morning the accused man looked more at ease than before. He even had the nerve to smile cheerfully at the chancellor. Angrily, Bek nodded at de Godfree to get on with the business at hand. The skinny proctor smiled obsequiously and rose.

'Since the adjournment of this trial due to the . . .' He turned to cast an accusing look at Falconer. '. . . the violent attack on one of his fellows by the accused, William Falconer, Chancellor Bek has learned that rumours are circulating concerning a treasonable conspiracy at the root of Ann Segrim's murder.'

He waited whilst cries of disbelief and horror echoed round the church. A proper sense of outrage was expressed by all present before he continued. As the bedlam died down, de Godfree pressed on.

'Chancellor Bek was aware of this conspiracy many days ago, and has spent time verifying if this exonerates the accused.' Another susurration travelled through the throng. And Bek smiled knowingly, accepting his proctor's lie as truth. 'He has discovered that, on the contrary, it ties Falconer in more firmly to the murder of Mistress Segrim. I call to witness Regent Master Edward Skepwith.'

There was a murmur of surprise from the assembled masters. Skepwith was known to be an undistinguished scholar, who despite some wildness in his student days, had settled down to a steady but unimaginative career as a teacher. He was deemed to be reliable, if a little boring. There was a certain nervousness in his bearing as he walked the length of the aisle, his shoulders stooped and his head bowed. When he finally stood in front of de Godfree, the proctor clicked his fingers and made him look up at his colleagues.

'Master Skepwith has something to tell which will horrify, but which needs to be revealed nevertheless.'

De Godfree stepped back and sat down. Skepwith coughed, shuffled his feet, and glanced nervously at the chancellor. Bek for his part smiled encouragingly, though his heart was thumping at having to rely on this weak man for the final piece of evidence. Edward Skepwith took a deep breath and began. It was a tale that went back nearly ten years to the Barons War, when King Henry was opposed by Simon de Montfort, and for a brief period lost his throne. The university at Oxford was divided in its allegiance and bitter disputes rocked its foundations. Skepwith's face became flushed as he recited his story.

'You will recall that Smith Gate in the north of the town was locked against us, and it took a concerted effort by the students, myself included, to pull down the gates and gain access to the fields beyond. King Henry was outside the town, and whoever locked those gates wanted to stop us showing our support. I was later told that William Falconer was instrumental in having the gates locked.'

Falconer smiled ruefully. There was some twisted truth in what Skepwith said. He had arranged for the gate to be locked, but it had been to stop a murderer escaping, not to keep the students inside. The near riot had been an unfortunate result of his decision. Some had even seen the event as the opposite to what Skepwith was suggesting. That the students had been locked in to prevent them showing their support for de Montfort. But time and the defeat of de Montfort by Henry had distorted the view. Half-truths could be used to support both sides of an argument. As a scholar, Falconer was used to this. He waited with resignation as Edward Skepwith concluded his accusation.

'William Falconer supported the barons against his rightful king. And now he has murdered the wife of the man who was in a position to reveal this latest treason to us. He was involved in conspiracy before, and is besmirched with it again.'

Bek smirked as Skepwith made his way back to his seat at the rear of the church. It had all been well arranged by Henry de Godfree, and he was sure of the verdict he would get from the assembled masters. He could have concluded matters there and then, but wished to give his bid for power the best possible chance of legitimacy. Besides, he felt like savouring the feeling of control for a while longer. He rose to speak.

'Regent Masters of the Black Congregation of the University of Oxford, you have heard all the evidence available. Your decision should not be hasty, however. We shall reconvene after the dinner hour at nones in the afternoon.'

Peter Bullock decided to ride out to Godstow nunnery as it was too distant for his ancient legs. As he cleared the ramshackle outskirts of town, and the White Friars monastery at Beaumont, he could see clearly all the way across Port Meadow to the north. The sun was already making the view hazy, but he detected a figure dressed in green crossing the meadow on foot in the same direction. He thought he recognized who it was and spurred his rouncey on to a canter. As he closed the gap between them, the shimmering figure soon resolved itself into the shapely form of Saphira Le Veske. When he was a few yards behind her, she took note of the advancing horse and stopped. She turned to see who it was, tucking her burnished, unruly locks more firmly into her snood. Bullock reined in beside her and dismounted.

'Mistress Le Veske. What are you doing out here so early in the day?'

'I might ask the same of you, Constable Bullock.'

'I have business in the vicinity. And you?'

Each was aware of the guarded tones of the other, though Saphira was not clear why Peter Bullock had recently clammed up on her. If he was reluctant to be open with her about his investigation, she decided he would not have the chance to accuse her of the same. While he hesitated, she explained her business.

'I am here, Peter, at the behest of William. He is otherwise engaged, after all, and has asked me to go to the nunnery on his behalf.'

Bullock was puzzled. How did Falconer know about Odo de Reppes's sister having died in the nunnery recently?

'The nunnery? Then we are both going in the same direction. Shall we walk together?'

Saphira nodded, and side by side they walked along the footpath across the meadow, Bullock leading his nag by the reins. It took only a few moments of studied silence on Saphira's part to get the constable talking.

'How did William find out about the death of Odo's sister?'

Odo's sister? This was news to Saphira, but she didn't let on to Bullock that neither she nor William knew that. This was getting more and more interesting.

'Ann Segrim told William of Sister Marie's death. I think she wanted confirmation that she had made the right deduction in calling it suicide. But you know William. Any death following close on another is cause for deep suspicion.'

For his part, Bullock was now intrigued. He hadn't known that Ann had looked into the death of Odo's sister on Gwladys's behalf. How did this fit in with Odo's possible involvement in Ann's death? His mind was whirling and he suddenly stopped in his tracks. Saphira walked on a few paces before she realized her companion was transfixed. Turning back, she knew they both had to be honest with each other, if they were to help William. She took Bullock's arm and squeezed it firmly.

'Peter, we must share our knowledge, if we are to get anywhere.'

Bullock cast his eyes down to the dusty track unsure what to say.

'Do you still trust me, Peter?'

He took a deep breath and voiced his fears.

'I did not know what to think when I discovered you were learning the art of poisoning. And then Falconer told me it was you who prepared the potion he took to Ann. I even have a message you wrote telling Falconer you knew all about poisons and for him to beware.'

He pulled the scrap of parchment he had found in Falconer's solar from his purse. It was crumpled and stained from his regular rereading of it, but the writing was still legible. Saphira, who had forgotten all about the note, read it out loud.

'Take care! This preparation is dangerous. I should know, because I now have learned how to poison someone!'

She laughed uproariously.

'And you think I poisoned Ann based on this piece of parchment?'

Bullock's face went red, and he began to bluster his way out of an embarrassing situation. Saphira put her warm fingers over his lips.

'Peter. I wrote this half as a joke when I found William had taken something very dangerous simply to see if he could tell what it was. It was henbane, if I recall, and he might have killed himself. But he was always the empiricist.'

Bullock didn't know what she meant by the word, but he now believed that William trusted her. And therefore so should he.

'Saphira, I don't know what to say.'

'Then say nothing. Except to tell me what you know about Odo de Reppes's sister. Because neither I nor William knew who she was. Only that a nun had died recently. And Ann thought she had killed herself.'

They walked on, sharing what they knew. Bullock explained that he understood that Odo de Reppes had only learned of his sister's death after arriving in the area. Laurence de Bernere knew little about Odo, but thought his desire to speak to his sister must have been occasioned by a deep need. Here, Bullock quoted part of the Rule of the Templar Order by way of explanation.

'"Let them not have familiarity with women. We believe it

is dangerous for any religious to look too much upon the face of woman. For this reason, none may presume to kiss a woman, be it widow, young girl, mother or sister . . . ".'

'Perhaps he felt he was too deep in whatever conspiracy he had become involved in, and needed someone to confide in who could not or would not speak to others.'

'You may be right, Saphira. But only Odo knows that, and his sister is now dead.'

'Then what do you hope to find out at Godstow?'

Bullock gave a deep sigh.

'To be frank, I do not know. I confess I am out of my depth here. What I need is Falconer's guidance. Thomas is willing, but he is as lost in this maze of half-truths and lies as I am.'

'Then I can help. I told you that I spoke to William yesterday. And he has been thinking about this. I give thanks that he is almost back to his old self.'

Bullock grinned.

'You mean he is driving everyone around him mad with his damned incomprehensible logic?'

'That too, Peter. That too. But between us we have eliminated Covele the talisman seller from consideration.'

She explained to him how she had come to that conclusion, and he gladly accepted her opinion. Then she went on to describe what William knew about the death of Sister Marie. What Ann had told him before she died.

'She said she had spoken to all of the nuns, and examined the means of access to Marie's cell and the nunnery generally. As you probably know, the nunnery cloister where the cells are located can only accessed by the main door from the outer court, which is kept locked. There are two other doors apparently – from the days when nuns from rich families used to entertain their relatives – but these have long been closed and barred. No man is allowed into the inner cloister. Sister Marie must have died by her own hand. Or at the hands of another nun.'

'How did she die?'

'I think that is what left a little doubt in Ann Segrim's mind. She did not see the body, but was told the nun had been found when she failed to attend the Night Office in the early hours of the morning. They found her with her bedclothes cast aside and lying face down on the floor. Her eyes were wide open and she had a look of fear about her, apparently. There were some local herbs amongst the rushes on her cell floor, but these had been cleared away before Ann could look at them. She concluded that Marie had taken something poisonous quite deliberately, at a time when she would not be missed for several hours. The prioress had admitted that she was probably doubting her vocation.'

Bullock wondered if that was why Odo had come to Oxford. Had his sister got a message to him somehow asking him to free her?

'Does Falconer think Ann got it wrong? That the girl was murdered after all?'

'He simply doesn't know. And that is why he asked me to come here. Not knowing is an unacceptable situation for William. Until he knows why and how Marie died, he cannot tell if Ann's involvement in the sad business had any bearing on her death. And as we didn't know until now that Marie was Odo de Reppes's sister, I am not sure if that has anything to do with it either.'

They now stood at the rickety bridge that led over the stream towards the nunnery gatehouse. They paused for a while, staring at the stone archway.

'As a woman, Peter, it may be possible for me to gain access to the nunnery, where you cannot. Can I suggest we divide our resources. I will speak to the prioress, and you see if you can glean anything from the gatekeeper.'

'If he is sober. Very well, I must admit I was not relishing crossing swords with Mother Gwladys this morning. Hal Coke is by far a preferable witness to tackle. So let's get on with it.'

They crossed the bridge over the stream which sparkled and rippled under their feet, and entered the nunnery under the imposing stone arch. Bullock pointed Saphira towards the large door across the interior courtyard set with its own grille at head height.

'Knock there and someone will come. I'll deal with him.'

He tipped a thumb at the gatekeeper, Hal Coke, who rather belatedly was lumbering out of his office at the side of the gateway. Saphira strode across the yard, while Bullock grabbed the protesting Coke by the arm and steered him back to his office. She knocked tentatively on the door, and when there was no immediate response, hammered loud enough to waken the dead. The stony face of an old crone, wrinkled and

disapproving appeared at the grille. It peered short-sightedly
at Saphira and then, apparently unsatisfied with the inspec-
tion, it spoke through thin, sour lips.

'You have no need to hammer down the door, I am not
deaf, you know.'

A quieter, firmer voice came from behind the crone.

'Oh, yes you are, Sister Hildegard. That is why you are my
constant companion when I speak to people outside the
confines of this nunnery. You offer me an unenviable discretion based on your infirmity. Remember?'

Hildegard's sour face turned red and disappeared from the
opening. It was replaced by an almost equally old, but much
more serene visage. Saphira guessed this would be Mother
Gwladys, and detected a Welsh lilt in her voice. It reminded
her of the Bretons far to the north of her old homeland.

'Forgive me for disturbing your contemplation, Mother
Gwladys, but I need to speak with you. Confidentially.'

The eyes on the other side of the grille looked hard at
Saphira, examining her carefully. They took in the shape of
her face and the colouring of her skin which, despite the tint
of Saphira's hair and her green eyes, was a darker, richer hue
than that of the normal, pale-skinned ladies of England. She
felt as though the prioress was weighing her very substance,
assessing the nature of her soul. An attribute which no doubt
stood Gwladys in good stead when it came to seeing to the
heart of the nuns she mothered. The prioress smiled wryly.

'I do not suppose you are here to convert to our faith, are
you?'

Saphira smiled back, seeing the woman knew her for a Jew.

'Your supposition is correct. I am here at the behest of the
constable of Oxford to talk to you about the death of Mistress
Segrim.'

'Then you had better come in, so that we can talk privately.
Hildegard, dear, will you unlock the door. I think Master Coke
is busy.'

The crone's face reappeared at the grille, a look on it
betrayed extreme disapproval of both Saphira the Jew and the
subject she had come to discuss. A key grated in the lock and
the door swung open.

TWENTY-THREE

Mother Gwladys's chamber was austere but smelled sweetly of dried herbs. Saphira, even with her newly acquired medicinal knowledge, could certainly detect lavender, but was not sure of the other scents. The prioress invited Saphira to sit, and then sat down opposite her, leaving Hildegard to hover at her shoulder like some grotesque gargoyle.

'We were all shocked to hear of Mistress Segrim's death. She had been a friend to us all here. But tell me, why is the constable enquiring into her demise? Our chaplain told us that the university was trying one of its regent masters for her murder.'

'William Falconer, yes. But he was . . . very close to Ann Segrim. He is innocent of her murder.'

Gwladys nodded wisely.

'Ah, yes. It was no doubt him she spoke of once when she called on me. Nothing by way of a confession, I hasten to add, or I could not talk of it. But she said they had been estranged for a while, and blamed a certain person who had arrived lately in the town.'

Gwladys's look was directed straight at Saphira at this point. She blushed, knowing the prioress had correctly divined her own part in this triangle of disaffection. She looked down at her lap while Gwladys continued.

'I reminded Ann of her wifely duties and we said no more of it.'

'Yes. But I believe that there was another matter you discussed with Ann at the time. The death of a nun.'

Hildegard hissed like a snake roused from its slumbers. Gwladys, however, merely raised her hand to silence her companion.

'There was a confidential matter we discussed concerning the good running of the nunnery. Mistress Segrim was good enough to give us some advice from her point of view as a more . . . worldly woman.' Gwladys smiled ruefully. 'Sometimes our communion with God blinds us to the goings-on of the outside world.'

Hildegard crossed herself, as if warding off any evil Saphira might have brought from the world her prioress made reference to. But it was an evil that Ann had detected already lurking inside these walls that had caused the nun's death. Saphira was about to press the matter, revealing that she knew the circumstances of the nun's death, when a pale face was thrust round the door of the prioress's chamber. If she had been feeling uncharitable, Saphira might have assumed the nun, who now enquired if any sustenance was required, had been eavesdropping at the door. Hildegard would have waved her away, not wishing to waste good Christian food and drink on a Jew. But Gwladys suggested some watered wine. The girl ran off to fetch it, and was soon back fussing around Saphira. Gwladys gave her a hard stare, but continued her conversation nevertheless.

'Mistress Le Veske, I will be frank with you. Ann Segrim talked to the nuns here, and came to a conclusion that was most unpalatable concerning a poor member of our community who died recently.'

'That it was self-murder.'

The young nun serving Saphira her watered wine almost dropped the jug she was holding at this brutal statement. The wine splashed on Saphira's dress and the nun gasped out her apologies. She tried to wipe the stain away with her hand, her big, brown eyes filled with horror. Whether at the accident or the mention of suicide, Saphira could not tell. She lifted the nun's hand from her dress. It was trembling.

'It is of no importance, dear. Do not worry.'

She looked into the nun's eyes and detected a deep pain in their depths. What had frightened the girl so? Gwladys broke in and motioned for the girl to leave the room.

'Sister Margaret, do get a grip on yourself. Calm and contemplation on your misdeeds is what you need now. Go.'

Mumbling her apologies, the pale nun left. Gwladys continued the conversation as if nothing had happened, a homely smile on her face.

'Self-murder was too extreme an opinion, though we were grateful for Mistress Segrim's views. I am sure it was an unfortunate accident. The girl drank some concoction of her own, while confused about her state of mind. She was no doubt seeking a cure for some imagined ill, and took something that had the opposite of a curative effect.'

Saphira could tell that Gwladys was hiding the truth from her. She made one last attempt to uncover whatever it was the prioress was unwilling to reveal.

'There is a most pleasant scent in the room. I can detect lavender, but what are the other herbs you use?'

Gwladys, a little surprised at the change in the conversation, relaxed and detailed the aromatic herbs she liked to use. Saphira smiled and carried on her indirect inquiry.

'And do all the nuns strew their cells with them?'

'Some do. But I fear I have to admit their use is a vanity I allow mainly myself. I could give you some for your own house.'

Saphira held up her hands as if to fend off the generosity.

'Please, there is no need. I was just enquiring, because Mistress Segrim drew William's attention to some herbs on the floor of Sister Marie's cell. There was probably no significance to them.'

Gwladys's face turned frosty, as she realized that her visitor had tried to draw out more information about the dead nun.

'I fear our conversation is at an end, my dear. Divine offices call me.'

She stood, and just as Saphira moved towards the door, there came a great cry from somewhere outside the nunnery, followed by a clash of steel. All three women cast fearful looks at each other. Gwladys was the first to respond, rushing from the room to follow the unholy sounds. At the gate leading back into the outer courtyard, Gwladys pressed her face to the grille. She gasped in horror. Pushing past her, Saphira looked to see what had so shocked the prioress. In the middle of the courtyard, lying on the ground was Hal Coke with his hands over his head. He was quaking with fear. Astride him, but down on one knee was the bent figure of Peter Bullock. He held his rusty old sword in a defensive position across the front of his body. Before him stood the towering figure of a black-bearded knight dressed in white. As Saphira looked on in horror, he swung his gleaming sword in a downward arc. With great clanging of steel on steel, Bullock wearily parried the fierce blow as clearly he had done a few times before.

But his energy was spent and he was blowing hard. Saphira called out.

'Peter!' Then she turned to the prioress. 'Open this door.'

'What? And let this maniac in?'

'We must do something. He will kill Peter.'

She turned to look back through the grille and breathed a sigh of relief. A small wiry man garbed in a brown tunic was restraining the ferocious knight. He called out to him.

'Brother Odo, stop this. You cannot kill this man, he is the constable. There is nothing to gain now. She is dead.'

Odo de Reppes took a deep sigh and fell to his knees before Bullock, who carefully relieved him of his sword. Gwladys, with the danger over, at last unlocked the gate to the outer court. Saphira flew through and helped the panting Bullock to the gatekeeper's lodge, where he slumped on the stool. There was blood seeping from a head wound and he looked grey. Hal Coke, whose life he was protecting, also staggered in and sat on the floor. With a great commotion, Hildegard and Gwladys appeared in the doorway.

'Does he need any aid?'

Saphira nodded.

'Something for a head wound. A clean cloth and an astringent. I would suggest helichrysum if you have it.'

Gwladys hurried off with Hildegard in tow. The old crone cast suspicious glances around her as she crossed the outer yard. Odo de Reppes and his sergeant had mounted up and gone already, but she clearly felt the press of outside evil. Saphira looked at Bullock, staring into his eyes to make sure he had not taken a serious blow to the head. Both of them ignored Coke, who dragged himself over to a barrel of ale and tapped off a draught into a jug. He drank deep of the only medicine he required.

'Did you learn anything?'

Saphira shook her head at Bullock's question. She had some clues, but had got nothing precise from the prioress after all.

'No. How about you? And how did all that start?'

Bullock shrugged his shoulders, while trying to hide the fact that his hands were shaking. He did not like to admit that the whole encounter had deeply shaken him. Odo de Reppes's eyes had held murder in them.

'I was questioning Coke about who might have access to

the nunnery, when we heard the sound of horses. Coke was first out, with me following. We had no reason then to suppose that whoever it was had violent intentions. The next thing I knew was that the Templar had Coke by the throat wanting to know who had killed his sister. I stepped in to calm matters down and suddenly we were at swords drawn. One thing it does tell me, is that however Odo is involved with this whole mess, he is too hot-tempered to have solved it with poison.'

'I agree. There is something odd here in connection with Odo's sister's death. It concerns . . .'

Before Saphira could voice her doubts, Gwladys returned, not with Hildegard but the whey-faced Sister Margaret. The young nun held an iron-bound box in her hands. Gwladys pushed Margaret forward.

'Here is your patient, sister.' She turned to address Saphira. 'Sister Margaret is learning the skills of herbal medicine. She is quite a keen pupil, aren't you, Margaret?'

The nervous girl mumbled some response under her breath and opened the wooden box. Choosing a particular pot, she applied the contents with a clean cloth. Bullock gasped as the astringent oil staunched his wound, and Margaret mumbled an apology. She then closed the box and scurried back to the door of Coke's lodge. While Gwladys was engaged in questioning Hal Coke as to the cause of the fracas, Saphira took the opportunity to follow the young nun.

'I would like to know what you used on the wound. I am learning about remedies myself, you see.'

Margaret cast an edgy look around her, as if afraid of the outside world pressing down on her. She had not been beyond the gate of the nunnery for a long time.

'It is a preparation of helichrysum, which grows around the Mediterranean Sea. We cultivate it now in the garden here.'

Saphira smiled encouragingly.

'You are very wise concerning plants, then? Perhaps you saw what was on the floor of Sister Marie's cell the day she died. They and the rushes were cleared away by someone.'

Margaret looked as if she might faint and Saphira held out a hand to steady her. But the young nun recovered, stepping away from Saphira's proffered support. She looked away from Saphira towards the open gate of the nunnery. Her eyes betrayed her desire to be safely within its confines once again.

'I cleaned the cell myself at the behest of Mother Gwladys. I saw some dried herbs mixed with the rushes on the floor.'

'Could you tell what they were?'

'Yes. But it is not important. They grow around the nunnery in profusion. I am sure Marie picked them not knowing their properties. It is not true she killed herself.'

'If so, then you have no reason to avoid telling me what they were.'

Margaret was becoming more and more agitated, picking with a fingernail at one edge of the iron binding on the box she held.

'There was birthwort . . . and henbane.'

'Birthwort?'

Saphira and Peter Bullock were walking back to Oxford across Port Meadow. The constable seemed well recovered from his ordeal, though Saphira was keeping an eye on him. He was an old warrior, but the shock of an encounter such as he had experienced could come much later, when Peter had time to think about what might have been. For now, she was happy to distract him with an analysis of what they had learned.

'Yes, birthwort. It is that weed growing in abundance around the nunnery. The one with the small greeny-yellow flowers. And yes, it is used for what its name suggests. Both to encourage birth and, if taken early on, to cause a miscarriage.'

Bullock grimaced.

'Some might say that its link with a nunnery, with the repu-tation it had before Gwladys's days as prioress, spoke strongly of the nuns' behaviour. And maybe even after Gwladys's arrival, the presence of it in a cell where a nun died should not be ignored. It is too late now to know if Sister Marie was with child, but it looks like another avenue to follow. And the henbane? It's a poison, isn't it?'

Saphira didn't reply immediately as a stern-faced man dressed in black was approaching them from the direction of the town. She didn't want their conversation overheard, no matter how accidentally. As the man passed, both she and Bullock greeted him, but he did not deign to reply. His mien was stiff and awkward, and she noticed a bruise on his cheek. She stopped, thinking that she recognized him from somewhere.

But then, it was probably from the thronging streets of Oxford. She did ask Bullock if he knew him.

'Who, him? That's Regent Master Ralph Cornish. He bore witness against William and got that bruise on his cheek for his pains. Falconer punched him by way of preserving your honour.'

'Mine?'

Bullock blushed.

'He suggested something improper was occurring between you and William. So William hit him.'

Saphira laughed loudly.

'And what is he doing out here, I wonder?'

'Oh, Thomas Symon told me. He's the chaplain to the nuns at Godstow. He'll keep them on the straight and narrow will that one. He behaves like the world is a cesspit, and it's his duty to see it cleaned out. Goes around like there's a nasty smell under his nose and a poker up his arse. If you'll pardon an old soldier's language.'

'If he's a regent master, why is he not sitting in the Black Congregation? You don't think they have reached a verdict already?'

'We had better get back and find out.'

PART THREE
THE VERDICT

TWENTY-FOUR

Chancellor Bek rose from his seat and the Black Congregation fell hushed.

'The time for disputation is over. The facts have been presented in the case of Ann Segrim's murder, and they point in one indisputable direction. How do you find William Falconer? Guilty or not guilty?'

He scanned the assembled masters, whose faces were a pale and sombre crest bobbing on a sea of black. Bek heard but a few murmurs of dissent. He would note who they were for careful but persistent persecution in the future. His gamble had paid off. The overwhelming response was clear.

'Then I find William Falconer guilty of the murder of Ann Segrim.'

He turned to look severely at the accused and, tasting its sweetness on his lips, he repeated the sonorous word.

'Guilty.'

TWENTY-FIVE

I t was a glum Thomas Symon who met with Peter Bullock and Saphira Le Veske that evening.

'Guilty. What are we to do now? Can Master Falconer buy his freedom?'

Bullock shook his head.

'No. It is only the great of this land who may do that. And then only when the royal courts are involved. The king is more interested in raising funds than dispensing justice. Our only hope is that the king's justices reckon the chancellor has over-stepped the mark in holding the trial in the first place. Though it has to be said that the law is unclear on that. After Thomas Becket's murder, the mood was to allow the Courts Christian to try the clergy. And Falconer as a regent master is in holy orders. No matter how he might behave.' He glanced briefly at Saphira, not wishing to cast doubt on Falconer's celibacy in front of Thomas. 'But I have sent a message to the sheriff urging him to alert the king's justices to what is afoot.'

Thomas felt he had let his mentor down, and could not accept there was nothing more they could do.

'What of Odo de Reppes? Is not his behaviour at the nunnery a clear sign of his madness? What is de Bernere going to do?'

'Brother Laurence remains tight-lipped about his fellow Templar. They are a close-knit bunch. I should know – I served them for years. But I do believe they will sort the matter out within their own ranks. I do not think de Reppes will get away with it, whatever he has been up to. I do think, however, that we can wipe him off our list of suspects for Ann's murder. Saphira, you are right. He is too much of a warrior to meddle in slow poisoning.'

'But where does that leave us?'

It was Thomas's question that roused the so far silent Saphira to respond.

'I am convinced that the reason for Ann's death is closer to home than you thought, Thomas. And William thinks as I do too.'

Thomas frowned.

'Do you mean someone at Botley? Alexander Eddington? The servants say he was rebuffed by Ann when he tried to elicit her favours.'

The boy blushed at his own suggestion of improper behaviour on the part of Ann's brother-in-law. Saphira smiled and leaned over to pat his hand, causing him to redden even more.

'We must not ignore that possibility. But I was thinking more about the nunnery. There is something very wrong inside that place, despite Gwladys's best efforts. And I would like to speak to Sister Margaret again. She surely has something to hide.'

Bullock cut in.

'But how are you going to do that? You said your last conversation with the prioress ended on a very frosty note. How will you get back in again?'

'I was wondering if the chaplain might help me.'

'Ralph Cornish?' Thomas couldn't help being surprised at Saphira's suggestion. 'But he was a witness against Falconer.'

'Then I shall appeal to his Christian charity. But that is all for tomorrow. Tonight I propose to talk to William, and see if he has any more insights to offer. You know, he seems to work best in isolation. His mind does not get diverted by other mundane matters. Perhaps after this is all over, I should lock him away permanently.'

She shared a secret smile with Bullock, who saw the undertones in her words. But he could not be amused by her wanton suggestion. He was afraid his friend might not survive to enjoy the undoubted pleasures offered by Saphira Le Veske.

Sister Margaret could not sleep for the demons. They assaulted her senses as soon as darkness came. She kneeled by her bed in prayer, but they mocked her. They accused her of licentious and unholy acts with other women.

'No, I did not. There is nothing evil in an act of love.'

She spoke in a whisper, scared that others might hear and report her. She could be accused of being possessed. Of witchcraft. But they poked and prodded her, the voices. Hissing like a serpent in her ears until she tried to stop them with her hands pressed either side of her head.

'I loved her. And she loved me. But she was not strong enough. You broke her, not me. It was not my fault.'

She threw herself on the cold, damp floor of her cell, her arms stretched out in the shape of Our Lord's Cross. She mumbled prayers. But they would not go away. One voice silenced all the others. It whispered to her in the darkness. A voice no longer disembodied, coming from the dark shape lingering in the gloomy corner of her cell.

'You killed her. You alone killed her.'

'No. No. NOOOOO!'

Her voice wailed too loud to be unheard. She buried her head in the dirty rushes on the floor, feeling rather than seeing a shaft of light falling on her. Then as suddenly as it had come, she was in darkness again. Until the sister from the next cell pushed her door tentatively open.

'Are you having a nightmare, sister?'

Sister Margaret sobbed, and scratched at the stone floor until her fingers bled.

Saphira thought that Falconer looked remarkably calm for a condemned man. When she had arrived at the Bocardo with a supply of cold meats and a flagon of Rhenish, he had pressed his face against the grille and smiled cheerfully. He had taken the provisions, placing them carefully on the floor of his bare cell, before returning to the grille.

'I shall eat the meat tonight before the rats get to it. And the Rhenish will ensure a good night's sleep, I don't doubt.'

Saphira was astonished at his equanimity. She had dreaded this meeting, thinking she would have to be the one to be cheerful, when she felt everything but. He saw the surprise on her face.

'Don't worry about me. Peter has sent a letter to the sheriff, and he will not allow Bek to get away with it.'

'But you know Peter is not the greatest of scribes. And, as he would admit himself, nor is he persuasive when it comes to niceties of law. He only knows the power of the sword and a threat of bodily harm. Why would the sheriff listen to him?'

'Because I drafted the letter myself. And exercised all my subtle skills in ensuring the sheriff, as the representative of the king, sees how his master's law is being undermined. Along with his revenue from fines.'

Saphira could not help laughing, despite the desperate situation.

'So the convicted murderer has written his own letter to the justices pointing out the error of the ways of his judge.'

'Something like that. It would not surprise me to find that the king's justices were already riding hot-foot towards Oxford even now. I think Chancellor Bek's days are numbered, along with anyone who has aided and abetted him. So, tell me what you found out at Godstow nunnery, and perhaps we will have an alternative view on the murder to present to them when they arrive.'

Saphira laid before him her discovery concerning the poisonous herbs seen in Sister Marie's cell, which were cleared away before anyone could question their presence. Falconer's eyes lit up.

'Birthwort. Could the poor girl have been with child, and seeking to get rid of it?'

'It's possible. But no man can get into the nunnery, and the nuns do not come out beyond its walls.'

'What of Odo?'

'No, he was her brother, and besides this was his first visit in years apparently.'

'Hal Coke? I recall he is something of a rogue and he keeps the key to the nunnery gate.'

'He is a drunk and an old man.'

Falconer eyed Saphira ruefully through the grille that separated them.

'I am not much younger than he is. And if it were not for this cell door, I would prove to you that old men can still . . .'

Saphira hushed him and glanced around. The lane in which the jail stood was dark and narrow, but it was still a thorough-fare where anyone might pass.

'Be serious for a moment. The nun may have been with child, or merely imagined she was. We women are quite hysterical creatures, you know.'

Falconer played along.

'And prone to fainting fits when they cannot have their own way.'

Saphira pressed her body against the door.

'What? Like now.'

There was a quiet cough behind her and she started back from the cell door, blushing. Peter Bullock stepped out of the darkness, jangling some keys on a ring.

'I don't want to interrupt your sweet blandishments, but I have a plan to ensure William's safety.'

Saphira looked worriedly at the constable, then at Falconer.

'I thought you said you were confident the verdict would be overturned, William?'

'I am. But Peter seems to think otherwise.'

Bullock inserted a key in the cell door, jiggling it to make it turn.

'I do. I do not subscribe to your naïve trust in justice prevailing. No good you being exonerated later, if your neck is already stretched from a gallows tree. I just want to make it difficult for Bek to find you, should he take it into his head to hang you before the king's justices arrive.'

He swung the door open and Falconer went to step out. Then he stopped in his tracks.

'Saphira, you said that there was evidence of henbane in Marie's cell.'

'According to Sister Margaret, yes. I think the girl was suggesting her fellow nun took her own life. Even though in the very next breath, she insisted Marie did not.'

'But why would someone seek to abort their child and kill themselves at the same time? Self-murder would achieve both ends in one. This Margaret needs to be spoken to again. She knows something she is trying to hide.'

'I think so too. That is why I am going to speak to the chaplain of the nunnery tomorrow. You know him as one of your colleagues – Ralph Cornish.'

'Cornish? I knew he had a living locally, but I did not know it was so close. Bearing in mind how hard he worked to convict me, it will be quite an irony if he can help me prove my innocence in the end.'

Bullock pulled Falconer clear of the door and swung it closed behind him.

'Now, if you have finished your philosophizing, I would like to hide you away in St George's Tower before daylight reveals you are missing. And that I have committed a most heinous crime. Come.'

He hurried his prisoner and co-conspirator, Saphira, down

Bocardo Lane, past Trillock's Inn, and through into the court-yard of the castle. They met no one on the way, but he was still not happy until Falconer was safely ensconced in the uppermost room of the tower that formed his quarters as constable. It would be very hard for the chancellor, whatever he might suspect of the constable's complicity in Falconer's disappearance, to insist on searching there. He did make Saphira return to her own house, though, and exhorted her to behave as though she did not know William's whereabouts. He could not be sure how far Bek might push his luck, after all.

TWENTY-SIX

S aphira made sure she was in Sumnor's Lane first thing in the morning. The narrow lane ran close under the northern ramparts of the town walls. If Ralph Cornish were to be going to the nunnery, or to the schools nearby, he would pass along this lane. The early morning sun had not risen high enough to warm the lane, and Saphira shivered with the cold. Clouds heaving themselves darkly across the sky warned of rain. A break in the hot dry weather would be welcome, but she was not prepared for a downpour, if she had to wait too long. She need not have worried. Promptly on the sound of the terce bells, a stern-faced man garbed all in black emerged from Black Hall. A bruise marred his left cheek, and Saphira could tell it was the same man who had passed her and Bullock on Port Meadow yesterday. He walked briskly towards her, but as he went to pass, she stepped from the shadows.

'Master Cornish? May we speak?'

'I am a busy man, mistress. What is it you want?'

'It's a rather delicate matter concerning the nunnery.'

Ralph Cornish suddenly showed more interest in this apparently chance encounter. His eyes narrowed.

'As you clearly know that I am chaplain to Godstow, then you must also realize that any business concerning the nunnery is private. Or even subject to the confidentiality of the confessional. I cannot answer your question.'

He made to push past Saphira, but she grabbed his arm and stopped him. Surprised at this woman's firm action and vice-like grip, Cornish hesitated. Saphira continued.

'Don't you even want to know what the question is before you refuse to answer?'

Cornish gave an exaggerated sigh of exasperation, as if this nuisance was a mere fly that could be swatted and forgotten.

'Ask it.'

'Did you speak to Ann Segrim when she was at the nunnery the last time?'

'Before William Falconer poisoned her, you mean? I am afraid I didn't. I was engaged on my teaching duties here and had not been to the nunnery for a few days. I regret that now, for I feel I neglected the poor unfortunate child who died. She might have been alive if she had been able to confess her sins to me. Mistress Segrim's . . . involvement . . . in seeking the causes of her death were no doubt well meaning, but fruitless. It was an accident.'

'Do you know if Ann spoke to all the nuns?'

Cornish was beginning to get restless at Saphira's enquiries.

'No. I do not know for sure, though the prioress told me later that she had.'

'So, she must have spoken to Sister Margaret, for example. Perhaps she noticed something odd in her behaviour. Did Mother Gwladys mention that to you?'

'Sister Margaret? No, she did not say anything. And I am sure as her chaplain I would have noticed anything strange in the sister's behaviour myself. Now if you will excuse me.'

Saphira still held on to Cornish's arm, so he could not break away without using force.

'Then, do you not think there is something amiss with Sister Margaret now?'

'Just who are you?' Cornish wrenched his arm free of her grip, an angry look on his face. 'You are that Jew, aren't you? Falconer's whore.'

Saphira raised her arm, aiming to slap his face, but he quickly grabbed it. Then suddenly all the heat seemed to go out of him. His face, which had become a mask of anger, once more slipped into the solemn mien he had worn when he emerged from Black Hall.

'Mistress. Forgive me, but these events have disturbed me, and I feel guilty at neglecting my care for the nuns. You have touched a sore point. Though I am convinced of Falconer's guilt still, I will speak to Sister Margaret. If there is anything burdening her soul, I will help her. I can say no more than that. Whatever she tells me will be in confidence.'

Saphira, thrown off course by Cornish's swift turnabout, could only acquiesce. At least Margaret would get an ear to listen to her troubles. Saphira would have to find another way of discovering what those troubles were, though. With a godly smile on his face, Ralph Cornish took his leave of her, and she turned back towards Jewry. She had only got to the end of Jewry Lane, when she became aware of a commotion outside Samson's house. An old man, holding on to a steaming nag with one hand, was beating on the old man's door with the other. Knowing Samson's fear of abrupt and noisy hammerings on his door, she hurried over to see what the problem was.

'What in heaven's name are you doing?'

The old man turned to her and she recognized him as one of Segrim's servants. His face was pale and his breathing was heavy and irregular. She thought perhaps he was ill and was seeking Samson's aid. But she was wrong. Between rasping gulps of air, Sekston gasped out his mission.

'It's Master Eddington. He's took ill. Bad.'

Saphira was at once scornful of the urgency of the situation, recalling Alexander Eddington's propensities for drinking too much.

'Tell him to drink less and he will recover. Now stop disturbing good men in their own homes.'

She went to walk away, but Sekston called out after her.

'No. It's not that. He is sorely ill. The same as the mistress was. Please can you help?'

The same illness as afflicted Ann? Then Eddington's life was in danger. She made an immediate decision.

'Go to the Golden Ball Inn, tell them to saddle me a rouncey, and bring it here. I will gather some necessities.'

She went into her house and quickly scanned her notes made from Rabbi Maimonides's treatise on poisons that was Samson's trusted guide on such matters. The celebrated Spanish Jew recommended an emetic, and Saphira placed a stone jar of oil in a convenient box, along with some dried anethum, and some asafoetida, natron and cabbage seed. The rest of her needs could be supplied at Botley Manor. By the time she emerged from her front door with the precious box in her arms, Sekston was back with a sound horse, saddled and ready for her. They mounted up, and picked their way through the crowds that were beginning to throng the streets of Oxford. Once out through North Gate, they were able to encourage their horses to a greater speed. But despite the urgency of the errand, Saphira suddenly reined her rouncey in and slipped to the roadside. Sekston, who was barely keeping pace on his old nag, called out in horror.

'What are you doing, mistress. The master is dying.'

Saphira pointed to a feathery plant beside the track.

'Look. Fresh dill. It will be much more effective than the dried anethum I have brought.'

She grabbed up a handful of the aniseed-smelling herb, and climbed back on her mount. When they galloped into the court-yard at Botley, an anxious Sir Humphrey already stood at the door to let her in. She left Sekston to deal with the horses, and grabbing her box, ran up the steps to the manor house door. The old knight, trembling with shock, led her directly to a small solar at the back of the raised gallery above the old hall. Eddington lay on his bed, pale and still. For a moment she thought she was too late, but then he groaned and threshed his limbs.

'Please help him. He is my brother. I cannot bear the thought that he will die as Ann did.'

Sir Humphrey's face was grey and his shoulders bent, as if with a heavy burden. He had clearly been deeply disturbed by what had been happening around him for a long while now. This could be the final straw that broke him. Saphira murmured reassurances, even though she could not be certain she was in time to save Eddington. She opened her box and issued firm orders to the servants who stood, mouths agape, in the doorway.

'Fetch me fresh milk and cream if you have it, but first take this dill and steep it in warm water.'

Sir Humphrey turned to his servants, who were stupefied by the events. He growled out a peremptory set of commands.

'Sally, take the dill and boil it in the water on the fire in the kitchen. Margery, you go to the dairy and bring milk and cream. Now.'

It was not long before Sally returned with a cauldron of water smelling strongly of aniseed. She set it down on the floor and Saphira poured a good dose of oil into it, stirring it with her hand.

'Now. Give me a drinking cup.'

Segrim picked up a pewter goblet from the floor, tossing the dregs of red wine from it on to the rushes. He passed it to Saphira. She filled it from the cauldron, and sat beside Alexander Eddington. She lifted him easily with her right arm and held the goblet up to his lips.

'Here, drink this. All of it.'

Alexander groaned, shaking his head. But Saphira persisted.

'Imagine it is a fine Rhenish.'

Alexander opened a bleary eye and Saphira saw the redness

in them. Like devil's eyes. This was a clear sign of arsenic poisoning. He drank deeply, spluttering a little at the taste. She replenished the goblet and forced him to drink again. He did so, and then began to heave and groan. She stepped back from the bed, just as Eddington lurched upward and vomited noisily over the side and on to the floor.

'What have you done?' cried Segrim. 'He is worse.'

Eddington himself now saw who had been treating him and raised a shaky finger to point at Saphira.

'She is Falconer's accomplice. Why have you let her in here to finish the deed?'

Saphira stayed calm and smiled as the patient once more vomited over the floor. She steeled herself to observe what he had brought up. He obviously had had much red wine in his stomach from the watery spew that was spreading across the floor. But there were also semi-digested lumps of food. She explained what she had done.

'No, I have not finished you off.' She looked at Sir Humphrey. 'It is essential first to rid his stomach of whatever has poisoned him. That much we have achieved already. Then he will drink plenty of milk and fats to neutralize the poison and line his stomach, so there is a barrier between the poison and his tissues. I dare say he will begin to feel better soon.'

Eddington flopped back on his bed, holding his head.

'I am dying.'

'On the contrary, you are going to survive. Now you have rid your body of what poisoned you. Can you say what you have been eating recently?'

Sir Humphrey butted in.

'That is what is curious. He eats at my table, of course, and drinks of my wine. We have all shared the same food. What could have caused this?'

Eddington groaned.

'I know. The sweetmeats. Ann came back from the nunnery one day with a supply of dried dates and figs that the prioress had given her. I love sweet things. I could not bear to see them wasted after Ann . . . passed away. I have been eating them the last few days.'

There was a cry behind them and the crash of a heavy bucket hitting the floor. Margery had only just returned from the dairy with warm, creamy milk to hear Eddington's admission of greed.

The bucket had fallen from her grip and the rich milk was running across the floor in a bluish river.

'Oh, Lord. The sweetmeats. The mistress ate some every day. I even tempted her with some when she was ill. I took some to her on the day she died.'

She looked in horror from one startled face to another.

'I poisoned her.'

Having sent Sekston back to Oxford to summon Thomas and Bullock, Saphira rode as swiftly as possible up the river bank towards Wytham woods. She hoped that Cornish had not already said something that would send Sister Margaret over the edge. As she galloped, her mind was in turmoil trying to figure out what had driven the nun to poison Ann Segrim. It obviously had to do with Ann's questioning of the nuns about the earlier death. If Margaret was guilty of causing Marie's death, she would then have wished to silence Ann Segrim. But once Ann had come to the conclusion she did about the cause of Marie's death – that is, self-murder – was there any point? Margaret had seemed ambivalent about the slur on Marie's name when she spoke to Saphira. She had hinted to it as a possibility because of the herbs she had found. But then she had been vehement about Marie's purity. Self-murder was a terrible sin before God. Mother Gwladys had concealed the possibility in order to spare the dead girl, and the nunnery, the shame. But it appeared more likely now that Margaret had killed Marie herself, and then tried to kill Ann before she spoke to the prioress about her conclusions. It was unfortunate that the arsenic hadn't worked in time. Margaret must then have been horrified that Ann hadn't revealed her complicity, and she had been in the clear. More so because she saw she couldn't prevent Ann later eating the poisoned sweet-meats without giving away her guilt.

Saphira had barely reached this conclusion when she was in sight of Godstow nunnery. Her horse clattered over the bridge and she pulled on the reins in a strangely silent courtyard. There was no sign of Hal Coke and, more alarmingly, the door leading into the nunnery was ajar. She slipped off the horse's back and strode over to the entrance. Suddenly, Ralph Cornish appeared in the doorway, his face a ghastly grey, and shock showing in his deep-set, brown eyes.

TWENTY-SEVEN

Sister Margaret was hanging from one of the beams in her cell, a stout cord round her neck. Peter Bullock looked up at the way the cord was pinched tight round her throat, and at her bulging eyes speckled red with broken blood vessels. He cast a glance at Thomas Symon, who stood in one corner of the cell transfixed by the sight.

'No doubt, then?'

'What? Oh . . .' The young scholar tore his horrified gaze from the unfortunate nun's purple face, and the protruding tongue. 'No, Master Bullock. I am sure she died from asphyxiation caused by the cord.'

Bullock contained his impatience, knowing this was new territory for the youth.

'I mean, she inflicted it upon herself.'

'Ah. I cannot say for sure, but there does not seem to be any signs of violence.'

In fact, Symon had not inspected the body closely. Nor did he think it appropriate for him to do so. She was, after all, a nun who had dedicated herself – body and soul – to God. Bullock sighed and climbed on to the bed. He took his dagger out to saw through the cord. As he did so, the body rocked and began to swing.

'Thomas, take hold of her, for God's sake. I only have one pair of hands.'

Thomas blushed, and stepping forward, held the still-warm body around the waist. He was very conscious of her female form, though she felt a little bony. He prayed silently for God's forgiveness for any unclean thoughts. Suddenly the cord was sundered by Bullock's dagger and the corpse slumped over Thomas's shoulder. He felt her breasts pressing against his back and almost dropped her there and then. Quickly, he stepped forward and tipped Margaret's dead form on the bed of her cell. He wondered if he would ever be able to dissect a female in the same way his predecessor in Falconer's service, Richard Bonham, had. At that moment, he doubted it. Hearing a gasp from the doorway of the cell, he stood away from the body. Mother Gwladys hurried over to the bed and arranged Margaret's hands in a prayerful attitude.

'However will we recover from this? Two deaths in a few weeks, and this one self-harm without a doubt.'

Bullock refrained from reminding the prioress that the previous one – the death of Marie – had probably been no accident, as Gwladys had asserted at the time. In fact, it was now likely that the one had led to the other, together with the murder of Ann Segrim. Ralph Cornish was even now sitting in his office in the outer courtyard of the nunnery, after intimating that Margaret had as much as admitted to him that she had been responsible for Ann's murder. The constable would not be surprised if the girl had killed Sister Marie too. Though he was past caring about that. Leave that for the prioress to sort out, as she attempted to clear the midden that was Godstow nunnery. It was far more important for him to carry the news of Margaret's confession and suicide to Oxford, and the sheriff, in order to free Falconer.

When Peter had arrived at Godstow, he was first ushered into Cornish's presence by Saphira Le Veske. She had taken control of the situation well, even forbidding the prioress from doing anything to Margaret's body before the arrival of the constable. How she had managed that, Bullock did not know, but Gwladys's face was thunderous. She had also made Cornish return to his office to await the constable. The man was quite subdued, and Bullock could see he had not coped well with what had happened around him. After blaming himself for not seeing Marie's distress before her death, this second incident had obviously hit him hard. He had hardly been able to look Bullock in the eyes.

'She more or less admitted to me that she was responsible in some way for Marie's death. Though I could not get her to say exactly why. Either she killed her, or she gave her the potion that helped end her life. But she did say quite clearly that she killed Ann Segrim with arsenic, as she was scared that she would be accused by Mistress Segrim of Marie's murder. She was a very disturbed child.'

'If she told you she was the killer, why did you do nothing about it?'

Ralph sat up and looked Bullock in the eyes for the first time in their conversation.

'I did. I did what was necessary. I told her to return to her cell and pray for forgiveness. Then I examined my own conscience, trying to decide if I should tell anyone about her confession.'

Bullock was outraged.

'Tell anyone? Knowing that William Falconer had been found guilty of the murder – a verdict, you had been instrumental in affecting – how could you even think twice about not telling me.'

'Because I am her confessor.'

Bullock crashed his fist on the table that stood between the two men, and Cornish flinched. He held his hands up in supplication.

'I don't expect you to understand. And I feel ashamed that I was somehow misled into thinking Falconer guilty. But the man is his own worst enemy. And he is still a fornicator.'

Bullock wished his world was as simple as the one inhabited by Cornish. At one time it had been. As a soldier, he had seen only in black and white. Friend and foe. He wished life was like that now for him, but Falconer had opened his eyes to shades of grey, and he could not avoid the shadows that loomed around the edges of death. He pointed a horny finger at the priest.

'Stay here.'

He went off to view the body in situ.

Now, after dealing with the dead nun, and leaving her in Gwladys's care, he returned to Ralph Cornish. With Thomas hovering indecisively in the background, he let the man go.

'You can return to Oxford. In fact, you can do something for me.'

'What is that? Pray for your salvation?'

'No. You can tell your Chancellor Thomas Bek that I am releasing William Falconer, and will be advising the king's justices when they arrive that the case is solved. Sister Margaret killed Ann Segrim for fear of her involvement in the other nun's death being discovered. You can also tell Bek that I wouldn't be surprised if his days as chancellor are numbered when they find out what he has done. And how badly he has done it.'

Ralph rose and hurried from the room, glad to be released. Thomas Symon patted the constable on the back.

'That was a fearfully strong speech, Constable Bullock. It was worthy of Master Falconer himself.'

Bullock grinned broadly.

'It was, wasn't it? I was quite proud of myself. It is not often I get a chance to chastise a master of the university.' He looked over Thomas's shoulder. 'Where is Saphira?'

It was Symon's turn to smile.

'I think she wanted to be the first to tell Falconer the news.'

When Bullock and Symon got back to St George's Tower, the pair were waiting in his chamber. Falconer rose and took his hand.

'Congratulations, Peter. You have solved another case. And without my interference this time.'

Bullock almost blushed but took the plaudits well.

'Mistress Le Veske and Thomas, here, did their bit too, I will admit. I have sent a message to Bek, and I don't think he will bother you any more. The authority of the Black Congregation in murder was always dubious, anyway. As far as I am concerned, you are free to go.'

Saphira stood up and took Falconer's hand.

'Come. Rebekkah will have left some food for me, and she always prepares too much. You can share it with me and forget all about Agnes's little pleasures.'

There was a hint of a sparkle in Saphira's eyes as she spoke those final words. It was an invitation that Falconer could not resist. After a week in the Bocardo, he was a free man. He and Saphira left Peter and Thomas broaching open a new barrel of ale, and walked down Fish Street towards Jewry. A few curious folk eyed them, some no doubt recognizing Falconer as an accused murderer. He did not care what they thought. The gossip would soon catch up with reality. However, standing on the threshold of Saphira's house, he still hesitated. Her reputation mattered to him. She laughed at his uncertainty and dragged him inside.

'Come. No more skulking round back doors for you. Both our reputations have been torn asunder in the Black Congregation, and I am now a woman of ill-repute.'

'And I a fornicator in Holy Orders, and a seducer.'

'Hmmm, yes. You are Peter Abelard to my innocent Heloise.'
Falconer winced.

'I hope not. Wasn't Abelard castrated for his wickedness?'
They walked through to the rear room of the house, where
a fire burned in the hearth. A stew bubbled over the flames,
left there by Rebekkah. Falconer stepped up close to Saphira,
who suddenly wrinkled her nose. She pushed him away.

'You have a week's stench of prison on you.'
Falconer looked down at his crumpled and dirty black robe.

'I should go back to Aristotle's and change.'
Saphira took his arm, staying him.

'I have a better idea. Take that robe off, together with
whatever disgusting garments you have under it, and I will
cleanse your body. I will perfume you like the Queen of the
May.'

Falconer was embarrassed, but Saphira seemed unconcerned, and pulled her snood off her head to release her wild
auburn hair. She busied herself collecting clean linen and
setting a cauldron of water on the fire to warm, so he started
to undress. She produced a couple of pots from a box.

'Here is some jasmine and wild camomile.'
By the time she had stirred them in the warming water,
Falconer stood naked before her. She smiled and began to
wipe his body down with the scented linen cloth. She made
no objection when he began to untie her dress, stepping dain-
tily out of it when it fell to the floor. He marvelled once again
at her lithe, shapely figure, pulling her to him.

Afterwards, Falconer lay on her bed with his arms folded
behind his head. He looked at her sleek body, glowing with
a sheen of sweat.

'I still don't see where Robert Bodin fits into this.'
Saphira groaned, burying her head in his shoulder.

'Leave it alone, William. The matter is resolved, so be
satisfied.'

'No, but Margaret could not have got the arsenic from Bodin
herself. She was locked away in the nunnery. Nor, by the same
token, could she have killed him.'

Saphira's mumbled response was inaudible, coming from
somewhere below his armpit.

'What?'

'Maybe his death had nothing to do with Ann's. Perhaps it was a burglar killed him.'

'Perhaps.'

Saphira could hear the doubt in William's voice, and began to draw her nails down his chest, distracting him. But he still picked at the loose ends.

'I suppose it could have been coincidence. Odo de Reppes's involvement turned out to be a pure fantasy, existing only in Humphrey's head. The fact he was Marie's brother was a coincidence. But I don't like . . .'

'Coincidences. Where did you get this scar?'

Saphira was delineating a rough mark that ran from William's left side to near his belly-button. Falconer looked down.

'At Wiener Neustadt, I think. If my memory serves me right, it was from the sword of a ferocious Tartar from the east.'

Saphira slapped him lightly on the flank.

'That was over thirty years ago. You are teasing me.'

'It's true. I was but a boy, yet I was there. And now you are teasing me, with your hand being where it is.'

'Yes I am, aren't I?'

When Falconer next woke it was early morning, and Saphira was not in the bed with him. He sat up, hearing a sound from the kitchen below. He smiled and pulled on the long white linen shift he had borrowed from Saphira's clothes chest the night before. He stretched and yawned. The thoughts he had had about Bodin's murder and the sequence of events that led to Ann's death, still bothered him. And there was something else too. Something that Ann had said to him at their last conversation before Alexander Eddington had interrupted. He knew it was significant, but he could not bring it to the front of his mind. He walked down the stairs, meaning to talk to Saphira about what was niggling at him. Perhaps between them they could tease out the strands. He strode into the kitchen towards the figure bent over the fire.

'My dear, I need that sharp brain of yours.'

The figure turned round in shock, almost dropping the pan she held in her hand. When she saw the tall form of William Falconer, however, garbed in a white robe a few sizes too small for him, she burst into a fit of giggles. Falconer scratched his head, glad he had not grasped the girl lovingly in mistake for Saphira.

'You must be Rebekkah. Where is your mistress?'

Suppressing her amusement at Falconer's incongruous appearance, and thinking of the scandalous gossip she could share with her friends, Rebekkah replied.

'She has gone away, sir.'

'Gone away?'

Falconer was distracted. Ann's conversation was beginning to return to him. They had been talking of the awkwardness between them and how she regretted walking away from Saphira. Rebekkah's words reminded him of it. Ann had said she even confessed her petulance to Mother Gwladys.

'Where has she gone?'

Rebekkah stifled another giggle.

'She said if you asked, I was to tell you she has gone to a nunnery.'

Suddenly the truth dawned on Falconer. And he realized that Saphira was in grave danger.

TWENTY-EIGHT

Saphira had suddenly awoken knowing what the little worm was that had been gnawing at her brain. Despite diverting William from his niggling doubts about Margaret's guilt, she too had wondered how the arsenic had come into her possession. The only possibility was that someone had obtained it for her. And that limited the options for a nun enclosed in a nunnery for eternity. It also meant some sort of planning and complicity on someone's part. She could not imagine that Odo had anything to do with the plan. If he was not capable of slowly killing Ann with poison himself, then he was equally unlikely to have assisted Margaret in the same slow murder. That left only two men.

Sitting up in bed, she thought of waking William. But when she looked down at his head on the pillow next to her, she saw how serene his face was. He was fast asleep for the first time in a week, in all probability. Sliding out of the bed, and pulling on her clothes, she resolved to sort out the problem by herself. Soon after North Gate was opened for the first time, she was striding across a cool and pleasant Port Meadow towards the nunnery. Her first port of call was Hal Coke's lodge beside the gatehouse. The old man had only just risen, and sat on his stool bleary-eyed and half-asleep. He responded irritably to Saphira's question.

'No. There is only one entrance to the nunnery, and only the prioress and I have the key.'

'Do you run errands for the nuns like in the old days. Before Mother Gwladys tightened things up?'

Coke looked wearily at her, as if this question had dogged him for years and he was tired of it.

'No, I don't. I only wish I could, because they paid me well for it. And to turn a blind eye to the men some of them entertained. That Templar wanted access, saying he had seen his sister in her cell last time. But that was some years ago, and it is impossible now. I told him as such. Now, if you please, you are unwelcome here, and I have things to do.'

He pushed past her and crossed the yard towards the stables, disappearing from sight. Saphira followed him as far as the centre of the courtyard, scanning the covered way that ran the length of one side of the yard. Beyond the thick wall lay the nunnery cloister apparently only accessible through the central gate. There was one other door in the corner of the courtyard though. She approached it and tried the handle. The door was locked.

'It is the entrance to St Thomas's Chapel.'

She turned round to see Ralph Cornish had quietly walked up behind her. He explained the significance of the chapel.

'It once housed the tomb of Rosamund, the old King Henry's whore and mistress. It was a place of pilgrimage until the bishop insisted that the abomination should be moved elsewhere. Would you like to see inside? The nuns do not use it for their day-to-day devotions, preferring the domestic chapel.'

'You have a key?'

'Oh, yes. As chaplain I have a key to the chapel.'

He slid past her and inserted one of two keys on a ring into the lock, turning it easily. The door swung open silently and Saphira stepped into the cool, gloomy space. Cornish followed her, closing the door behind him. Plunged into darkness, Saphira's heart started beating fast. She felt Cornish slip past her in the dark, obviously sure of his footing.

'Let me light a candle.'

From a glowing pot of embers by the door, he lit a taper, and went across towards the altar. Having genuflected before the Cross, he lit two candles either side of the altar steps. The yellow glow allowed Saphira to see well enough to spot another door at the far end of the nave. She pointed it out.

'Does that lead directly into the nunnery?'

Cornish smiled, the flickering candles distorting his features with the shadows they cast.

'Yes, it does. And before you ask, yes, I have the key to that also.'

Falconer ran across Port Meadow as the sun began to rise up in the sky. A low mist still hung over the water-meadow and it made the world seem unreal. Between taking great gasps of air, he cursed Saphira for a headstrong woman, little recognizing her nature was just like his own. He also wondered what spark of new information had caused her to rise so early and make her way to the nunnery without rousing him. He knew how he had put the final threads of the tapestry together to weave a clear picture. It all came down to the words Ann had used in her private solar that last time. Her voice spoke loud and clear to him now.

'I regretted being unkind to Mistress Le Veske and I confessed so to Mother Gwladys. I was still hurting and called her your mistress in front of Gwladys and Hildegard. Even the little nun who served me with figs probably heard me. Gwladys soon put me right though.'

Later, Falconer had wondered how Ralph Cornish had known of his relationship with Saphira, exposed so crudely in front of the whole Black Congregation. He had thought he had been so discreet. The link must have been one of the nuns by way of the confessional. Ann had told the nuns about Saphira, and one of those nuns, probably Margaret herself, had told the chaplain. In the form of Ralph Cornish. And why had she told him this titbit? Because she was his puppet. Falconer surmised that Cornish had some hold over her in connection with Marie's death and used that to gather gossip. He might even have forced her to kill Ann for the very reason Falconer had assumed had driven Margaret. To obscure the real cause of the death of Marie. With Godstow almost in reach, Falconer set aside the myriad possibilities for the time being. All that mattered was securing the safety of Saphira.

The chapel was cold but Saphira resisted the urge to shiver. She did not want Ralph Cornish thinking she was afraid. Even if she was.

'I might not have guessed it was you, if I had not recalled where I had seen you before. It was the day before Robert Bodin the spicer was killed. I was watching his shop because he had been nervous about something or someone for a little time. He had sold arsenic to more than one person, and clearly was worried about its use in the murder of Ann Segrim. On that day, he was visited by two old women – who I will discount – a beggar boy – who I know now was innocent. And you. I recognized you from the bruise on your cheek.'

Cornish raised his free hand and felt the tender spot where Falconer had delivered his blow.

'Yes, your gallant knight did that. But I almost made him pay. For that, and a previous humiliation.'

'What I don't understand is how you got Sister Margaret to poison Ann Segrim. It must have been you made her do it, if you were the one to provide the arsenic. She would not have done it on her own, as I first thought.'

Ralph Cornish swung the keys back and forth as he spoke. He sounded almost pleased with himself.

'Of course I was the instigator. The girl was too weak to have arranged it herself. I wanted Ann Segrim silenced, but unfortunately I miscalculated the dose. It took too long. But the irony was that she didn't uncover the truth about Sister Marie's death anyway. She put it down to self-murder, a conclusion that was so appalling to Gwladys that she covered the whole matter up. Ann Segrim need not have died. But then I turned it to my advantage when Falconer was accidentally present at her death. It was almost divine providence.'

'And Margaret's death? That wasn't suicide either, was it?'

'No. I told you – she was a weak vessel. She would have told all eventually. So I visited her cell in the night by using this way into the nunnery. And strangled her. It was easy to make it look like self-murder.'

Saphira was almost mesmerized by the swinging keys in Cornish's hand, and didn't see his move. He took three rapid strides towards her, grabbing her arm in his tight grip.

'This place has become a cesspit of evil, like it was once before. And needed cleaning out. Now you will be swept away with all the other sinners, filthy Jew.'

Suddenly, the door behind Saphira swung open and light flooded into the gloomy chapel. A welcome voice boomed out.

'But you are the source and origin of all the evil yourself, Cornish.'

Saphira breathed a sigh of relief at the sound of William Falconer, at the same time as being a little nettled that he had once again appeared as her rescuer. She would never live it down. If she lived. Cornish swung her round, encompassing her waist with his arm.

'Master Falconer. Welcome. How is it you make me the evil one? Do you know what started all this? It was those two girls and their evil. I could see that something had troubled

Sister Marie for a good while. Finally, I persuaded her to confess. She told me that little Margaret had told her of her strong feelings for Marie. How she had persisted in whispering enticements in her ear. How she had touched her. She said Margaret had spoken of love, and that she had given in. How they had lain together. What could be more evil than two nuns sinning in such a way together after devoting their bodies to Christ?'

Falconer stepped inside the chapel, moving slowly and cautiously towards Cornish and his captive.

'But then why was Marie murdered? Because she was, wasn't she? By someone else, I mean. It was not self-murder.'

'Margaret killed her with henbane.'

Cornish was backing away from Falconer towards the inner door of the chapel and the nunnery. Falconer still niggled at the truths.

'Why would she kill a woman she loved? Unless she felt betrayed, or forced to do so. By you.'

Cornish's voice rang out loudly through the chapel as he finally lost his temper.

'Yes, yes. I had her kill Marie, and she did it willingly.'

Saphira suddenly saw it. The source of all the horrors that had taken place had their stem and origin here, with Ralph Cornish. She spoke calmly, though she was scared, and could not break free of Ralph's grip.

'She killed her with henbane. But why did Marie willingly take the henbane? She took a mixture of herbs thinking she was taking birthwort to kill the child that was growing inside her. A child Margaret could not have helped create. You fucked Marie because you could. You had heard her confession of sin and used it to get her to give in to you. Margaret agreed to give the fatal herbs to Marie because she felt betrayed by her. And was scared of you. You. The putrid source of all these unnecessary deaths.'

Saphira felt the door behind her open. Cornish must have unlocked it as she was talking. He pulled her through the opening into the cloister. He made to lock the door again from the outside, but Falconer must have grabbed the handle from the inside. A battle of wills took place before her eyes, but Cornish still did not release her. He finally gave in to Falconer's greater strength, and backed away from the door and along the cloister.

Falconer burst out of the chapel, stopping dead in his tracks when he saw Cornish holding one of the keys close to Saphira's eye.

'I will blind your pretty whore, if you come any further, Falconer. In fact I might blind her anyway.'

Saphira winced as her captor pressed the end of the key into the edge of her eye. She believed he was capable of doing it. He had lost control, shouting out his contempt for William.

'This is all your fault, Falconer. You persistently humiliated me in front of others at the university with your clever arguments. Then, when I had triumphed in argument, you behaved like a child and threw that firecracker at me. You should have been humiliated by your action. But everyone thought it was highly amusing, and it was I, who was the butt of all the jokes. My reputation was ruined. And I made sure you paid for that.'

Saphira squinted at Falconer, her eye watering with pain. But William didn't seem concerned at all. Annoyingly, he was smiling, his arms folded across his chest. Why wasn't he rescuing her?

Falconer watched as Cornish backed away, feeling with his leg along the edge of the stone bench that ran the length of the inside of the cloister. What he could see and Cornish and Saphira couldn't was that, standing on the bench, was the small figure of Mother Gwladys. In her hand she held a heavy, iron-bound Bible. When Cornish got close enough, she swung the Bible with all her strength at Cornish's head. As he slumped to the ground, stunned, Gwladys called out loudly for all to hear.

'And God was displeased with this thing; therefore he smote Israel.'

Saphira stepped away from the unconscious figure on the ground and looked up at the prioress.

'Actually, I am glad you smote him, Mother, and not Israel. In the form of this poor Jew.'

For the first time ever, the startled nuns, who had poured out of the small domestic chapel, heard the strange sound of their prioress laughing heartily.

EPILOGUE

Four people sat in the house in Fish Street comparing thoughts over some nice Frankish wine. Saphira Le Veske had already teased William over the fact her life had been saved by another woman.

'Gwladys had the presence of mind to secrete herself from Cornish's view. While you, William, had to confront him. Just like a man.'

Falconer laughed.

'Oh, remind me, then. Did she get him to give himself up by using her female wiles? Or did she hit him over the head with a heavy weapon? Just like a man.'

'It was a Bible. She persuaded him with God's words.'

Falconer raised his hands in defeat, and drank deep of the wine. Bullock poured him some more from the jug and walked back to his own chair. Slumped in it, he nursed his own replenished goblet.

'Ralph Cornish is locked safely away and the king's justices are on their way to Oxford. I don't think Chancellor Bek will dare try him at the Black Congregation. Cornish has killed too many people, or caused their deaths with the help of the poor little nun. I will wrench a confession out of him about Robert Bodin too. I won't let that pass unsolved, not while I'm constable.'

Falconer mused on Bek's fate.

'I think Thomas Bek will not last long as chancellor as soon as the king hears of his ineptness. A successful murder trial might have aided him, but as his attempt at grabbing power was so ill-shaped, I am sure he will have to go.'

Thomas leaned forward, all fresh eagerness.

'Perhaps they will elect you chancellor, Master Falconer.'

The other three burst out laughing at such an incongruous idea, and Thomas blushed to the roots of his well-cropped hair. To divert attention from his ill-judged words, he asked another question of Falconer.

'And what of Odo de Reppes? Was he really part of a

conspiracy against the king and his family? Or was Segrim confused about it all?'

Bullock and Falconer exchanged glances. They had spoken to Laurence de Bernere about the Templar, but the master of Temple Cowley had been quite tight-lipped. He had talked of Odo's sister, as Falconer explained.

'It seems that Odo had long been impressed by his sister's piety, and more than once had sought to speak to her about matters that troubled him. His journey to England seems to have been just to talk to her again. It was probably coincidence that his path then happened to cross Sir Humphrey's. As for the great conspiracy, will we little folk ever know what happens at court? It is true that Segrim is convinced he saw Odo at the Church of Saint Silvester where Henry, nephew of the king was murdered. And Odo was in Berkhamsted when Richard died. But Segrim was already obsessed with the Templar and may have seen what he wanted to see. Besides, Richard was a very old man with the half-dead disease. It is perhaps all coincidence.'

Thomas grinned wolfishly, catching his master out at last.

'But haven't you always told us that you don't believe in coincidence?'

Laurence de Bernere sat in the chapel at Temple Cowley singing the psalm *Venite* as commanded in the Templar Rule. He prayed with his brothers, speaking softly so as not to disturb the prayers of others. When it came to sing the *Gloria patri*, everyone rose and bowed to the altar in reverence for the Holy Trinity. When the service was complete, he walked slowly towards the cells, deep in thought. He peered in the dark and stinking cell where Odo de Reppes lay heaped in chains. He had sought guidance from God for what he was about to do, but he knew the Rule was clear on the matter.

Auferte malum ex vobis.

Remove the wicked from among you. It was necessary to remove the wicked sheep from the company of faithful brothers. And the letter from Guillaume de Beaujeu, Templar preceptor in the County of Tripoli in the Holy Land, expressed no doubt over Odo's guilt. He would simply disappear from the earth.

Laurence de Bernere crossed himself and returned to the chapel to pray.